BURN BRIGHT

AN ALPHA AND OMEGA NOVEL

PATRICIA BRIGGS

Orbit
An imprint of
Little, Brown Book Group
Carmelite House
50 Victoria Embankment
London EC4Y 0DZ

An Hachette UK Company
www.hachette.co.uk

www.orbitbooks.net

ORBIT

First published in Great Britain in 2018 by Orbit

1 3 5 7 9 10 8 6 4 2

Copyright © 2018 by Hurog, Inc.

The moral right of the author has been asserted.

A CIP catalogue record for this book
is available from the British Library.

ISBN 978-0-356-50600-5

Printed and bound in Great Britain by
Clays Ltd, St Ives plc

Papers used by Orbit are from well-managed forests
and other responsible sources.

For Michael, my heart, who taught me to follow my dreams

A Tale Without an Ending

Once upon a time, there was a small spring that, touched by the earth's spirit, bore a sparkle of magic scattered in its cold, pure water. It was only a little magic, but it brought good things into the world— tiny bits of goodness born of the tiny bits of magic.

There is a certain sort of evil that cannot abide happiness, even such humble joys as lived in that spring.

Such an evil came to dwell at the spring, culling victims from those who came to seek the little surcease it offered. Eventually, even the earth's magic could not cleanse the evil from the water, and the spring's small magic was turned to darker uses.

Thus died a little joy in the world, and evil was satisfied for a time.

This evil held the now-polluted spring, one way or another, for a very long while. Time changed, and the evil changed with it, grew more clever about drawing prey to it. Sometimes it fed upon innocence, sometimes magic, sometimes beauty—but the evil always took satisfaction in robbing the world of any good it could find.

It became aware of one who sought, like the spring once had, to do a little good in a world now bleak and dark. On the evil one's webs came whispers of a monster who fought other monsters. The evil deemed it no more of a meal than a thousand others like it. Still, it could not, by virtue of what it was, allow such a one to live. It set a snare to catch one who was a hero—for heroes are delicious when they fall. It set a snare to trap a monster because even evil fears monsters, a little.

The one who sprang the trap was truly a monster. The one who triggered the snare was also a hero.

But this one was an artist, too, and not just any artist. Such an artist, he was, as found beauty and joy in the world and shared it for all to see. An artist who, like the spring had, spread little magics around and left happiness where there was none before.

An artist such as that was a bigger mouthful than evil, even such an old and wicked evil as this, could swallow easily.

Much was lost in the battle, and it cost both sides dearly. As far as anyone knows, the fire of the battle burns still.

1

This was bad. This was so very bad.

He ran full tilt, ghosting through the trees. The branches and brambles reached out and extracted their price in blood and flesh for running at such speed through their territory. He could feel the ground absorb his blood and his sweat—feel it stir at the taste. *Dangerous.* Feeding the earth with his blood when he was so upset was not wise.

He almost slowed his feet.

No one was chasing him.

No one had even known he was there. They'd seen the trees who'd obeyed his will, but they had not seen him. The trees . . . he might have to answer to her for the trees.

She'd told him to run, and he had paused to call the trees. That was not how their bargain was supposed to work. But he couldn't just let them take her, not when it was within his power to stop it.

Think. Think. Think. The words were his, but he heard them in her voice. She'd worked so hard to give him rules. The first rule was *think*.

It was funny that everyone believed that she was the danger, that she was the crazy one. Very funny—and his lips stretched in a grin only the forest could see. It wasn't amusement that caused his feral smile. He wasn't sure exactly what the emotion was, though it was fueled by an anger, a rage so deep that the earth, aroused by his blood, rose eagerly to do his bidding. The earth, out of all the elements, was the hardest to wake but the most eager for violence.

He could just go back. Go back and teach them what they got for touching someone he loved . . .

No.

Her voice again, ringing in his ears with power. She was his dominant, though he was so much older, so much stronger. As such, she wielded power over him—a power that he'd given her out of love, out of despair, out of desolation. And their bargain, their mating bond (her word, then his) had worked for a very long time.

Anyone who cared to look around would know how well her hold on him had worked—there were still trees on this mountain, and he could hear the birds' startled flight as he ran past them. If that bargain had failed, there would be no birds, no trees. Nothing. His was an old power and *hungry*.

But their mating had given him balance, given him safety. His beautiful werewolf mate had brought love to his sterile existence. When that hadn't been enough, she had brought order to his chaos as well.

Order . . . that word . . . No, *orders* was the word that sifted through his roiling thoughts. She had given him *orders* for this situation.

He vaulted over a deadfall with the grace of a stag.

Call the Marrok, she had told him. And also, *Right the hell now.* That was the correct task. Call the Marrok for help. But the reason for his speed—his *right the hell now*—was because if he allowed himself to slow, he would turn around and . . .

The mountainside groaned beneath his feet. A soft shift that only someone like him—or like his true love—would feel.

His fleet footsteps . . . which had slowed . . . resumed their former speed. She was alive, his love, his mate, his keeper. She was alive, and so he had to call the Marrok and not raise the mountains or call the waters.

Not today.

Today, he had to call the Marrok and tell him . . . and his mate's voice rang in his head as if she were running by his side.

I know who the traitor is . . .

CHARLES TIPPED HIS father's computer monitor so that it was at a better angle and wiggled the keyboard until it felt right.

He'd told Bran that he could run the pack just fine from his own home while Bran was gone, just as he had the last dozen times that the Marrok had to be away. But this time had looked as though it might last awhile, and his da had been adamant that it was important to keep the rhythms of the pack the same.

It wasn't that he didn't understand his da's reasoning—some of the hoarier wolves under his da's control weren't exactly flexible when it came to change—but understanding didn't make it any easier for Charles to function in his da's office, his da's personal territory.

Charles couldn't work in the office without making it his own—

and wasn't that just going to set the fox among the hens when his da got back and had to reverse the process. But Bran would understand, as one dominant male understands another.

Charles had to admit, if only to himself, that he'd moved the mahogany bookcases to the other side of the room and reorganized the titles alphabetically by author, instead of by subject matter, just to mess with Bran. Anna, he thought, was still the only person on the planet who honestly believed he had a sense of humor, so he was pretty sure he could make his da believe the rearrangement was a necessity.

Charles hadn't moved the bookcase until Bran called him this morning, not quite a month after he'd left the pack in Charles's keeping, to let him know that his initial business was concluded—and Bran had decided he would take another week to travel.

Charles couldn't remember the last time Bran had taken a vacation from his duties. Charles hadn't realized that his da was *capable* of taking a vacation from his duties. But if the rearrangement of Charles's life was no longer essential, just required, then he felt free to make some changes to make his life easier. And so he'd rearranged his da's office to suit himself.

Even in the redecorated room, it took Charles longer than normal to lose himself in his work, his wolf restless in his father's place of power. Eventually, the hunting game that was international finance grew interesting enough that Brother Wolf let himself be distracted.

It was a complicated dance, to play with money at this level. The battle pleased Brother Wolf, the more so because they were good at it. Brother Wolf had a tendency toward vanity.

Eventually, drawn in by the subtle hunt for clues in the electronic data on his screen, he sank into what his mate called "finance space," chasing an elusive bit of rumor, stocks rising for no apparent reason, a new company seeking financing but there was something they weren't saying. He couldn't tell if what this company was hiding was good news or bad. He was running down the background of an engineer who'd been hired at what looked to be an abnormally high salary for his title when he was pulled out by the sound of the door hitting the wall.

He looked up, Brother Wolf foremost at this interruption to his hunt. It didn't help his temper that it was his da's mate who'd barged into (what was now) his territory without permission.

"You have to do something about your wife," Leah announced. She didn't react to his involuntary growl at her tone. When she spoke of Anna, she would do better to talk softly.

He didn't like Leah. There were a lot of people in the world he didn't like—most of them, even. But Leah had made it very easy not to like her.

When his da had brought her back with him, Charles had been a wild thing, lonely and lost. His da had taken his much-older brother, Samuel, and been gone for months off and on. Half-mad with grief at the death of Charles's mother, Bran probably hadn't been the best person to raise a child when he *was* home.

Charles's uncles and his grandfather had done their best, but Brother Wolf had not always been as willing to ape being human as he was now. A werewolf child born instead of made, Charles had been (as far as he knew) unique; no one, certainly not his mother's people, had any experience dealing with what he was.

A good part of the time Bran had been gone, Charles had roamed the forest on four feet, easily eluding the human adults tasked with raising him. Wild and undisciplined as he'd been, Charles had no trouble admitting that his ten-year-old self had not been a stepson that most women would have welcomed.

Still, he had been very hungry for attention, and Leah's presence meant his da was around a lot more. If Leah had made even a little effort, his younger self would have been devoted to her. But Leah, for all her other personality flaws, was deeply honest. Most werewolves were honest by habit—what good is a lie if people could tell that you are lying? But Leah was honest to the core.

It was probably one of the things that allowed Bran's wolf to mate with her. Charles could see how it would be an attractive feature—but when someone was mean and small inside, it might be better to keep quiet and hide it, honest or not, rather than display it for the world to see. The result was a mutual animosity kept within (mostly) the bounds of politeness.

Charles honored her as his da's wife and his Alpha's mate. Her usual politeness to him was brittle and rooted in her fear of Brother Wolf. But, since she was a dominant wolf, the fear she felt sometimes made her snappish and stupid.

Brother Wolf recovered his temper faster than Charles. He told Charles that Leah was agitated and a little intimidated, and that had made her rude. Brother Wolf didn't like Leah, either, but he respected her more than Charles did.

Other than the growl, he did not respond immediately to her request (he refused to think of them as orders, or he might have to take an action about them that did not involve anything she would appreciate). Instead, he raised a hand to ask her for silence.

When she gave it to him, he spent a moment leaving himself clear notes about the suspicious engineer that he could follow up on later, as well as highlighting a few other trails he'd been investigating. He concluded the other changes he wanted to make, then backed out of his dealings as quickly and thoroughly as possible. Leah waited in growing, but silent, indignation.

Finished packing up his business, he looked up from the screen, crossed his arms over his chest, and asked, in what he felt was a reasonable tone, "What is it that you wish me to do with my wife?"

Apparently, his response wasn't what Leah had been looking for because her mouth got even tighter, and she growled, "She seems to think that she's in charge around here. Just because you have been placed in charge temporarily doesn't allow her the right to give orders to *me*."

Which seemed out of character for his wife.

Oh, the disregard for pack hierarchy, traditional or otherwise, was typical of his mate. Anna would not, Charles thought with affection, know tradition if it bit her on the ear. His Anna had carved out her own, fluid place in the pack hierarchy—mostly by ignoring all the traditions completely. It did not, however, make her rude.

Nothing good had ever come from sticking his nose in business that had nothing to do with him.

"Anna is Omega. She doesn't have to obey the Marrok," he told her. "I don't know why you think she would obey me."

Leah opened her mouth. Closed it. She gave him an exasperated growl, then stalked off.

For a conversation with his stepmother, he thought on the whole it had gone rather well. That it had been short was the best part of it.

One of the reasons he had resisted moving into Bran's home while the Marrok was gone was because he knew Leah would be in, harassing him all the time. He paused to consider that because, until this very moment, she hadn't done that. This was the first time she'd interrupted him at work. He wondered, as he began playing with the numbers on the screen in front of him, what it was that his da had said to Leah that had kept her out of his hair this effectively.

Before he was seriously buried in business again, Bran's phone rang.

"This is Charles," he said absently—as long as it wasn't Leah, he could work while he talked.

There was a long pause, though he could hear someone breathing raggedly. It was unusual enough that Charles stopped reading the article on the up-and-coming tech company and devoted all his attention to the phone.

"This is Charles," he said again. "Can I help you?"

"Okay," a man's voice said finally. "Okay. Bran's son. I remember. Is Bran there? I need to talk to the Marrok."

"Bran is gone," Charles told him. "I'm in charge while he is out of town. How can I help you?"

"Bran is gone," repeated the man's voice. It was unfamiliar, but the accent was Celtic. "Charles." He paused. "I need . . . we need you to come up here. There's been an incident." And then he hung up without leaving his name or where exactly "up here" was. When Charles tried calling him back, no one picked up the phone. Charles wrote down the number and strode out, looking for his stepmother.

He hadn't recognized the voice, and if one of the pack members had been in trouble, he'd have felt it. There was another group of wolves who lived in Aspen Creek, Montana, though they were not part of the Marrok's pack: the wolves Bran deemed too damaged or too dangerous to function as part of a pack—even the Aspen Creek Pack, which was full of damaged and dangerous wolves.

Those wolves, mostly, belonged to the Marrok alone. Not a separate pack, really, but bound to the Marrok's will and magic by blood and flesh. "Wildlings," Bran called them. Some of the pack called them things less flattering, and possibly more accurate, though no one called them the Walking Dead in front of Charles's father.

The wildlings lived in the mountains, separate from everyone, their homes and territory protected by the pack because it was in everyone's best interest for no one to intrude in what peace they could find.

Bran had given him the usual list of names and a map with locations marked. Most of them Charles had met, though there were two wolves he knew only by reputation. The wildlings were, as a whole, both dangerous and fragile. Bran did not lightly allow anyone else to interact with them.

The list had not included phone numbers.

He found Leah with Anna in the stainless-steel-and-cherry kitchen. Anna had her back to Leah, whose face was flushed. His Anna was mixing something—he could smell chocolate and orange—and paying the Marrok's mate no attention at all. He recognized Anna's tactic for dealing with people she felt were too irrational to discuss anything with. She'd used it on him often enough.

Leah was tall, even for the current era, when women of five-eight or -nine were more common. She was several decades older than Charles, and in the eighteenth century, when she'd been born, she would have looked like a Nordic giant goddess. Her natural build was athletic, an effect enhanced by a life spent running in the woods. Her features were even and topped by large blue eyes the color of a summer lake at noon.

His Anna was, as she liked to say, average-average. Average height, average build, average looks. Her curly hair was a few shades darker and a hint redder than Leah's dark blond. Anna considered her hair to be her best feature. Charles loved her freckles and her warm brown eyes that lightened to blue when her wolf was close.

Objectively, Leah was far more beautiful. But his Anna was *real* in a way few people were. He'd tried explaining that realness to his da once, and his da had finally shook his head, and said, "Son, I think that's one of those things that your mother would have understood without trouble, and I never will."

Anna connected to the world around her as if she instinctively understood his maternal grandfather's view of the world: that all things in the world are a part of a greater whole, that harm to one thing was harm to all. She had coherence with the world around her, while most people were fighting to be connected to as little as possible because that was safer. He thought Anna was the bravest person he knew.

He understood that other people would consider Leah the more beautiful of the two. He even understood why. But to him, Anna was—

Ours, said Brother Wolf. *She is perfect, our soul mate, our anchor, the reason we were created. So that we could be hers. But we have other business to attend to.*

He didn't know how long the silence between the two women had held—it hadn't been that long since Leah had stormed out of his office. His father's office.

"Leah," he said, because there was no time to wade into the deep waters between the two women even if he'd been stupid enough to want to do so. "I just received a distress call from one of the wildlings, I think. Do you know this phone number?"

He held the paper out to her.

Leah demonstrated one of her shining qualities. She dropped

whatever fight she was trying to pick with Anna and took the paper he handed her, setting aside her personal business without hesitation when duty called.

"Hester and Jonesy," she said immediately. "They live up Arsonist Creek about twenty miles. What did she say?"

And that was why he hadn't recognized the voice. Jonesy very seldom spoke when his mate was available to do it. Hester . . . Hester was old. In that category of old that meant neither she nor anyone else was entirely sure how old she was.

"Jonesy called me," Charles said. "He said there's been an incident, and he wanted me to come to them."

"*Has been* an incident?" Leah frowned, glanced over her shoulder at Charles's mate, and frowned harder. "Hester isn't easy even for Bran. The last time he went up—last fall—she was lucid and seemed to enjoy singing with him. But then she tracked him halfway back to the road, and he had to call Jonesy to lure her back to her home. If there has been *an incident*, having an Omega wolf there might be a good move for everyone."

Charles frowned. "An Omega wolf isn't always a good thing when dealing with the wildlings."

Initially, Bran had been very excited about what Anna might do for his wildlings. And she'd helped a couple of them. But one spectacular disaster that ended with the wildling dead and three of the pack damaged had taught them to be cautious. That the wildling had been under a death sentence before Anna tried to help him hadn't kept her from feeling terrible.

Charles was unwilling to expose Anna to such trauma again. He and his da had had several heated arguments about that recently— arguments that both of them were careful to keep from Anna.

"Tracked?" Anna asked, taking a spoon and sinking it into her bowl.

Leah nodded. As long as the topic was important, her voice stayed professionally brisk. "She took wolf form and tracked Bran as if he were prey. He said he wasn't sure he shouldn't have let her catch up with him." Leah's brisk voice traveled right over what that would have meant: Hester's death. "But she'd been lucid for the better part of two days—and Jonesy seemed well enough. Bran thought it could have been just having a dominant wolf in her territory that had set her off, so he let it lie."

She pursed her lips, and said, "You aren't your father. Hester might not be willing to let you approach her at all by yourself. Unless you want to have to put Hester down, you should take Anna." She saw Charles's hesitation. "Unlike the wildling who had such a bad reaction to Anna, Hester's personality is a strong one. It is her wolf that is her problem—not the human half." She gave a little biting laugh at his expression. "You can ask your da, that was his assessment."

"I can put this in the fridge," Anna said briskly, breaking into the conflict Leah was about to start. "Or someone else can. How much of a hurry are we in?"

The problem with the wildling Anna had tried to help so disastrously had been that the wildling's wolf half had been the sane part of that pairing. When Anna sent it to sleep, all that was left was the crazy human—who still had had a werewolf's fangs and strength.

"I don't intend to dawdle," said Charles, giving in. "But any emergency is going to be over before we can make it there. As Leah said, Hester's place is twenty-odd miles away—and most of that is rough country."

"Okay," Anna said. She took the spoon she was stirring her dough with and filled it, handing it to Charles to taste as she reached for the plastic wrap with her other hand.

"It's Mercy's recipe." Anna wrapped the bowl with an efficiency that belied the relaxed-chat tone of her words. "I put some orange peel in, too. What do you think?"

The chocolate was rich and bitter in the sugar-butter-and-orange matrix—a brownie batter, he thought, though it might be some sort of soft cookie dough. His foster sister, Mercy, had always had a genius for baking things with chocolate. She'd also had an uncanny knack for driving Leah to unpredictable heights of craziness.

His Anna was really annoyed with Leah if she would go so far out of her way to bring up Mercy. He grunted and dropped the spoon-sans-dough in the dishwasher.

Anna could read his grunts. "Good." She put the bowl in the fridge and turned off the oven. "Ready when you are."

Leah had been watching Anna's performance with narrow eyes, but when she spoke, it was only to say, "Hester's old enough that a gift is a pretty good guarantee she'll treat you like a guest instead of an interloper. Bran usually brings fruit because that's one thing they can't grow or kill. Give me a minute, and I'll put a basket together for them."

She left the room at a brisk trot, presumably to find a basket, because there was plenty of fruit on the counter.

Charles knew Leah well enough to know that whatever Anna had done to raise her ire wasn't over. Leah didn't let go of a battle—but she wouldn't bring it up again until the situation with Hester was resolved.

He eyed his mate. To the untrained eye, she looked relaxed and calm.

Charles's eye was not untrained. He murmured, "Trouble?"

His mate leaned against the granite counter and heaved a put-upon sigh that was only half-feigned. Then she straightened and shook her head. "It's hard for her to have us here. She has no idea how to handle me in her personal space. She is finding it incredibly frustrating. And you don't help."

He raised an eyebrow.

She laughed despite her tension. "It's not your fault. You don't do anything wrong except exude Charlesness, but that's enough to set her off."

He didn't know what Anna meant by "Charlesness"—he was who he was. He couldn't help that. But there was no question that his presence had an effect on Leah.

"This seemed to be a more specific problem," he said.

"Yes," Anna agreed. "Tag stopped in while you were wrestling rhinos in Bran's office."

"I was moving bookcases," he told her. "No African animals involved."

She grinned at him briefly. "Sounded like rhino wrestling to me—complete with animal grunts and bellows. Anyway, he stopped in—apparently to tell us he was bored." She hesitated. "He came in the middle of a discussion Leah and I were having. I think he had other business, but we distracted him."

Anna was an Omega wolf. That meant that any dominant wolf felt the need to make her safe—which was the reason Leah thought she might help with Hester. If Tag had come into the room while Leah and Anna were having some sort of heated discussion . . . yes, the big Celtic werewolf would have done what he could to interrupt it.

"Tag suggested we reinstate the Marrok's musical evenings,"

Anna told him. "Apparently, they were a community staple before the Marrok allowed them to lapse a few years ago."

"Almost *twenty* years ago," Charles said, more than a little taken aback. What had brought that into Tag's head? Surely there were things more likely to come to mind than events coated in decades of dust when someone walked into the middle of a fight between two women. "More than a few years."

"Twenty?" Anna frowned. "That's not what Tag said when he suggested it."

"Tag's sense of time isn't anything I would rely on too much," Charles told her dryly. "Ask him about Waterloo. He talks about it like it happened a week ago."

She grinned. "Only if you are the one to tell him that the French lost the battle this time. I'll sit on the sidelines and eat popcorn."

Tag's real name was Colin Taggart. He identified as Irish, Welsh, or Scot depending upon the day and the accent he was using. He'd fought for the Little Corporal during the Napoleonic War. Tag was still particularly bitter about "the English."

"Anyway," Anna said with a glance toward the doorway Leah had used to exit the room, "I thought that it would not be a good thing to institute sweeping changes while Bran is away. Leah disagrees."

Charles blinked at her. It was not like his Anna to come down on the side of caution. Nor was Leah in the least musical. Not being interested in anything that wasn't centered upon her, she'd been more relieved than almost anyone when they'd stopped.

"*Leah* thinks that the pack would benefit from some kind of social gathering beyond the moon hunts," said Leah, emerging from the depths of the house with a basket in her hand and a bite to her voice.

"*Anna* thinks that the pack won't fall into despair and boredom if we wait until Bran comes back," said his Anna mildly, in a tone he had heard his da use on his recalcitrant sons. "She also believes that referring to oneself in the third person is absurd."

Charles bit back a smile. Somehow, he didn't think a smile would help the situation, particularly because he could tell by Leah's pinched expression that she recognized the origins of that tone, too.

Leah restrained herself to a wordless grimace. Then she loaded the basket with apples, peaches, and bananas, which somehow, in her skilled hands, took on an artistic shape.

"Here," she said to him, handing him the basket. "I hope this helps." Despite the edge in her tone, she wasn't lying.

Charles nodded gravely. "Thank you."

"I DON'T UNDERSTAND that woman," said Anna, getting into the driver's seat of his old truck. She had finally given up offering to let him drive unless there was some real reason that she didn't want to or he needed to. "Why is everything a battle with her?"

Charles made a *hmm* noise. Evidently, she was going to blow off all the steam she'd been building up with Leah onto him. That was okay. He had broad shoulders. He liked that she gave him her secrets—even if those secrets were only about how frustrating she found Leah. Not much of a secret, really, but it was his.

Anna turned her irritated frown on him before backing the truck carefully out of the driveway. Anna drove like an old grandmother. He thought it was delightful. So was the frown.

"Aren't we in a hurry?" she asked. "Shouldn't you be driving?"

"Whatever happened has already happened," Charles said. "We

shouldn't waste time, but I don't think ten minutes one way or the other will make much difference."

"All right, then," she said. "Am I going the right direction? I was so upset with Leah that I didn't ask. I don't know where Arsonist Creek is. Why don't I know where Arsonist Creek is?"

"This is the way," he said. "And the pack lands are riddled with creeks and brooks and puddles. No reason you should know them all—especially when Arsonist Creek is in a part of our territory we leave to the wildlings."

"Okay," she said, then she was quiet. Trying, he thought, to contain her irritation with Leah. She stewed a little more before her frustration bubbled enough to be given voice.

"It is a good idea," she told him. "Tag should be able to say, 'Hey, let's do this thing.' And she should say, 'Hey, that is an amazingly good idea, let's do that thing you suggested.' And it could be just ducky for everyone. Instead, after I made the mistake of saying it sounded like fun, she was all 'we should wait until Bran gets home.'"

So she'd switched sides, he thought, his clever wolf. He'd seen her do that before. Sometimes to him. Anna would have brought up all of Leah's objections until there was nowhere for his stepmother to leap except exactly where Anna wanted her to go. If Leah had been smarter . . . but she wasn't. As his da had once told him, it was not fair to blame her for being exactly what Bran needed in a mate. Someone his wolf would accept—and the man would not love.

"I can't see a world in which Leah would use the word 'hey,'" he said. "Except, perhaps, if it was the homophone 'hay,' instead. And only then if she had a horse she needed to feed."

Anna let go of the steering wheel and waved her hands. "It's a barbecue, not a rite of passage or a county fair or anything requiring much organization. Just a 'bring food, bring instruments if you want to; we're going to have fun tonight' kind of thing. We're a musical bunch here. Enjoying that shouldn't take an act of Congress." Anna put her hands back on the wheel about a hundredth of a second before he'd have felt compelled to do the same.

"Turn here," he told her. "Then take the turnoff as though you're headed up to Wilson Gap."

He let silence flow between them for a moment. Brother Wolf thought that Anna was fully capable of getting along with Leah if she wanted to. She usually did, in fact. Leah was no exception to the effect that an Omega wolf had or to Anna's sincere friendliness. If Tag had interrupted a fight, it was one that Anna had allowed to happen.

Brother Wolf didn't know why she'd do that, but Charles put two and two together for them both. Maybe, he thought, it hadn't been anything his da had said that had kept Leah out of his hair since Bran had left.

"Have you been picking fights with Leah so that she forgets to pick fights with me?" he asked.

Anna raised her chin.

"Thank you," he said.

"My job," she said—and there was a little grimness in her voice—"is to make your job easier."

He thought about the grimness and the subtle emphasis when she'd said "my job." Brother Wolf stirred uneasily. In matters pertaining to their mate's happiness, Brother Wolf sometimes had insights that Charles, distracted with human things, could overlook.

His Anna, whose talent for music had burned so brightly that she'd had a full-ride scholarship to Northwestern University, should have been playing her cello on a stage under spotlights. Instead, she was trapped in Aspen Creek, Montana—where the closest thing to spotlights within a hundred miles were probably the ones on the top of his truck.

"You were going to look into finishing your degree," he said. He'd been meaning to ask her about it for a while. But Anna could be a private person, and he tried to give her room to breathe. It was a difficult balance between Brother Wolf's sometimes overwhelming desire to protect/love/defend and Anna's need to be herself and not be overwhelmed.

She didn't say anything for a while.

"I can get an online bachelor's in music theory," she said finally. "But I'm starting to think maybe I should go into therapy or counseling."

"Is that what you want?"

She sighed a little and shook her head.

"Then why are we talking about that?"

She was looking for a purpose in her life.

Us, said Brother Wolf. *We should be her purpose as she is ours.* Then, when Charles disapproved of the wolf's narrow-mindedness, Brother Wolf offered, *But if she wants something more, we need to provide it for her.*

That, Charles was in wholehearted agreement with.

He had been working with his da to see how he and Anna might go about adopting a child. It was complicated by the low profile Bran was trying to keep for Aspen Creek and the pack.

But Anna's dissatisfaction wasn't something a child would fix. She wasn't a person who lived through other people.

"What do you think about Tag's suggestion?" Anna asked, changing the topic. "Don't you think it would be a good idea to have some sort of get-together that isn't just pack but the whole community?"

"Not to take Leah's side—" he began, but had to laugh at the look she gave him. "Just listen up, Anna-my-love. The musical evenings were the center of a battle between my da and Mercy—and you know how Leah feels about anything that had to do with Mercy."

"I do," she said. "I even understand it, much as it pains me to say so. Bran is funny about Mercy. If you were that funny about Mercy, I would feel the same way Leah does—no matter how likable I might find her."

"Bran's not funny about her," he told Anna, feeling uncomfortable. "He thinks of her as his daughter, and he doesn't have any other daughters still alive. There's nothing strange about it."

"Or so everyone is much happier believing," agreed Anna blandly. "Including Bran. We'll leave it at that. So the musical evenings were *a thing* between Bran and Mercy?"

"Not like that," Charles said, feeling defensive because Anna put her finger right on something that he'd been ignoring for a long time. He took a deep breath. "All right. All right. You might have a point about Da and Mercy."

She smiled, just a little.

He threw up his hands. "Okay. Yes. I saw it, of course I did. As did Leah. But my da would never have moved on Mercy. Say what you will about him—but his wolf has accepted Leah as his mate, and he will not cheat on her. And Mercy has never seen him as anything except a father figure and her Alpha. That's what she needed, and that's what he gave her. I don't think Mercy has ever recognized that it could be more than that."

"Yes," Anna agreed, to his relief. "That's how I read their relationship, too." She paused, then said in a low voice with her eyes firmly on the road in front of them. "Do you think she's okay?"

"Mercy?" Mercy had been taken. For that reason, Bran had left the pack in Charles's hands. Luckily, that situation had been quickly resolved—at least Mercy's part in it had. He had the feeling that the shake-up from it would be playing out for a long time.

"Yes, Mercy."

He pressed a fist to his heart. "If she were not, my da would have brought down the fiends of the ages to wreak vengeance. Since he decided to go visit my brother in Africa, of all places, and 'take a vacation,' I expect that she is fine. You could call her."

Anna blew out a breath. "Okay. I tried calling her today, but her cell number isn't working, and the house phone was answered by some boy who said that she was outside trying to figure out how to get Christy's car functioning, quote, 'well enough to make Christy go away again,' unquote. He advised me to let her cool off for a day or two before trying again."

He smiled wryly. "Have you met Christy?"

Anna shook her head. "Who is she?"

"Adam's ex-wife. Beautiful, fragile, a little helpless—just the kind of woman most Alpha wolves gravitate toward." He smiled a little wider as Anna let out an impassioned huff of air.

"I am not helpless," she said. "Nor fragile."

"No," he agreed. "And neither is Christy, really. I give thanks every day that my da found Leah as a mate and not someone like Christy. Leah is a lot more straightforward."

"Nor am I beautiful," Anna continued, undeterred.

"On that," he said peaceably, "I think we'll have to agree to disagree."

"Tell me about the music nights?" Anna asked after a moment, though he noted with pleasure that her face had flushed a little because she would have heard the truth of his words.

"Mercy and Bran engaged in a feud over those musical nights," Charles said. "You've met her. 'Stubborn' doesn't quite cut it."

Anna frowned. "Something has to set her off, though."

He nodded. "Mercy doesn't like being front and center. She is a fair musician. She sings on key, but she doesn't have a real voice, and she knew that. But she was pretty decent on the piano."

"She told me she hates piano," Anna said.

"I think it all got caught up in the mess of Leah's feud with Mercy," he told her. "Leah was merciless in her torment of Mercy, restrained by two things."

He held up a finger.

"My da made it clear that anyone who actually physically harmed her was answerable to him. And Mercy's foster father, Bryan, was a scary bastard when he was angry. It took a lot to get him there, though, and Leah was very careful to skirt just on the edge of that. Mercy made it easier for Leah because Mercy always retaliated—and that muddied waters that would otherwise have shown Leah clearly at fault."

Anna grimaced in sympathy, so he added, "And there is this, too—usually everyone ended up feeling sorrier for whoever had pulled Mercy's wrath down upon their heads than they did for Mercy herself."

She laughed. "The shoe thief." And she lowered her voice conspiratorially. "The chocolate Easter bunny incident."

"Exactly," Charles said. "To be fair, my da, he believes in trial by fire. No one will ever again be able to maneuver Mercy into being blamed for something that wasn't her fault. Leah taught Mercy that revenge has to wait until the right moment but that justice can be satisfied without dying for it."

"That's *fair*?" Anna asked.

Charles nodded. "Mercy wanted to believe that the world was a just place—and she can turn into a coyote in a world filled with werewolves and vampires. She has no quit in her. She had to learn how to survive—and Da let Leah teach her how to do it. Not that Leah knew she was helping Mercy." He wasn't completely sure that his *da* had known that he was helping Mercy.

"What did you do?" she asked.

Brother Wolf wanted to roll in her confidence that they had not left their little coyote sister alone to face off with Leah.

"I could not override my father's decision," he said. "Which was that we not interfere between Mercy and Leah. Leah, he told me, was his mate—and thus dominant to me."

"So what did you do?" she asked again.

"Whenever there was a chance that Leah would find Mercy alone, without a witness between them, I was there." It had taken work—and if his da ever found out just how many of the pack had made it their business to help him in his self-appointed task, there would be a reckoning. What he had done undermined Leah's authority in the pack, something his father would not have stood for had he known about it. But Charles had learned something from Mercy, too—it's all good as long as you don't get caught.

"So how does that tie in to the musical nights?" Anna asked.

"Mercy finally figured out that Bran knew about Leah and had no intention of interfering. Bryan—"

"Her foster father."

"That's the one," he agreed. "He told me about it because he was worried about what Mercy would do. We both knew she wouldn't just let it alone."

"Of course not," Anna agreed.

Charles smiled. "The evenings started sometime in the 1960s. My father was a victim of a self-help book some idiot gave him for Christmas one year. He decided the pack . . . the town needed some kind of bonding experience. He's a musician—so he turned to music. All of the kids over the age of five would perform on a rotating schedule—pack-related or not." Aspen Creek was tiny, but there had still been five or six children at every performance. "They would be followed by a couple of volunteers, willing or not, from the pack. And finally, he would cap off the night with a performance of his own: music usually, but sometimes storytelling. It made the rest worth sitting through for the adults not related to the kids. By the time Mercy came to the pack as a pup, the evenings were an established tradition." He slanted a look at his mate. "Some of us might have felt that they were a tedious tradition."

Anna considered that solemnly. "There's a lot of talent here, no question. But I've been a part of performances with kids. Heck, I've been a kid in performances. I bet some of those nights were longer than others, especially if none of those kids were yours."

Charles grinned. "Mercy thought so, too. As soon as she hit eight or nine, she rounded up the littles—the youngest, the ones who couldn't carry a tune in a bucket, and the kids who made the mistake of looking at her too long—and made them do a 'special performance.'"

He shook his head. "Some of them were really memorable. Not

always musical, but memorable. The first benefit was that those evenings got a lot shorter because we got through most of the kids—and all of the ones who were really bad—at once. But after a while, she got the hang of it. I think Samuel helped her in secret, because I recognized a few of the songs as his. But she started competing with Bran for best performance—invited the audience in to judge for themselves. He loved it."

"Bran?"

"My da, for all of his faults, has very little ego. He is dominant, not competitive." Anna made a noise, so he had to correct himself. "All right. I give that to you. He's competitive enough. Let me say, then, that he doesn't feel that he has to wipe the floor with a group of children in order to feel like an Alpha. He took pride in her efforts and encouraged her—the way he does. Blink and you miss it—just like this road to our left. Turn here."

She did, and the truck slowed because although the road was paved, it was only just.

"Then she found out that Bran knew about Leah's attacks," Anna said thoughtfully.

"Right. Let me just say that Mercy is fiendish with her punishments. Never get on her bad side. She'll figure out the thing that will irk you the most."

"What did she do?"

"She played the first movement of Beethoven's Pathétique Sonata."

"Number Eight," said Anna. "Opus 13?"

He nodded. "For almost two years, she played it every music night."

"What's wrong with that?" Anna asked. "It's a beautiful piece."

Charles grinned. "You'd think that. And it is. But I hear it in my nightmares, and I imagine Da does, too. You can't play a tuned piano out of tune, but that's the only thing she didn't do to that poor piece of music.

"Every performance was something new. Once she performed with a blindfold. Once she set a metronome up and never once played at the speed of the metronome. Once she played it at a quarter speed and added the other two movements." He laughed at the memory. "People would think she was done, start to clap, and she'd play another note. A very slow note. It felt like it went on forever. But she never quite tipped my da into anything but white-lipped anger." He closed his eyes, re-membering, the smile dying down. "It's not often when Da does the wrong thing—and most of those moments in the last thirty years have revolved around Mercy."

"He's funny around her," Anna said, deadpan.

He opened his eyes to give her a mock glare, but she was paying too much attention to the road.

"Yes," he said. "Funny. Anyway, these were real performances. Boys wore ties and white shirts, girls wore dresses. For what was to be her final performance, Mercy came dressed in cutoffs and a T-shirt with paint on it. The T-shirt was emblazoned with Mickey Mouse giving the world the middle finger." He sighed.

"What did he do?"

"My da knows how to fight dirty, Anna, he just usually chooses not to. He turned to Mercy's foster mother—a shy, sweet mouse of a woman who had just been diagnosed with some horrific human disease—and ripped into her in front of everyone for not seeing to it that Mercy had clothing fit to wear. She cried. Bryan wasn't there—I like to think that my da forgot that he had sent Bryan off on some task that night, but he might have planned his actions that far in advance. Mercy didn't say anything. She got up off the piano bench, took Evelyn by the hand, and led her out of the room."

Anna considered it a moment. "Bran attacked a sick woman who couldn't defend herself in front of the whole pack? Wow."

"Don't let my da fool you, Anna," he said. "Push comes to shove, he is a mean bastard."

"What did Mercy do?" Anna asked. "The Mercy I know wouldn't have just let that stand."

"No," he said. "Of course not. She peanut-buttered the seat of my father's new Mercedes and tricked him into sitting in it."

"Hah!" Anna's voice was satisfied. "Good for her. I'd have paid to see it."

Charles wondered why the memory made him feel melancholy. Probably because he'd liked Evelyn—and watching his father brutalize her, even with words, had been gut-wrenching. And he, like the rest of the pack, had just stood there and watched. Only Mercy had defied the Marrok.

He and Brother Wolf had long ago conceded that they had been wrong not to do something, too.

"The peanut butter," Charles said, "reminded my father that he'd been doing battle with a child. Someone he'd sworn to protect. And because he had felt he was losing that war, he'd hit someone who couldn't defend herself. My da is not humbled very often, but Mercy managed it that time. He brought flowers for Evelyn and apologized in person, then in public. To her, to Bryan—to Mercy, too. After that, Mercy would come to the evenings in that same outfit every time. She would sit at the piano for five minutes with her hands folded in her lap. My father would thank her gravely for her performance, she would bow her head like a samurai warrior, and they were done. It lasted until Evelyn died—about two years, I think—then Mercy sat in the audience, and my da quit asking her to play."

"Is that why he ended the evenings?" Anna asked.

He shook his head. "It was when he sent her away."

Anna knew the story, so he didn't repeat it. His brother had decided that a sixteen-year-old coyote-shifter Mercy might be a way for him to have children who survived and set about courting her. Bran had intervened before Samuel had done irreparable damage to her—or to himself. But it had cost them all anyway.

"We had a couple more musical nights after she went to live with her biological mother. At the second one, Bran concluded by saying that they had served their purpose, and it was time to move on."

"Without Mercy to battle, it wasn't fun anymore," said Anna.

"That's what I think," Charles said. "No one ever had the nerve to ask my da."

"No wonder Leah thinks reestablishing that tradition would be bad news," Anna said thoughtfully. "Maybe we should make this barbecue a onetime event."

"This event Leah thinks you don't want," Charles said, unable to hide his amusement. "She's probably ready to make it a daily thing at this point."

"I can't cancel it altogether," Anna told him after a moment. "If I switch sides again, even Leah will know that I'm playing her. But I think I can get her to make me do all the work for it. I can make it as different from those nights as possible. Maybe no children." She paused. "Or if we never want to repeat it—only children."

Anna was pretty good at getting people to do what she wanted. Once in a while, she stepped on toes when she did so because the instinctive deference that most wolves felt for the more dominant was just missing in her. She was getting much better at dancing around the dominance thing, though.

Leah wasn't smart, but she'd been around a long time. And if she'd trained Mercy—well, Mercy had trained her back. She might see through what Anna was doing because of that. But if Leah made a fuss, he'd take care of it. Brother Wolf liked that idea.

"Stop it," Anna said firmly. "I can take care of myself."

"Of course you can," he said, surprised. "That doesn't mean I can't do it, too."

She shook her head at him, but he knew she was laughing inwardly because Brother Wolf told him so.

"And you tell everyone you don't understand people," she said.

"I don't," he told her contentedly. "I just understand you."

It took Anna the better part of an hour to drive twenty miles.

Since she had become Charles's mate, most of the time she felt as though she belonged here, in the wilds of Montana. Then she'd take a drive with Charles in the mountains and be forcibly reminded that she'd been raised in a city.

True, some of Chicago was a wilderness in its own right, but even in the bad areas, roads could be relied upon to be paved, wide enough to get at least one car through, and she'd been able to trust that there wouldn't be a freaking tree growing up in the middle of the road, hidden by a sharp bend.

If she hadn't been wearing her seat belt for that one, she might have gone through the windshield. Charles, who hadn't been, had braced himself just before she hit the brakes, and she wondered uncharitably if he'd known about the tree.

"No," he said, as if he could read her mind. "I just saw it the same time you did."

"Why is there a tree in the road?" she grumbled.

"That's one of those questions without a correct answer, right? Like when a woman asks if her pants make her look fat." There was no amusement in his voice or eyes, but she knew he felt it all the same, and her lips curled up in response.

She edged the truck around the tree. "At least you didn't say, 'When a mommy tree and a daddy tree love each other very much . . .'"

Charles laughed—and she felt proud of herself, because he didn't laugh easily.

"I haven't been up this way in five or six years," he admitted. "There wasn't a tree growing here then. But it's not a big tree, and aspen can grow three feet a year."

"No one has been up this road—and I use the term loosely—in five years?" she said. "I thought Bran was up here last fall."

"There's another road," he said. "It's probably in a little better shape for most of the way because it's traveled more—but this way is faster."

"As long as we don't hit any trees," she said.

The tree wasn't the only obstacle. Though the road apparently wasn't traveled much, there were long stretches with deep ruts. There were rocks—some the size of her fist, with sharp points that might bruise a tire and cause it to go flat; some the size of a bowling ball, which could puncture the workings on the underside of the truck. In a couple of places grass and bushes had grown so thick that she could only guess where the road was. She'd slowed down so much that she thought they might make better time on foot.

"Get your wheels out of the ruts," Charles advised her in that even voice he had that told her he'd been fighting those words for a while. "You could lose an axle if the hole in the road gets too deep."

She knew that. She'd just forgotten.

"This isn't a road," she told him indignantly, with a growl she hadn't meant to use. "It's just wagon tracks through rocks and mud."

But she pulled the wheel to the left, and the truck tipped a little as the wheels climbed up on the side of the track. Their bumpy ride got a lot bumpier because the bottom of the ruts were a lot smoother than the sides, but the scrape of rock on the underside of the truck happened less frequently.

The road got drier as it climbed out of a ravine, then got mushy again as it dropped over a ridge in the mountain they were, as far as Anna could tell, circumnavigating.

Charles came to alert. Reading his body language, she brought them from a crawl to a full stop before he said anything. She didn't bother to try to pull to the side because there wasn't a side to pull off onto; besides, they hadn't seen another car since she'd turned off the main road.

Charles was out of the truck before she'd come to a complete stop. She turned off the engine and got out to join him.

"Hester and Jonesy don't drive," he said. "So why am I seeing fresh tire tracks?"

Anna looked down, and there they were—tire tracks. She should have noticed them.

She tried to redeem herself. "ATVs, right?" The odd-to-her-city-eyes vehicles were as common in the rugged country of Montana in the summer as snowmobiles were in the winter. "Four-wheelers." Because there were older three-wheeled ATVs. "At least two of them because there are two sizes of tires."

Charles nodded.

"Wait," she said, waving a hand with one finger extended. "Wait. There are at least three. Because this guy"—she pointed to a set of tracks where they cut into the dirt because the four-wheeler turned—"is heavier, his bike digs in deeper in the same kind of soil. All going in the same direction."

"Right," he agreed, and waited.

She frowned at him, looking at the tracks again to see what she'd missed. But no matter how intently she looked around, she didn't see any boot marks, or convenient scraps of fabric bearing scent, empty beer cans, or cigarette butts that might hold vital clues as to who had been traveling this road before they came here.

She narrowed her eyes. *What would Gibbs see?* She might have a minor addiction to a certain police-procedural TV show.

"A week ago we had rain," he told her before she could get too frustrated. "You can see there is still some mud under the trees where the sun doesn't reach. These tracks were made after the soil dried—you can tell by the loose dirt. I expect these were made today."

"And because you got a call today," she said, "it's highly probable that these tracks and the call are related."

"That did lead me to look for reasons those tracks might be more recent," he agreed. Tracking, he'd told her, was not just about what your senses told you; it was also about using what you knew.

He took a deep breath of air. She did, too. She smelled the pines, the firs, and a hint of cedar and hidden water. There was a cougar nearby. She glanced around, looking up in the trees, but couldn't spot it. They were good at hiding, but sometimes their tails twitched and gave them away. Not today.

Somewhere within a mile or so, but not much nearer than that, either, there was a small group of blacktail deer. She caught the scent of the usual suspects: rabbits, various birds, and what Tag liked to call tree tigers because the squirrels were brave and made a big uproar when someone entered their territory.

None of those were what was making Charles look so intent.

"What is it?" she asked.

He looked around again. Breathed in again. Then he shook his head. "I don't know. Something."

"Your spidey senses are tingling," she said.

He gave her a blank look. He had weird cultural gaps, as if there were entire decades during which he had not turned on a TV or talked to anyone. She hoped he had just not paid attention, but the "not talking to anyone" was a distinct possibility.

"Intuition," she said. "Your subconscious knows something that you can't put into words yet."

"From *Spider-Man*," he said in as serious a voice as he would have used if she'd been quoting from Shakespeare.

She nodded.

He took one last deep breath, then headed around to the driver's side of the truck. "Get in. I'll take it from here. My spidey senses," he said, his voice a touch dry on the unfamiliar syllables, "are telling me that we should hurry after all."

"Oh, thank the hairy little men in the moon," she said sincerely, climbing gratefully into the passenger seat.

It wasn't that she was afraid she'd kill them—they were werewolves; killing them in a car wreck at ten miles an hour would take some doing. It was that the old truck was something Charles loved—and every time she heard the scrape of tree branch on paint, she could see him not-wince.

But she understood why he'd preferred her snail's pace and the damage she'd dealt to his truck—he hadn't really wanted to get to their destination.

When there were incidents involving any of Bran's wildlings, it usually meant that Charles had to kill one of the old wolves. She knew, better than anyone, that her mate was very tired of being his father's executioner.

She hopped into the truck and impulsively slid over, rose up, and kissed his cheek. As she settled back and put on her seat belt, she said merely, "Remember not to drive in the ruts."

THE LAST THING Charles thought he would do, on his way into the mountains to (probably) kill one of his da's beloved wildlings, was laugh.

But life with Anna was like that.

Once she was safely belted in, he set out getting to Hester's as quickly as possible. His wolf spirit's growing unease—something separate from his dislike of killing wolves who needed to meet death—rode the back of his neck and told him that they needed to be at Hester's now.

He navigated the track that wound around the mountain with a speed that could have been fatal (to the truck, anyway) if he didn't have a werewolf's reaction time and a familiarity with the area. Anna made small sounds now and then and kept a death grip on the door that made him grateful for the Detroit steel that held up under her hand.

As he'd told Anna, it had been some years since he'd been up here. Once Hester and Jonesy moved in, his da had decreed that this area was off-limits for casual runs. After that, he'd only traveled this road by necessity. But he'd been here often before that, in the truck this one had replaced nearly fifty years ago. He knew where the road turned and twisted, though he had to maneuver around a few more trees that had not been here the last time he'd traveled this way.

The truck roared and growled and occasionally, when he found some of the mud left over from the rainstorm, howled. But he piloted it to the top of the ridge at the edge of Hester's valley without coming afoul of anything larger than a few aspen fingerlings that gave way under the pressure of his bumper.

He paused there on the top of the ridge—a strategic move. He noted the clear-from-the-truck-cab marks that told him the four-wheelers had turned off the track here. Charles hesitated, but the path the other people had woven through the trees was too narrow for the truck. So he turned down the track to the little valley where Jonesy and Hester lived.

As they bounced down the road toward the still, small building, Charles noted absently that the windows were old-fashioned double panes that they should replace with vinyl soon. Other than that, the structure was in good shape. For all that it had been cobbled together over years, the house appeared all of a piece. There were flower boxes on either side of the door, filled with the black-eyed Susans that grew wild in the mountains around here. Those hadn't been here when Charles had helped put in solar panels the last time he'd been up.

He stopped the truck and let it idle for a moment, unhappy with the quiet. But as soon as he turned off the engine, the front door of the house opened and Jonesy emerged.

Hester's mate looked like a throwback to a bygone time, mostly an effect of his hand-spun clothing. His pinesap-colored hair was rough-cut to stay out of his eyes. There were a few leaves and a twig or two tangled in its ragged length.

His feet were bare and mottled with dried blood, though he walked evenly enough. Once Charles was looking for it, he noticed that there were small tears in Jonesy's shirt. He was clean-shaven, though, with skin that looked as smooth as a woman's. Maybe he, like Charles, didn't have much of a beard to shave.

It was impossible to read his expression or his body language, and that made Brother Wolf unhappy. Charles hopped out of the truck and met Jonesy halfway between truck and house. He made a slight gesture with his hand, and Anna dropped a little behind him. He knew, without looking, that she was keeping a sharp eye out for trouble so he could concentrate on Jonesy.

When in the company of the dynamic woman who was the fae man's mate, Jonesy hadn't made much of an impression on Charles. Brother Wolf's intent wariness made Charles think that perhaps that lack of attention had been confined to his human self.

"Charles," Jonesy said, his unhurried voice carrying a Welsh accent stronger than Charles's da's, stronger than it had sounded on the phone. "*Diolch*. Thank you for coming."

He smelled like the fae that he was, a scent so overpowering that Brother Wolf couldn't make heads or tails about his state of mind—not from his scent, anyway. His body language was meek, an effect not detracted from by his slender frame.

He was everything that Brother Wolf would normally be protective of, which made Charles's wolf's reaction that much more strange. Brother Wolf thought they should pin this one to the ground so that he would understand that they could kill him at any time. Charles couldn't figure out why Brother Wolf thought Jonesy was such a threat, but he wouldn't dismiss his other self's instincts. Even if Brother Wolf had never reacted to Jonesy this way before . . . but then Hester had always been present.

Hester kept the fae in line, agreed Brother Wolf.

"*Croeso,*" Charles told Hester's fae mate. "There is no cost to our help for you this day," he said carefully, because exchanging words of gratitude with the fae was dangerous. Having the fae owe him a favor was as dangerous as owing the fae a favor. "My word on it. This is my mate, Anna."

Jonesy glanced up at Anna's face, glanced away, then back, squinting his eyes as if she were too bright to look at. Then he took two quick steps that brought him within reach, and raised his hand suddenly to touch her face with fingers that trembled. Anna didn't move.

Charles had to fight Brother Wolf to keep from knocking Jonesy to the ground.

Anna could protect herself—and, other than the speed of it, Charles could see nothing threatening in Jonesy's action. He had enough magic in his own bloodline to feel it if the fae tried anything with power.

"Oh," Jonesy said, wonder in his voice. "Oh, and haven't I heard that the mate of the old one's son was an Omega wolf? And haven't we all been overjoyed that such a wolf ran in our woods." The look he turned on Charles was pure hope. "Maybe she can help? Hester hasn't been herself lately."

Jonesy might not be a wolf, but there was no question that he felt something from Anna. Charles reviewed all he'd ever heard about Jonesy—which wasn't much. Jonesy was . . . different, even for a fae. Slow, Charles had heard, but watching him now, he could tell that wasn't it. More that he interacted with the world a little askew from how most people did.

Anna smiled at Jonesy and let him touch her. But her eyes were wary. Maybe she was picking up some of Brother Wolf's wariness—or maybe she sensed something herself. But that heartfelt plea for his mate's safety . . . that was something Charles and Brother Wolf understood.

"She saved *me*," Charles told Jonesy. "I don't know what she might do for Hester. Da thinks she might be of some help."

Jonesy frowned. "I don't know if Hester needs saving . . ."

Charles stepped forward a little to put himself in a better position to protect Anna if he needed to. "What happened? Why did you call me?"

Jonesy blinked a couple of times and let his hand fall away from Anna as he turned his now-vague attention to Charles. "Did I call you? I called the Marrok, I thought."

"I answered the phone," Charles reminded him.

Jonesy frowned. Cleared his throat, and said, "You are Charles. Yes. That's right. I remember. Why did I call you?"

He shivered, as if a wind that Charles couldn't feel blew across his shoulders. He bowed his head, closed his eyes, and said, clearly, in a crisp British accent, "She's my caretaker, you know. Hester is."

"I didn't know," said Anna, putting a hand on Charles's arm to ask him to leave the interrogation to her. "What happened to Hester, Jonesy?"

Jonesy's eyes snapped open, and he reached for both of Anna's hands.

Dangerous, said Brother Wolf. *He could hurt her even if he doesn't mean to.*

Charles tensed but managed not to move when Anna linked her fingers around Jonesy's hands. The touch seemed to steady Hester's mate. Charles could see alertness and intelligence stir in the other man's eyes.

Dangerous, said Brother Wolf, but quietly, as if he didn't want to attract Jonesy's attention.

Dangerous, whispered the spirits in the trees. *Ours. Dangerous.* There was a gleeful, spiteful enjoyment in the voices of the spirits who spoke to Charles—spiteful and half-afraid.

Charles would definitely have a talk with his da when Bran got back. They would have to see who else was a lot more dangerous than he'd already accounted them to be. Charles seldom underestimated people, but he damned sure should have been paying more attention to Jonesy than he had. And so should Bran have.

"What happened?" asked Anna, her voice low and sweet. She couldn't hear the warning voices of the spirits, but she was smart about people. She'd know to tread lightly.

"We heard motors," Jonesy said after a long pause, as though whatever lived inside him had trouble with English. "They rode all over. They couldn't find us, not through my glamour, but they wouldn't go away. Hester went wolf, so I followed her. In case someone needed to be able to talk."

He hesitated. "I thought they were just kids, you know? We get them now and again—and usually Hester can frighten them off without much trouble." Then his voice grew lighter, almost feminine, as he obviously imitated someone. "A giant wolf is scary out in the woods. If people have a good way to leave—like a motorized vehicle— they do. Failing that, we can retreat all the way to Canada without crossing a major road." He cleared his throat, rocked back and forth a little, then bent his knees suddenly, dropping a foot or two in height with the motion. Balanced lightly on the balls of his feet, the fae looked up into Anna's eyes. He gently pulled his hands out of hers.

In a hungry and rough voice, he said, "Hester says not to kill anyone." His hands fell to the earth and dug into it. "That is the first rule if we are to stay here. I cannot kill anyone."

And there it was, revealed, the predator that Brother Wolf had sensed from the time they'd gotten out of the car.

Anna held Jonesy's gaze as carefully as she had held his hands. It was something another werewolf would never have done. Looking a stranger in the eyes was the first habit new wolves learned to break.

No matter how tough you are, there are other people who are tougher. Even Charles didn't meet a stranger's eyes unless he had a very good reason—and there wasn't a werewolf outside of his immediate family he'd ever found who could stare him down. But Anna was an Omega wolf who could meet the eyes of any without arousing another to challenge, her gaze warm and caring, like a blaze of peace in a world of war.

Under Anna's peculiarly effective sympathy, Jonesy's body relaxed, and his hands stilled, though he was still bent low in a posture that would be awkward if anyone less graceful had held it.

"These people weren't frightened off?" Anna asked.

Jonesy shook his head. "There was something about them that made Hester say they were connected to the people who've been flying over us."

"Flying over you?" Anna repeated.

He nodded, a gesture that began with his head but continued to his shoulders and traveled through his body to his knees.

"Hester has been worried lately." He turned his face, pulling away from Anna's gaze as if it took a little effort. When he had freed himself, he met Charles's eyes. "She says that there have been too many flying things. Spying things watching our woods."

Maybe it was that Brother Wolf lived inside him, or that his mother had been a magic handler and his da witchborn, or just the summer sun's illumination, but in the fae man's eyes, Charles could see Jonesy revealed for what he was.

The outer man, who was simple and . . . sweet, and the creature that lived inside him, who was not sweet. And that *something* inside Jonesy was powerful, his magic a dense ball of fire imprisoned within. How much power, Charles could not fathom. A lot. The monster saw Charles looking and grinned a bloodthirsty grin, though Jonesy's rather anxious expression didn't change at all.

"Too many aircraft?" asked Anna, glancing at Charles. Either she was oblivious to the monster she spoke with or unfazed by him. With Anna it was a toss-up.

"Normally, there isn't any air traffic up here," Charles told her. He used her words, her gaze, to allow him to change the focus of his attention from Jonesy to Anna—to drop Jonesy's eyes. Brother Wolf had no reaction to that other than relief. Jonesy and what Jonesy was would be his da's problem as soon as Bran returned. "Too remote and the air currents are rough."

But, like Hester, Charles was bothered that they had been getting flyovers. Mostly because if it had been someone just randomly flying over the camp, they would probably have passed over Aspen Creek, too. And Charles would have noticed if there had been an unusually high amount of air traffic over town.

There was a certain amount of drug running that tried to get through to Canada via the back roads of Montana. Sometimes that engendered a few unexpected flights over their territory. But Charles kept track of such things and hadn't heard any chatter from his contacts at the DEA since they broke up a drug-trafficking ring out of Spokane two years ago. There were a few pot farmers, but that was legal in the state now—and no one was currently hounding them.

"Helicopters or airplanes?" he asked Jonesy.

"Flying things," said Jonesy, sounding stressed. "I don't know 'helicopter' or 'airplane.'"

"Okay," Anna said, and Brother Wolf wanted to roll over and bask in the wave of comfort and quiet she sent out. "That's okay."

He didn't think she meant to direct it at him. Anna was still working on controlling that aspect of her Omega powers. There were times when Charles needed Brother Wolf to be alert, especially when his mate was standing so close to Jonesy.

When she got worried about someone, she tended to soothe them whether she wanted to or not. Even nonwerewolves felt the effects if they got too close to her.

Jonesy's face lost the lines that had gathered around his eyes, and the monster inside him became less ferocious.

"How long has Hester been worried about the flying things?" Charles asked.

"A month," Jonesy said. "Maybe a little more."

Shortly before his father had left.

"So what happened?" Anna asked. "Where is Hester?"

Jonesy's face was suddenly twisted and inhuman, and the monster who lived inside the innocent said in a voice that could have come from the throat of a mountain, "WE LEFT HER. WE COULD HAVE

STOPPED THEM. STOPPED ALL OF THEM, AND SHE SENT US AWAY."

Jonesy dropped to all fours, and Charles thought that perhaps his real fae form was something with four feet. On Hester's mate, that posture was a position of strength.

Anna was too used to living with monsters to do more than flinch at Jonesy's volume, and even that had been very slight. The spirits that had been slowly gathering closer as Anna and Jonesy spoke vanished, frightened by the monster's raw appearance.

Charles didn't move, though he felt the vibrations of that voice rising from the ground beneath his feet. Jonesy was too close to Anna, and even Brother Wolf knew better than to increase Jonesy's stress when she was vulnerable.

"Hester sent you home?" said Anna in a soft voice. "That's rough. We need to go help her, right? You need to tell us the rest, so we can do that."

And just as quickly as it had come, the beast left Jonesy's face.

He nodded and rose to his feet ungracefully. When he spoke, it was a half mumble. "She said, 'Go home, Jonesy. Go home. Call Bran. No, he's gone. Call his number and tell whoever answers to come up here. Then you wait behind your glamour for them to come. You go, Jonesy.'"

Charles was aware, because Bran had told him, that Hester could talk to her mate when she was in wolf form. What he found most interesting was that her words—he had no doubt he'd been given what she said word for word—didn't sound like a wolf who had gone feral after she'd killed a bunch of intruders who had invaded her territory.

"Why couldn't she come?" asked Anna. She was still sending waves of comfort—it would take a while before she could get it under control again.

Charles had learned to deal with that. Her power made Brother Wolf rest, leaving the human part of him completely in charge. Sometimes it was wonderful. Sometimes, like when he was in the middle of a fight, it was very inconvenient. But it was no longer enough to throw him for a loop. He wondered if she was helping Jonesy's control, wondered what would have happened if Charles had come here without his mate.

Jonesy rubbed his upper arms as if he were cold, then he took a step closer to Anna and relaxed a little. Brother Wolf didn't like the change in proximity. Not at all.

"She was in a cage," Jonesy said. "An iron-and-silver cage. She couldn't break the silver, and I couldn't break the iron. A trap. They didn't see me." He whispered, "She sent me home."

Jonesy was fae, and whatever kind of fae he was, was powerful. Charles was willing to believe that if Jonesy didn't want someone to see him, they wouldn't be able to. He also believed he could have stopped a bunch of people who caged Hester.

"Where?" asked Charles.

Jonesy pointed to the far side of the valley. "There. Up on the mountain. About two miles from here as the crow flies." He turned to look up into Charles's face, his own bearing an expression of sorrow. "She said I was to wait here because under no circumstances could I be captured."

He looked at them, and said in a whisper, "I could destroy them, you see. But to do it I would have to break my word."

Dangerous, said Brother Wolf, again.

"We made a bargain, she and I. A bargain with your father. A home here in return for never using my power for harm."

So Bran did know what Jonesy was. Charles was going to have a talk with his da about that.

Jonesy dropped his head. "I cannot help you. I cannot go back with you. If they have harmed her"—he looked up, and the monster was back in his eyes—"I would kill everything in my path of vengeance. There would be none who was safe from me."

Anna, brave Anna, reached out and touched Jonesy's face. "She is not dead now," she said. It was a statement, but her tone made it a question.

Jonesy shook his head. "I would know. And they have not taken her from our forest. Not yet."

"Okay, then," she told him. "We will stand as your proxy. If it is within our power, we will bring her out safe. If it is not, we will cause them to regret what they have tried here."

Jonesy nodded jerkily. He caught Anna's hand and brought it to his lips. Charles saw the other male's eyes and knew it was the monster who lived inside Jonesy that kissed Anna's hand.

Charles had to fight Brother Wolf to breathe evenly.

"We should go," he told them.

Jonesy nodded. "I'll wait," he told them. And Charles heard the promise in his voice. "I don't want to disappoint her," Jonesy said honestly.

Hester, he meant. Charles understood the need not to disappoint one's mate.

Charles changed to Brother Wolf's body. The truck would be useless without roads through the trees, and Brother Wolf was quicker than he was running on two legs. It hurt, but he pulled the change as fast as he could. And that meant faster than any other werewolf in the world. He twisted and expanded into Brother Wolf's true shape in the time it took to draw a deep breath.

Not being a werewolf born, Anna changed at the same speed as most werewolves. Given that she could run at inhuman speed even on two feet, it wouldn't be worth it for her to try.

Anna felt it necessary to put this into words anyway. "Go," she told him. "I'll follow. But you'll be faster. Go ahead."

By his rough reckoning, it had been at least an hour and a half since Jonesy had called. He wasn't sure that the speed he had over her would matter, but he wasn't sure it wouldn't, either. He dug his claws into the dirt as he sprinted into the forest.

Brother Wolf chose to take the trail Jonesy had left. Charles felt it was reasonable to assume, since the trail traveled through underbrush and rocks and other woodland obstacles in an unusually straight line and followed no worn footpath, that it had been Jonesy's quickest way home. Which meant that it would be the shortest way from Jonesy's home to where Hester had been taken.

Brother Wolf was a little appalled that Charles had had to work out something so inherently obvious.

The direct route took him across two streams—or the same stream twice. The first crossing was narrow enough for him to jump, but the other, too wide to clear in a single leap, proved to be deep as well. Deep and swift.

That crossing slowed him.

To make up for it, he redoubled his speed—and almost ran right into the small clearing where Hester and her four-wheel-driving invaders had holed up. He managed to stop, but only by making enough noise that it attracted the attention of the trapped wolf.

The kennel that held her had been placed as far from the forest edge as possible. It was constructed of thick metal plates with small, heavily barred openings, presumably to let air in. If he had been making a kennel to hold a werewolf—that would be exactly the kind of kennel he would choose to make.

The thing had taken considerable damage, assuming that the sides of the box were supposed to be flat. All of the sides Charles could see sported bulges where something inside had hit them hard. Through the small opening facing him, gold eyes examined him without favor.

Hester in wolf form was, like Anna, pitch-black, though Anna's eyes were ice blue. In build, Anna's wolf was lithe and graceful. Hester was made for war—though for that much he had to rely on memory. Only a part of her face and her eyes were clearly visible, the rest of her hidden behind dented metal.

But she didn't need anything more than her eyes to convey her cool disapproval—like a librarian catching the gaze of a child popping bubble gum. It had been a long time since anyone had given him a look like that—and he deserved it for making so much noise.

Even though they had not attracted the attention of anyone except Hester, Brother Wolf was humiliated. Charles's chagrin was tempered with amusement and relief.

He'd been afraid he would be too late. That, with Hester captive, the men on the four-wheelers would have already left with her, despite Jonesy's confidence that she was still there. This kind of operation depended upon speed. Assuming Hester was the target, they should have been in the next county already instead of hanging around waiting for Hester's pack mates to show up and take this battle to a different level.

As Charles carefully moved back deeper into the shadows of the underbrush, the wind shifted a little, and he smelled gasoline. He moved a little farther to the side and saw why they hadn't been able to leave with Hester.

The four-wheelers were trapped in the aspen trees that had somehow grown up *through* them while they had been parked. One of the vehicles was six or seven feet in the air.

It wasn't just the aspens, he noted as he gave the sight a more thoughtful look. A fir tree had gotten into the act and punctured the gas tank of one of the vehicles, leaving the sharp smell of gasoline in the air.

He usually kept his awareness of the other part of the world, the spirit world, as closed as he could. He couldn't afford to wander around distracted. If something wanted his attention, it could nudge him—and if there was something bad around, Brother Wolf could sense it.

Seeing the unnatural actions of the trees caused Charles to instinctively open his senses. The land was shivering with joyous anxiety, like a dog whose master has just come home. Power ruffled the hair along his back, and Brother Wolf forgot his humiliation and came to alert, though they both knew that the one who had innervated the land, who had caused the trees to put on a hundred years of growth in minutes, was waiting for them back in Hester's cabin.

Jonesy.

The amount of power that would have been required to shape trees with that kind of speed was staggering.

Dangerous, Brother Wolf reminded him, over his irritation for the urgency Charles had fed him that had made them lose face in front of Hester.

Once he'd accepted the quivering, excited eagerness of the forest, other things came into focus. Beneath the stench of gasoline, Charles could smell meat and blood and the beginning of rot. Someone had died here. He closed down his mother's gift because it was too distracting.

Instead, he relied only on himself and Brother Wolf and reevaluated the clearing. As he and Anna had seen earlier, there were three four-wheelers. Assuming one of them had been carrying the heavy cage that now contained Hester, each of the vehicles had had only one person on it.

That meant that the two men in biking leathers—standing as far from the cage as they could get—were the only ones between Hester and safety. Brother Wolf slunk lower toward the ground and carefully began moving around the clearing with the intention of closing in and taking them by surprise. Still flinching under Hester's reproof, Brother Wolf was utterly silent.

"You should call again," said the bigger of the two men.

They spoke in hushed whispers, as if they thought someone might be listening. Charles thought of the trees growing through their four-wheelers, and Brother Wolf smiled. That would give a person pause, wouldn't it? To be stuck in the middle of a wilderness with someone who could do that would be pretty terrifying. If he were one of them, he'd be wondering what else a person like that could do.

"Helicopter is coming," responded the other man in a soothing voice. "But this clearing isn't big enough now, and our second-choice landing zone is too far for us to carry the wolf all the way. Extraction team is coming to help."

"I heard all that, too," said the big man—he sounded thoroughly spooked. "But Boss will be crazy mad that we only have the one and not both. Wanted both. This one and her fairy mate. Maybe Boss'll just leave us up here for the Marrok to take."

"Edison, just be cool," said the other man, his voice calm and authoritative. "We got the female that's wanted. Not our fault that the male was more powerful than we were told. Information wasn't our task. Someone else's head will roll for that."

And the wind shifted directions just enough to slide past them, bringing their scent right to Charles. Brother Wolf pricked his ears in rage. These were werewolves.

Werewolves attacking Bran's people in Bran's territory.

In the distance, Charles heard the distinctive thrum-thrum of a helicopter. He was out of time.

If they had been humans, he would have handled them differently. But there was only one answer for werewolf intruders.

Even so, it was hard.

He and Brother Wolf were built to make the submissive wolves safe, that was their *purpose* in this life, and the big man was clearly a submissive wolf.

Under any other circumstances, he would have killed the dominant and given a submissive wolf the benefit of the doubt. A submissive wolf might feel he had no choice but to follow the orders he was given. But this one had become involved in a raid in the Marrok's territory. For that there could be no forgiveness.

Tactically, he should have taken the other, more dominant and thus more dangerous, wolf first. But Brother Wolf would have none of it. They could not save the submissive wolf, but they could kill him as quickly and cleanly as possible—would see to it that he never had a chance to be afraid.

Silently he stalked them, using pack magic and his mother's magic and his own skill. When he launched himself out of the trees and landed on the big man, that one's muscles didn't have a chance to tighten before Charles's fangs tore through tendon and into bone that cracked beneath the pressure of his jaws.

While he was killing the first man, the second raised his weapon—a gun that looked wrong somehow—with wolf-quick reactions. Charles had considered the second werewolf in his plans but had calculated that the surprise of his attack would buy him the few seconds he needed to take care of the first wolf.

Someone had trained the surprise out of this soldier. Charles hadn't counted on that, and that was going to get him killed.

Brother Wolf tried jumping aside but let Charles know what he already knew, there wasn't a werewolf on the planet fast enough to dodge a bullet. They could only hope that it wasn't a silver bullet or something big enough to kill him anyway.

But these men had come into this land hunting werewolves, hunting Hester. It seemed likely that whatever they carried would be able to take care of werewolves.

There was an instant of blazing pain so big it had a sound that vibrated his bones, followed by silence.

CHAPTER

3

Charles woke to the sound of stone banging on metal and the human snarl of his mate. Assuming, from the words she was using, that she hadn't joined him in Heaven, he decided he wasn't dead, though he couldn't figure out how he'd survived.

He raised his head—and didn't that feel all sorts of lovely. But there was no blood, so, wincing against the thought-scattering pain, he rolled upright and saw Anna hitting the door of Hester's prison with a rock. He also saw that the man who had shot him was very dead.

He couldn't have been out long because he could hear the helicopter, much nearer now but not yet on top of them, over Anna's chant, "Break. Break. Break. Damn it." She wasn't beating on the kennel itself but the sleek, tough-looking padlock on the door.

A human wouldn't have stood a chance at opening that lock with a rock, but Anna was a werewolf. He rose to his feet, all four of them, as the lock on the kennel door broke.

Ignoring the wobbliness that threatened to pull him back to the ground, he trotted unsteadily to Anna's side and put himself between Hester and Anna as Anna pulled the padlock arm free of the hasp, releasing Hester.

He got a bite in his shoulder for his trouble. It wasn't a nasty bite, but Hester's fangs dug in, driven by anger at needing a rescue. Hester was not the kind of wolf who dropped to the ground and crawled on her belly in gratitude.

"Stop that," Anna said, smacking Hester on the nose with enough force that the old wolf released Charles and snarled at his mate.

Anna jerked her hand back from Hester with a hiss, then shook her hand out. The silver in the padlock and the cage had left blisters on her hands. Hitting Hester had hurt her further. Seeing them, Brother Wolf growled at Hester and drove her away from his Anna with a lunge that the other wolf reacted to reflexively.

Hester growled at *him* this time, her eyes narrowing with rage, compounded by her involuntary reaction to his dominance.

"Charles," Anna said. "Please. Hester—we're trying to help you. Jonesy called us in. Let's get under the trees, where they can't just shoot us from the helicopter before you try to kill each other, okay?" She glanced up at the sky as the helicopter flew directly over them, low over the trees but fast. "Why are they just buzzing us instead of landing already?"

She'd missed the notice that the clearing wasn't big enough for their chopper to land in—probably because the chunk that now held the trapped four-wheelers was filled with big trees instead of a clearing.

But she had a point. Charles had flown enough helicopters to have a pretty good idea of what kind of sitting ducks the three of them were here in the open.

But the helicopter hadn't even paused as it flew overhead.

Hester eyed Anna. Charles saw her weighing the benefits of teaching Anna better than to slap her on the nose while her mate was distracted watching the helicopter.

Charles regained his human form before Hester could do something stupid. She yipped and jumped back. He didn't know if it was the suddenness of his change or the fact that he was fully clothed that had startled her. Neither was something any other wolf could do because no one else was a werewolf born instead of made—and born of two people who both carried magic in their veins. Anna had once pointed out that with his heritage, he was lucky he hadn't been born purple or with a unicorn horn; instead, he got to change in the blink of an eye and emerge clothed all the way down to his footwear.

He decided to ignore both the blood trickling from his shoulder and the fact that Hester had even thought about biting his mate. The pain in his head had subsided, the change speeding the healing with a thoroughness that told him Brother Wolf had decided to draw upon the pack.

He frowned at the clearing thoughtfully. He thought about how the helicopter had acted, searching for something or someone but flying over them as if they were not interested in their people or the werewolves. Or as if they hadn't seen them.

"Did Jonesy put a glamour over this place?" he asked Hester. "And could Jonesy hide your cabin from them without hiding it from Anna and me this morning? Maybe make it difficult to locate from the air?"

Hester snorted and gave him an "of course, idiot" face.

"So," Charles continued, "they can't see us, can't see a place to land, no matter what their instruments are telling them—if they are telling them anything," Charles told Anna. "We'll be okay here for a few minutes. Let me do a quick search of the bodies. I need to find out what he shot me with."

"This," Anna said, pulling the weapon he'd been shot with out of the hollow between the small of her back and her waistband. Up close, it looked like a cross between a gun and a Taser.

He took it—there was still a smear of blood on it.

Anna looked at him with eyes that shifted from brown to her wolf's blue. "I killed him," she said, her voice hoarse. "He hurt you."

Then she wiped her hands on the legs of her jeans, and he noticed that there were bloody marks on the fabric that showed she'd done that before.

She, both woman and wolf, knew how to kill because he'd taught her. The best way he knew to protect his mate was to teach her to protect herself. Charles and Brother Wolf between them had kills numbering in the hundreds if not more . . . but Anna did not.

Ignoring the bodies waiting to be searched, the weapon, and the helicopter, which was for the moment not an issue, thanks to Jonesy, he touched Anna's cheek. With an effort, he let Anna and her wolf see inside him through their mating bond. He left himself vulnerable to his mate, so she could know that he understood what her actions had cost her.

"He hurt you," she said, and this time her eyes were Anna brown and not wolf blue. She smiled, only a little grimly, and told him, "These men came to our territory and attacked us." Her voice tightened, and she said, "Attacked *you*. I have no regrets."

She heard the lie in her own voice and gave him a rueful smile. That was his Anna, tough to the bone.

He'd thought it was a gun when the man had pulled it. Even waking up without a bullet hole wasn't a surety that it hadn't been. He could sometimes heal an ordinary bullet wound pretty fast.

But this wasn't a gun that shot bullets. He took it from her and examined it. Up close, the device looked more like a beefed-up Taser, but there was no sort of cartridge or projectile.

"Right?" said Anna. "It's weird. I thought it might be a Taser—the way it dropped you. A kind of super-duper-charged one or something." Because a normal Taser didn't do much besides make a werewolf angry. "But it doesn't look like a Taser—and there were no wires or anything hooked into you."

He pointed it at the ground and pulled the trigger—and darn near dropped the thing as it grabbed energy from him and turned a small plant into powder. He took his finger out of the trigger and glanced at the pinprick left where something sharp had cut him to fire the magic. He rubbed it a couple of times because there was a numb spot right where the pin had gone in. He'd have worried more, but the spot was returning to normal.

The gun itself felt no more magical than it had before he pulled the trigger.

"Blood magic," he said to Anna—and Hester, who was watching him out of careful eyes. "Witchcraft of a kind I've never seen nor heard of. Isn't Da going to be very, very interested in this?"

He tucked the weapon in the small of his back, just as Anna had. The lingering pain that shivered through his joints was subsiding enough that it wouldn't slow him if he had to move quickly. The dead plant made him wonder why he was alive and kicking—not that he was complaining about it. Maybe it had something to do with the difference in size between him and the plant. Or maybe just the amount of power it was able to draw from him—magic born on both sides of his parental heritage.

He looked at Hester. "Is Jonesy around here?"

The wolf raised her head and turned until she was back where she started. She shook her head.

That surprised him. When the helicopter had overflown them, he'd assumed Jonesy had followed them. A glamour that big was difficult to maintain from a couple of miles out . . .

I told you—dangerous, said Brother Wolf.

"He's holding the glamour over us from your cabin?" asked Charles, just to be sure.

She shrugged and looked around as if to say "the evidence points to yes."

Somewhere to the west, the helicopter finally found a place to land. Unless Jonesy's magic was different than other glamours Charles had seen, the enemy would probably be able to follow whatever trace or GPS had gotten them this far despite Jonesy's spell. Only the Gray Lords working great magic together could confuse technology until it wouldn't work at all. He considered the reach of Jonesy's magic. Maybe their enemy was using witchcraft instead. Though witchcraft and werewolves were uneasy bedfellows, he had evidence in the odd gun a werewolf had used on him that their enemy was willing to mix power.

Under other circumstances, Charles would have waited for the enemy to find him. But the weird blood-magic weapon pushed him into caution. He'd never even heard of such a thing before. He didn't take on enemies without more intelligence about their capabilities.

He did a cursory search of the three dead bodies and discovered no more than that the first dead body, the one Hester presumably had killed, was human. None of them carried ID or had useful clues like insignia or easily discoverable tattoos. Their body armor and weapons (there was only the single witch-blood gun) were good but not custom-made.

It would have been nice if they could call the pack and get reinforcements, but neither he nor Anna had brought phones.

Twice since he and Anna had tangled with the government in Boston, they'd had to go out and rescue federal agents who got themselves stuck in the mountains. The first pair of agents hadn't been his fault, he and Anna had found them wedged in a rocky outcropping on their way back from a horseback ride. Since there hadn't been anything up that old logging road except for a few hikers and horseback riders since the 1960s, he figured they were hunting for him and Anna. They seemed suitably embarrassed when he got them out—and unsurprised by his ability to lift the front end of their truck, which confirmed his suspicions.

But after them, he'd been paying attention to his back trail. The second pair he allowed to discover why native Montanans don't drive over broad, flat meadows high in the mountains unless it's been below zero for a few weeks. Charles got the people out—but he imagined that the SUV might be sinking deeper in the mud even now.

After that, though, Bran had made a rule that anyone heading into the wildling territory could not carry a cell phone. People who disturbed Bran's special wolves tended not to live to regret their mistakes. Bran preferred not to kill government agents unintentionally.

"Let's get back to Jonesy," Charles said when he'd finished searching the last body. "We can make a decision then whether to hole up in the cabin and call for reinforcements or just pick him up and head to Da's house."

* * *

THEY WERE ALMOST halfway back to Hester's cabin when the sound of a gunshot echoed in the trees. Charles flattened himself on the ground as a second shot fired, noting that Anna and Hester had done the same without hesitation. There was something odd about the motion the two of them made, but he'd worry about that after he took care of the immediate danger.

Brother Wolf's hearing told him where the bullet hit in the tree behind where they had been standing. Because it had scored the bark rather than hitting in the middle, Charles also had a nice line of broken bark that pointed back where the shot had come from—downwind, which was why he hadn't scented anyone.

He divested himself of the witch-worked weapon, leaving it on the ground. Then he rolled to his feet and shifted to wolf in the same moment. The next time he changed, it would be slower, but with the adrenaline in his system, he was still plenty fast.

The shooter had climbed a tree to get the best shot at them. But that left her stuck in a tree with a werewolf coming after her. Not that it mattered. As far as Charles was concerned, as soon as she fired the first shot, she was dead. The tree swayed under his weight as he leaped from one branch to another. The unpredictable movement meant the two shots she aimed at him missed—as he'd calculated they would.

She looked startled more than frightened. She had probably thought that werewolves couldn't climb trees. Hunters said the same thing about grizzlies—and that was wrong, too. A grizzly could climb as far up as a tree would hold him. Which was pretty much true of werewolves, and Brother Wolf might be big, but he was a lot smaller than a grizzly.

The shooter was human, and she died quickly, dropping from the tree to the ground with a crash of underbrush. From the tree, Charles saw two more people, presumably more of the team who had been pursuing them. They were taking separate paths toward the place where the woman had been shooting.

Separated by no more than thirty feet of forest, he thought. Only one of them looked up, but it was obvious from his expression that he didn't see Charles, nearly three hundred pounds of werewolf, in the tree. Evergreens were good at breaking up solid shapes. Both of the men had a hand to their ear in a classic I-have-a-communication-device pose.

Charles dropped to the ground much more quietly than the body had fallen. Brother Wolf had identified the one who looked up as the more dangerous of the two, and this time, Charles decided it would be a good idea to take that one out first.

His familiarity with the lay of the land—even if it was half a century old—allowed him to approach his chosen target from the side and downwind. Like the two earlier in the clearing, this one was a werewolf. He was comfortable in the forest—he moved like someone who was used to combat missions.

He went down easily, though, the only sound being the crunch his spine made between Charles's fangs.

The third in what Charles's senses now told him had been a three-person strike team (just as the initial group had been made of three people) had found the body of the sniper. There were too many trees, and the underbrush was too thick for Charles to see him, but he could hear him speak into his communication mic.

As he slid through the woods, approaching the man from behind, Charles estimated about two minutes had passed between the time he'd heard the first shot. He took note of the information the man fed his . . . superior? Or maybe just someone on the helicopter Charles could hear. The copter was still on the ground, but, from the engine sound, it was ready to take off immediately.

"That's the report she gave me just a few minutes ago," the man said. He'd moved away from the dead female shooter and was running now, a path that was designed to take him in a straight line to the helicopter. Charles could have told him that he'd have trouble getting across the wide, swift-running stream that ran between him and his goal.

Not that Charles would let him make it that far.

"Two new players have joined up," the man said, his breath even, despite the speed he was running. "One is almost certainly Charles Cornick unless you can think of some other Indian who would be up in these woods. My team is gone. Presume the other team lost. Pick me up. We are FUBAR."

Charles could hear the helicopter lift, engines purring. Perhaps the man knew about the stream. There was a clearing (Charles was pretty sure) about a quarter of a mile from where he was tailing the man.

Unlikely that Charles could pull down the helicopter. But the man was easy prey.

He'd capture this one, Charles thought. This one was human, so not a werewolf intruding on their territory. Brother Wolf wouldn't insist on his death. This one would be full of interesting information. He slid silently through the forest, he and Brother Wolf on a hunt.

And then the earth rumbled, and the spirits of the earth rose with a howl of anger and loss. Next to Charles, a lodgepole pine that was older than he was, maybe seventy feet tall, fell with a crack that shook the ground again.

It took a moment for Charles to realize what had happened.

Charles understood that some of his choices had just been made for him. Brother Wolf would not allow any of the attackers to live now. The meaty noise as Brother Wolf tore into the last of their enemies on the ground must also have made it through the device the man wore because the helicopter abruptly changed directions, the noise it generated growing softer and disappearing to the east.

Brother Wolf dropped the body, finished with his task. Charles stepped into his human shape and frowned down at the dead man. He had needed to save one of them. One. So he could question him and find out who was sending teams with helicopter backup into the Marrok's territory.

But he would have to find that information elsewhere. Inside him, Brother Wolf snarled back, still raging. The earth roiled again, a lesser quake soon over. Charles took a deep breath and starting walking back.

ANNA DROPPED AS soon as Charles did. She belly-crawled to where he'd tossed the witchcrafted weapon and grabbed it. It was important both as a clue and as a weapon that someone could use against them—as evidenced not only by common sense but because Charles dumped it before he changed so that it wouldn't go wherever his clothes went when he shifted.

A rifle sounded twice. She was fairly certain the sound came from the same place as the initial shots had. Charles had found their shooter. A moment later, she heard a thud as something heavy hit the ground with significant force. She hoped it wasn't Charles.

But worry or not, she kept moving. Once the weapon was securely tucked back in the waistband of her jeans, she crawled to where Hester had dropped in the shelter of the underbrush, where her black coat made her virtually invisible.

"We should get deeper into the shadows," Anna whispered, her attention on the forest around them. She could hear the soft sounds of movement approaching their position. She wasn't as good as some of the old wolves yet, but she could tell distance and direction pretty well.

Scent should be useful, too, and she took a deep breath of blood-scented air. About that time, Anna noticed that Hester wasn't just being still—she was *still*.

She grabbed the wolf by any hold she could find and pulled her deeper into the bushes, where the leaves would give them some cover from any sniper fire. Anna dragged Hester into a bed of old leaves that smelled of coyote and mulch tucked in the lee of a rock the size of a small house.

Sheltered in the overhang of the rock and the leafy branches of a strand of aspen, Anna looked for the wound that left Hester limp and unresponsive. She found it, a darker hole in the darkness of Hester's black fur, a hole in the center of her forehead. Hester wasn't going to walk out of this one.

The wolf's ribs moved, air hissed out, then Hester . . . Hester's corpse, was still. A moment later the earth rolled, dirt sifting down from the rock above. Anna gave the rock a worried look, but, like an iceberg, she was pretty sure the biggest part of it was buried underground. If that rock rolled over, it would be a sign that the end was near and nowhere was safe.

Anna crouched beneath the rock, buffeted by the earth and by the death of the wolf she'd only just met, a death she could feel sliding through Bran and into the pack bonds like the icy burn of a dental probe that left numbness behind. Not as bad as when one of the members of the Marrok's pack itself died, but it was bad enough.

After a breathless second, the earth rolled a second time, then stilled. It was a waiting stillness. Almost, Anna thought she could see the wood as her mate sometimes did, alive with spirits, all of them watching . . . something. Waiting.

She waited, too. But when nothing more happened, Anna turned her attention back to Hester. Anna found the slug caught in a mass of blood and fur at the back of Hester's neck. She untangled it, a small, mangled thing. It burned her hands.

If it had been lead it probably would have killed Hester anyway. Werewolves were tough but not indestructible.

Anna closed her fingers around the slug. Such a small thing to end the life of a creature who had been alive when the *Mayflower* set sail. Powerful . . . ugly . . . and sad.

The fingers of her other hand worked their way into black fur, caressing the wolf who would not care. Anna could hear the faint sounds as the enemies around her died, and she could not feel sorry for them. They were the ones who had brought death here.

But the lumpy weapon in the small of her back made her worry for her mate. She could still see, in her mind's eye, the moment he fell—and only her mating bond had attested that he was still alive. Hester, old and clever, lay dead beside her. In a world where such things happened, Charles could die, too.

It was only five or six minutes after the last tremor before the leaves rustled and Charles, in human form, crawled into her refuge. Light trickled shyly through the canopy of foliage over their heads and touched his braid and the edge of his cheekbone.

This time his T-shirt was black. Usually, the shirts he wore when his magic clothed him were red. The black one meant that he'd known about Hester, Anna thought, either from the eerie *knowing* of her death through Bran's bonds with the pack or from the strange waiting feeling that had followed the last earthquake.

Earthquakes weren't as common here as they were in California, but the heart of the Rocky Mountains was a living thing, and sometimes it moved. But the rumble of the ground beneath her had felt more personal than that.

"First shot took her in the head," Anna told him, her voice sounding abnormally calm to her own ears. "She dropped before the second shot."

Charles's eyes, dark and liquid, watched her carefully.

She cleared her throat. She was a werewolf, she reminded herself sternly, someone who was used to death, the proper mate of Charles Cornick, son of the Marrok. She held out the slug to Charles and pretended her hand wasn't shaking, that her free hand wasn't buried in the ruff of Hester's thick, black coat, clutching the other wolf as if letting go would signal the end of something important.

Her voice was steady when she spoke. "This is what killed her—it looks weird to me. Not like the bullets we shoot."

She forgot to warn him that it was silver. He hissed and dropped the slug, then he took his focus off her face and dropped it to her hand.

Her skin was blistered, she noticed, following his gaze, but that had happened when she opened the cage door for Hester. Now, though, the palm of her hand was blackened and crusted, oozing a clear fluid. She hadn't noticed the pain of it until she saw the burns.

She would heal. She turned her palm away from Charles's gaze and hid her hand in Hester's fur.

"I picked up the witch gun," she told him. "Before I noticed that Hester was in trouble."

He closed his eyes and took in a deep breath, and she shuddered from the sadness that he felt, emotion that bled over through their mating bond. Marrok's son, death-bringer, bogeyman of the were-wolves was Charles Cornick—but he was no monster. He mourned Hester's passing, too.

He murmured something in Welsh, his father's native tongue, then translated for her. "Heaven keep us from the fate we deserve." When he opened his eyes, they were dry.

He touched her face with his naked hand, and she could breathe again. "Are you hurt?"

Yes. Hurt by thinking he was dead, if only for a moment, when the witchcrafted gun dropped him. Hurt by killing a stranger. Hurt by having Hester die without a chance to defend herself.

But that wasn't what he was asking. She didn't think that was what he was asking.

"No one shot me," she told him because that was the truth. "Just Hester. What about you?"

He shook his head. "Not a new scratch." He gave her a searching glance, then ripped off the bottom of his shirt and wrapped it around his hand. Skin protected, he picked up the malformed slug he'd dropped into the leaf-litter mulch that covered the ground.

Silver didn't mushroom like lead; it was too hard. Silver bullets, then, were not as deadly to werewolves as legend would have it. The wounds they made were more like the wounds from arrows than from lead bullets: a neat and tidy hole. Werewolves mostly healed human slowly from such wounds—but as long as the hole wasn't in the wrong place, they survived.

Right between the eyes was the wrong place. Especially when the bullet inexplicably behaved more like a lead bullet than a silver one.

"That's silver," she told Charles. "So why did it mushroom?"

It hadn't really mushroomed, exactly. Instead, it had opened up like a flower with sharp-edged petals. But she figured he'd understand what she was asking.

He frowned at it. "Winchester had a bullet they called a Black Talon that deformed like this." He looked at her. "About the time you were born. It looked scary but wasn't any more lethal than a standard hollow-point round. Less lethal, actually. But scary-looking sells to a certain segment of the gun market." He gave her a rueful look. "When the bullet was famously used by a serial killer, Winchester decided they didn't need that kind of notoriety and took it off the market."

He glanced at Hester, and ghosts moved in his eyes. "Someone figured out how to use that design to make a silver bullet that expands. I remember something about . . ."

He closed his eyes for a moment.

One of problems people whose age was in the three digits had was that they had a lot of memories to sort through. She'd noticed that sometimes important items didn't shake out until later.

Anna wasn't hampered by the weight of too many years. "Remember the vampire in Spokane, the one Mercy dealt with a while back? Didn't he make specialty ammunition intended for the supernatural communities? Did his company produce something like that?" She'd remembered the reference to the bullet from the nineties that had been discontinued because a serial killer had made it famous.

Charles opened his eyes and smiled at her. "Yes. That's what I was looking for. You are useful to have around."

"Back atcha," she told him. "And there was some connection between that vampire and Gerry Wallace—the one who paid Leo to make werewolves." She thought she got the name of her first Alpha out in a steady voice, but every muscle in Charles's body stiffened, and he growled.

"Leo's dead," she told him firmly. "But the moneyman, the guy with the money and some kind of political clout who seems to be lurking in the background . . ."

Charles nodded. "Because Gerry didn't have that kind of money— or those kinds of connections. Gerry used those poor wolves Leo made to try to find drugs that work on us. That part was all Gerry. But the person who knew that Leo had been trying to keep his mate alive by changing beautiful men—and you—and killing the pack members who objected, the person who knew Leo would be willing to supply the wolves with a little blackmail and money—that person we didn't find. He's a ghost—assuming he's all the same person. I get a whiff of him now and then. He was involved in that group of ex-Cantrip people who attacked the Columbia Basin Pack. He might have been a part of the Boston business we ran into last fall."

He tossed the bullet in the air and caught it, his eyes a pale gold. And then he whispered thoughtfully, "And here he is again, what did you call him? The moneyman."

Anna looked down at the wolf they had both been trying not to think about too much. Or that *she* had been trying not to think about too much even as her hands tried to comfort Hester and herself.

"Why are we taking time now?" she asked. "I mean, you don't usually talk while there are things to do."

Things like bringing Hester's body back to her mate.

"I'm giving him time," Charles said. "Jonesy."

"He knows she's gone," Anna said.

It hadn't been a question, but he nodded anyway. "The earthquakes. Those were him, I think. We should wait here a little longer. Old creatures are unpredictable when they are grieving."

Anna nodded and untangled her hands from Hester's fur. "Why did they kill Hester?"

Her voice sounded too small, but she couldn't help it. Hester wasn't the first dead person, dead werewolf, she'd been around. Anna had killed another person today. Shouldn't she be getting over death by now? She was a werewolf, right? She didn't get to be shaken by the deaths of near strangers.

She cleared her throat and tried to sound . . . unshaken. Or at least less shaken. "They tried so hard to take her away with them. Why not wait to see if they could capture her later?"

The question he answered wasn't the one she had voiced. "It is all right to mourn Hester. She is worth the weight of your sorrow."

"I didn't know her," Anna said. "How can I be so sad when I didn't know her? I mean, why mourn her and not that guy I killed? I didn't know her any better than I knew him."

Charles raised an eyebrow. "Aren't you mourning him, too?" he asked perceptively. But he didn't wait for her to answer his question.

He looked at Hester, and said, "I don't know why they killed her. I don't know why they came here or what they wanted. But they were looking for her—for a female werewolf. Maybe because she was female, maybe because she was Hester—and maybe because she and Jonesy were up here isolated. They knew too much, our enemy. They knew that Jonesy is fae, though they didn't have any idea how powerful he is. My da has been worried about the threat Hester and Jonesy represented—maybe he should have been a little worried about how vulnerable they were. If Jonesy hadn't called us, it would have been months before someone came up to check on them."

"We need to know if this was an isolated incident, if it was aimed at Hester and Jonesy only. Or if someone—the moneyman, maybe— is targeting werewolves living in isolation," Anna said, grateful for something to focus on besides the dead werewolf, the man she'd killed, and Jonesy, whose mate was dead.

"Yes," Charles told her gravely. "All of that." He frowned. "I could have captured the last one. He was human. But Brother Wolf—" He looked at Hester's body and shook his head. "Brother Wolf thought that it was better to make sure they were all dead."

He raised his chin and looked around them, his head tilted a little as if he could hear something she did not.

"I think we can go now." Charles rose to his knees and hefted Hester's body until he had her in a fireman's carry. He backed out of the underbrush and stood as soon as he could. He waited until Anna was beside him, then started back toward the cabin.

Her mate had grace in the steep terrain, never faltering as he stepped over downed timber or around rocks. He didn't slip, didn't make an unintentional noise, while carrying the huge old wolf.

Anna had been raised in suburban Chicago. The closest she'd gotten to mountains were the hills in Wisconsin, where she'd gone to a few summer camps in middle school. In wolf form, she was almost competent. But her human toes liked to stick themselves under tree roots and thunk into rocks, especially when she couldn't see because stupid tears kept welling up whenever she let her eyes linger on the dead werewolf.

"Should we be worried about Jonesy?" asked Anna. "As we approach the cabin, I mean?"

Charles hesitated, then said, "We should always worry about anyone as old and worn as Jonesy."

Any other day, Anna would have pursued that not-answer. But she was feeling as though she'd been knocked off her feet and couldn't quite find her balance, so she let it pass.

But he clarified his answer anyway. "You should probably stick close. As much for me as for you. Leah was right, bringing you was a good idea. It seemed to help Jonesy."

"How is that?" she asked his back. "I noticed it, too. Usually, I only have that kind of an effect on werewolves."

"No," Charles said. "I would have said that you affect werewolves most strongly. But watching Jonesy with you—you affected him as much as you affect any werewolf. It might be because he's the mate of a wolf. Or some of the fae are shapechangers . . ."

Anna looked ahead to see what had distracted him. They had just topped a rise, and the trees had thinned, so she could see the valley with Hester and Jonesy's cabin.

The happy sunflower-looking flowers that had been only in the flower boxes had now popped up all over the valley, not densely, like the poppies in *The Wizard of Oz*, but in small patches here and there. Maybe she just hadn't noticed them.

"Are those flowers new?" she asked.

"Yes."

They were pretty, gathered together like natural bouquets, not elegant enough to be beautiful but sort of homey and lovely. Warm and welcoming. They shouldn't have caused the dread in her stomach.

The little cabin was quiet. No soft-spoken fae came out to greet them. Charles walked right past the cabin without slowing. He just took Hester to the back of the truck and waited, without saying anything.

She dropped the tailgate, expecting him to lay Hester's body down, then push it in the rest of the way. Instead, he hopped into the bed himself, then set the body of the wolf down as if she could still be hurt if he didn't take care.

Anna wrapped her arms around her midriff, watching him. "He's dead, too," Anna said in a low voice. That's why they had waited. That's why he hadn't really worried about Jonesy when they were bringing his dead mate back to him.

Charles jumped out of the truck and landed lightly beside her. When he spoke, his voice was heavy. "Probably."

And she remembered that his father had left Hester and her mate in Charles's capable hands. Their lives had been his to protect, and Charles took his responsibilities very seriously.

He walked them unhurriedly back to the cabin. She noticed he didn't step on any of the flowers, so she took care not to as well.

The door was unlocked.

The interior of the cabin was tidy and cozy. A couple of rocking chairs near the fireplace, bookcases stacked with worn books, some of them leather-bound antiques, others modern. There was a small loom with the beginnings of cloth woven only a few inches long, a pale sea-foam green.

She could smell them here—Hester and Jonesy—but the only sounds were the ones she and Charles made. The house felt empty, as if no one had lived here in a very, very long time. No breathing, no heartbeat, none of the small, shuffly noises that come with movement and living. That lack didn't keep her from feeling like she was violating the private space of someone she didn't know.

The main floor was all one room, but there was a loft over half of it. Charles climbed the rungs on the wall that gave access to the loft, but when his head cleared the ledge and he could look over, he just shook his head and dropped to the ground without bothering to use the rungs on the way down.

"Here," said Anna. She whispered because it seemed appropriate— as if she were in a library or private garden, where noise might disturb someone else.

Here was a trapdoor in the corner of the room farthest from the door, next to the bathroom door. It was closed, but not in an attempt to hide it.

Charles passed a hand slowly over it, close, but not touching. Looking, Anna thought, for a trap, magic or otherwise. Once he'd finished, he opened the door and used an eyehook on the wall to hold it open.

A narrow, winding stairway dropped into the darkness below. All of the rungs and stringers were carved with fantastical beasts, the stringer was pine, and the rungs were a similar light wood with a different grain. It was a work of art.

It was not so dark that Anna's wolf couldn't see as she followed Charles into the basement. As with the main floor, there was only a single room in the basement, dominated by a large bed in the corner. She heard the sound of a match striking.

There was an oil lamp sitting on a small bookcase next to the stairway. Lighting it seemed to be a complicated matter, but Charles had no trouble. She supposed that he'd lit a lot of oil lamps before electricity became common.

The lamp was brighter than she expected, and, when Charles held it high, it shed enough light to illuminate the whole room.

The bed had no head- or footboard. The bedspread was a hand-made quilt, an old-style crazy quilt, the kind the pioneers used to make when every scrap of fabric had been precious, so every bit had been put to use.

On one side of the bed was a swath of deep-black soil of the sort that would make Asil, the pack's rose-obsessed gardener, hum with pleasure. She could smell as much as see that mixed into the soil were some still-green leaves and flower remnants.

Lying askew and half-buried in the soil on the bed and into the mattress below was a sword.

The sword was no pretty movie prop. It was made for killing things rather than impressing an audience. The blade, short, broad, and leaf-shaped, was nearly black, and so was the cross guard, maybe from age—but it looked as though it might have been charred in a very hot fire.

The grip looked like leather, old and cracking, like some long-abandoned relic. On the very end of the pommel, a rough gemstone the size of a walnut gleamed, a thing of beauty that contrasted with the grim fierceness of the rest of the weapon. It could have been sapphire, blue topaz, or some other deep-blue stone.

Charles set the lamp down and pulled the sword free of soil and mattress in a careful movement, shedding all of the particulate matter back onto the quilt. When he had it free, he laid it back down, parallel to the dirt but a handspan apart, careful to touch only the leather of the grip. There was a solemnness to his action that confirmed her suspicion.

"Jonesy?" she said. Upon death, the bodies of some of the fae, especially the very old fae, did unexpected things—like become earth and plant matter.

Charles nodded.

"You knew he would do this?" she asked. "That's why we waited?" She didn't know how she felt about that.

Charles met her gaze. "No. Yes. Maybe. I think I expected that he would destroy this mountain and possibly much more than that—especially if he had an audience. I wanted to give him time to make a different decision, to keep his word to Hester, that he would not harm anyone."

CHARLES CALLED HIS da's house from the house phone and organized a cleanup crew. He'd been lucky that Sage had answered: she was all business; there was none of the political maneuvering that Leah was prone to.

Because he was talking to Sage, he could watch his mate through the largish picture window in the main room of the cabin. Anna was leaning up against the truck staring at Jonesy's parting gift of flowers—or the flowers that the earth had given Jonesy as a parting gift.

She had been hurt—and he wasn't talking about the wounds she'd taken from the silver or the ones she hadn't taken from the flying bullets. His mate had been hurt, and, for all his best efforts, he had not been able to stop it.

If she had never become the victim of the Chicago pack's desperation, who would she be?

Would she have found someone else? A boy her age? Sweet and strong, full of hope—unfouled by centuries of killing? Could she have made a home with some other man? Had a dog, a couple of cats, and 2.3 children?

The only thing that he knew for sure was that Anna wouldn't have been crying over a pair of dead werewolves, one whom she'd tried to save and the other whom she had killed herself.

Brother Wolf huffed at Charles's self-indulgence. *And maybe she'd have been crying over the death of someone else she couldn't save. Grief is not the sole purview of werewolves.*

Even more indignantly, Brother Wolf continued, *Maybe she'd have found a serial killer to marry, maybe she'd have married a gentle soul like herself and always wondered why she was so bored. But she didn't. She found us. She didn't need to find anyone else.*

Charles felt Brother Wolf stir restlessly inside him until he found some surety amidst Charles's guilt.

She would have found us even if she had never met Leo or Justin. There was no doubt in Brother Wolf. *She has always been ours. She will always be ours.*

"Charlie?"

Sage's voice was a tentative question where she'd been all business before. The change brought his attention back to their conversation.

"Yes?"

"Have you heard from Bran? I mean, we all felt her die through him. Leah thought he'd call the house to see what happened, but he hasn't. She tried his cell, but it went right to voice mail. I know he's supposed to be out of the country, but his phone is a satellite phone. It should work wherever he is."

Charles frowned. "Both of us left our cell phones at home. They're in the office—you can check to see if he called."

"We know, we did. And there's been nothing. We were hoping that maybe he'd gotten in touch the other way."

If something had happened to his phone, Bran could talk to his pack mind to mind. He couldn't hear them in return, but it was still a handy thing.

"No." And wasn't that odd? And unlike Bran. Almost as unlike Bran as taking a vacation in Africa.

Sage squeaked, then Tag's soft voice said, "What are you doing with Hester's body and Jonesy's . . . leftovers? He was the sort who wouldn't leave a body."

Charles paused. He'd been going to bring Hester back for cremation and burial—the same as for any pack member who had no other family to make decisions for her. Tag sounded like he knew Hester and Jonesy a lot better than Charles did, better enough to know what would happen to Jonesy's body.

"What do you think we should do?" he asked, because Tag wouldn't have voiced the question without having an opinion.

"Hester's people burned their dead with their homes and possessions—freeing their spirits from the mortal world." Tag was enough of a Celt to make that sound poetic and stubborn enough that he would insist on it now that Charles had asked him his opinion.

Charles shouldn't have asked.

"It's high summer," he told Tag. "The cabin is in the middle of the forest. If we start a fire here, we'll have the whole forest up in smoke."

Tag made a negative sound. "All due respect," he said, "but that cabin had a firebreak all around it. I recleared it this spring myself. We had rain last week, so the underbrush is damp. If we light it at night, we can keep an eye out for stray sparks."

Tag had been Bran's contact with Hester and Jonesy, Charles realized. Bran liked to do that. Give the wildlings some contact in the pack other than himself in the hopes of helping the wildling to remain stable. Usually, that other person was Charles, Leah, or Asil. If not one of them, he should have at least picked a wolf more stable than Tag, who was nearly a wildling himself . . . but if the two wolves had known each other from an earlier time, it would make some sense.

Outside, Anna pulled the emergency blanket out of the truck and climbed into the truck bed. She shook the blanket out, then, with a graceful flick of her wrists, flipped it to cover Hester.

"She was old," Tag was saying. "And tough. She survived things that would make your red fur turn gray—and she did it with style. On her own terms. She deserves what we can do for her."

"I agree," Charles said. "Tell Sage I've changed my mind. We'll still gather all the pack up here to check things out—but it will be a funeral, too. We'll need food and drink. Fuel enough to burn the house to the ground."

"Gasoline and diesel?" Tag asked as Anna came into Hester's living room.

"Ask Asil," said Charles.

"Asil?" Tag said doubtfully. "He's old. Older'n me. What's he know about setting a house on fire?"

Sage said something that Charles couldn't quite catch.

"Oh, okay," said Tag. "That's all right, then. I'll make sure Asil knows he's in charge of the fire. No worries. We'll organize this end of it."

Sage took the phone back. "Don't worry," she said dryly. "*Leah and I* will organize this end of it."

The pack came by twos and threes, on four-wheelers, on motorcycles, or in various four-wheel-drive vehicles. Tag came on his backhoe.

They retrieved the invaders' bodies first. Those went into Charles's truck, all six of them, while Hester's body was removed to the cabin. By the time they'd finished with that, the whole pack was present.

Charles put Leah in charge of figuring out how to get the four-wheelers, now grown into the forest, out, without leaving obvious signs that magic had been worked there. It was obviously the most difficult job and, to his surprise, she tackled it with enthusiasm.

He'd flattered her, he realized, in front of the pack. And as a result, she hadn't even resented his giving her orders. Maybe Anna was right when she said that Leah wasn't the only reason he and his stepmother had a difficult time with each other.

Leah grabbed a half dozen wolves and, eventually, several chain saws. It had taken a few hours, but Sage's SUV held the cage Hester had been trapped in as well one of the four-wheelers. Leah's truck held the other three—chopped up into parts. Even removed from the forest, the mangled vehicles were an odd sight. Desultory leakage of various fluids attested that they had been running, but all of them had freshly sawn tree bits growing through the metal.

Charles didn't know exactly what he was going to do with them. What he wasn't going to do with them was stage them in his father's backyard as art pieces—as Sage had advised.

Tag's suggestion of finding out who they belonged to and giving them back was a better one, though the manner Tag wanted to do it in seemed a bit complicated. And violent.

Brother Wolf was in agreement with Tag.

While Leah's team took care of the four-wheelers, Charles set most of the rest of the pack clearing the area around the cabin of anything burnable. He sent the rest out to find any evidence of the invasion, anything that would hold a clue as to who these people were and what they had been about. He didn't expect them to find much; the people he'd killed today had seemed pretty professional. Professionals don't leave clues if they can help it.

That's why he was surprised when Asil came back almost immediately to report that he'd found electronic surveillance equipment up in the trees. Charles asked Asil to let the other evidence-hunting wolves know to look for more electronics. Once that was done, Charles pulled Tag off his backhoe and recruited Anna to help the two of them.

He and Tag because they knew what they were looking at when it came to tech. Anna because she kept him balanced.

The events of the day—the fact that Hester and Jonesy had died while under his protection—had left Brother Wolf beside himself.

Most of the pack were afraid of him for one reason or another. Normally, it would not have been a problem, but now the others could sense Brother Wolf's anger. Their increased fear enraged Brother Wolf more, creating a nasty snowball effect.

Anna took the edge off everyone's emotions, so he didn't end up killing some idiot for the crime of stepping in front of Brother Wolf at the wrong time. Some idiot that he was supposed to be taking care of for his da, who had not contacted anyone about Hester's death.

Brother Wolf didn't like that they hadn't heard from Da, either.

On the good side, as it turned out, none of the battery- or solar-powered surveillance equipment they found was functional.

"Jonesy probably zapped them," said Tag from twenty feet up in a lodgepole pine, where he was using a battery-powered drill to extract a camera from its perch in the tree. "He should have told Hester, but he didn't always tell her everything. He didn't like to worry her. Having awesome godlike power meant that nothing much worried *him* even if it should have."

"Zapped," said Charles dryly.

Tag made a popping sound with his mouth. He liked to sound dumb, even in front of people he knew were wise to him. "Zapped. That's why the innards are all melty-like and the out-ards are untouched. Only way I can think of to do that is magical zapping."

He'd gotten the camera off the tree by that point and opened up the casing. None of the electronics was store-bought. This was equipment built from components by someone who knew what they were doing. That meant that someone, some person, had touched the insides with their hands.

Tag brought the opened camera to his nose for a good smell, reclosed the casing to preserve the scent, then tossed it down.

Charles caught it, then took a moment to reopen the casing and get a good smell of the ruined camera himself. Outside, it just smelled of the forest, but inside . . . the faint ozone of zapped electronics and the peppery smell of the man who'd put this one together.

All in all, there had been three people who had worked on the custom electronics placed around Hester's cabin. All of them human—and one of them lay dead in Charles's truck bed. But the other two were still at large. He'd know them by their scent when he ran into them again. Tag's nose was pretty good; he'd know them, too. So would Anna.

But he didn't bother handing her this camera—she'd already gotten the scent of the three people from the other equipment they'd found. If he could count on Tag's letting him know if he found someone different, Charles wouldn't have to have Brother Wolf check each one out. But Tag was Tag. Tag took great pride in letting you fall if you leaned on him too much.

"You knew them pretty well," Anna observed to Tag in a gentle voice. "Hester and Jonesy."

Tag had been ready to drop down, but at Anna's gambit, he paused, hanging from a branch, like a nearly seven-foot-tall orange-maned monkey, swinging gently. He nodded at Anna's comment without looking at her.

"You could say I knew them," he said, dropping a hand to scratch at his head, his body as relaxed as if he were standing in the living room—or, Charles thought, dangling a thousand feet over an abyss. You didn't get a permanent spot in the Marrok's pack if you could function properly on your own.

"Hester better than Jonesy," Tag told Anna. "Hester and I were lovers a few centuries ago." He paused to consider that, his body stilled—so the swinging had been on purpose. Eventually, he added, "Give or take a few centuries, I guess. She tossed me back in the sea, figuratively and literally speaking as it happens, but we stayed friendly anyway, mostly because she fished me out so I didn't drown. Then she found Jonesy."

He loosed his grip with seeming carelessness that nonetheless gave him a clear drop despite the hazards of the proliferation of tree branches and small trees between him and the ground. He landed lightly on his feet for such a big man jumping from thirty feet up, though he took a little hop like a gymnast who hadn't quite stuck the landing.

An accident of position had Tag meeting Charles's eyes, just as he landed.

Brother Wolf thought it would be interesting to pit himself against Tag. In Tag's suddenly gold eyes, Charles saw the same desire. Tag was a little bit afraid of him, Charles knew. Other wolves might have let that fear cow them, but not Tag. Fierce joy and love of battle sparkled through the pack bond they shared. *Wouldn't it be fun?* Tag's wolf asked, and Brother Wolf agreed heartily.

Sometimes Brother Wolf was as crazy as all the rest of the wolves in his da's pack.

"Another time," Charles told Tag and Brother Wolf both. "Someday when there isn't a job to do."

"Just for fun," agreed Tag.

Anna looked back and forth between them and rolled her eyes.

"I guess since Hester fell for both Jonesy and me, she had a thing for dangerous men," Tag told Anna. He grinned, but there was an edge to it that might have had something to do with the exchange with Charles, or it might have been grief. Or both. "Jonesy was all right back then," he said. "Mostly. Mostly all right. But there was a dustup with some of his people, some of whom died who shouldn't have. He went from being wobbly at times to full out tilt-a-whirl. Hester took care of him."

"I thought Hester was supposed to be wobbly, too," said Anna. "Though she seemed pretty sharp today."

"Hester is . . . was as stable as me," Tag told her. "Well, no. Better than I am." He looked at Charles for a moment, then shook his head. He tipped his chin toward Anna. "As sane as you are."

"She tried hunting Da down last time he was here," Charles said dryly. "Sane people usually don't try that."

Tag gave him an agreeable look under his brow. "Hester and Bran, they went out of their way to make Hester sound crazier than she was. Especially if Jonesy was having troubles, more than usual. Make sure that no one except he or I came up here. Keep everyone wary of Hester. Like all the wildlings, they were here on sufferance, and the Marrok's power kept the other Gray Lords from bothering Jonesy. If Bran made them leave, they would have been on their own, and that would have been disastrous. For everyone."

"*Other* Gray Lords," Charles said.

Tag made a noise. "Well. Well. He wasn't a Gray Lord, not really. Not by his choice, anyhow. But with his parentage, it wasn't something he could easily get out of. And if any of the fae with an ounce of sense had talked to Jonesy this past fifty years, they'd have hunted him down and killed him. Had to. They take care of their problems, same as us."

"Would they?" asked Anna. "Did they? Do you think this was something aimed at Jonesy because one of the fae found out he was here?"

Tag pursed his lips, but before he or Charles could say anything, Anna was already shaking her head. "No. Sorry. This was a werewolf thing—werewolves working with humans and technology." She indicated Charles's already mostly filled backpack. "A Gray Lord wouldn't need technology to spy on someone."

"Maybe, maybe not," said Charles. "It's too early to rule anything out. It doesn't look like it from where we are standing, but that could change."

"A Gray Lord might put all the cameras in place and zap them himself, just to watch us run around like half-wits," muttered Tag. "Some of those guys are really off-kilter."

Charles took pride in the self-control that allowed him not to respond to the maybe-unintentional irony in that statement. His self-control was aided by the short time it had to stay strong because, from somewhere out of sight, Asil called, *"I've got another one up here for you techies.* Está roto. *What is it you said about the last one, Tag? Pretty borked. This one is pretty borked, too."*

"Coming," Tag called back.

The three of them headed toward Asil. Ducking through some underbrush, they came upon a fresh break in the ground some three feet across, fifteen feet long, and maybe twelve feet down. Probably the crack was due to Jonesy's earthquakes. Roots were stretched from one side to the other, the damage from the sudden wrenching obvious. One tree leaned precariously, its root ball rising out of the otherwise stable side of the tree.

Next storm or heavy snow, and it would fall, Charles judged. Several hundred years of life now dying a slow death. It was not the oldest fatality this day, nor the only tree to fall. But Charles was tired of death, and the trees were entirely innocent.

Brother Wolf wasn't tired of death, just tired of the deaths of those who had belonged to them, who were theirs to protect. He would be happy to kill all of the ones responsible for this attack on their territory. Very happy.

Anna slipped her hand under Charles's tee, just at the small of his back, and let her fingers rest against the skin there. Brother Wolf relaxed. Anna made Brother Wolf happier than killing their enemies would have.

"Not sure it wouldn't have been smarter to have put Jonesy down when he went funny," Tag said thoughtfully, looking at the damage. "Lugh's children are too damn powerful by half to let run around without the sense God gave a goose. But he was Hester's mate, and she wouldn't have survived his death any more than he survived hers." On the last word, he jumped across the broken ground.

Charles waited for Anna to make the jump. She had no trouble with it, and he didn't expect her to, but some things were ingrained. And he liked to watch her move. She was economical, so much so that it was easy to underestimate just how strong she was. He liked that about her, the way she could pass for human. It made her safer.

As he jumped, part of him was locked onto how well Anna's jeans showed off her muscular curves, part of him noted that she still had that witchcrafted gun tucked in the waistband of her jeans, but the biggest part of his attention was still stuck on Tag's rambling dialogue. "Lugh's children," he'd said.

There was only one Lugh Tag could have been talking about when referring to a fae. Charles had met a son of Lugh once. In Boston. He'd rather that none of the ancient fae god's progeny had ever been located within a thousand miles of his home.

He regretted Jonesy's death, but the chasm, small as it was, gave evidence of how much more Hester's death could have cost his pack. He thought of what he would do if someone killed his Anna—and part of him, Charles and Brother Wolf both, thought the less of Jonesy for not defying Hester's wishes and laying waste to the world for her sake.

"Finally, children. I had despaired of you reaching me in this century." Asil's voice came from somewhere in the mass of evergreen branches directly over their heads. "Your slowness has not been without benefit, however. It allowed me leisure to locate three more devices of some sort in a direct line from this one in this tree. Our enemies were *very* industrious."

OVER THE COURSE of the next few hours, if they didn't find all of the electronics the invaders had left, they probably found everything within a mile of Hester's house. Charles was, at least, absolutely certain that the pack left nothing any human-based investigators would be able to find.

"You seem to be awfully worried about human authorities," commented Asil, dusting off the dirt and debris that an afternoon of tree-climbing had left on him. "Do you think this might be the US government who dropped in to visit?"

Sage, who was seldom to be found too far from Asil if he was present, looked at Charles, echoing Asil's question without speaking a word.

"I don't," Charles said. "At least not directly. As far as I can tell, the government is as happy with werewolves as they have ever been. But a government is made of individuals, and there are plenty of those who are afraid of us, of the fae, and all the other things they know are out there in the night."

"Can't blame them," said Sage softly. "They call us monsters for a reason—and werewolves are just the tip of the iceberg. I could tell you some stories . . ."

Sage had her own nightmares suffered at werewolf hands. That his da had found out about her and rescued her as soon as he heard didn't mean that she loved being a werewolf any more than most of those who'd been Changed against their wishes.

Anna—who, as far as Charles could see, seemed to have embraced her wolf without bitterness—gave Sage a sharp look. "Hating all werewolves or fae makes as much sense as hating all humans," she said mildly.

Asil smiled at her, a smile both patronizing and affectionate. "Ah," he told her. "But you are a child of your generation. Raised by people who grew up in the 1960s and taught that people are not to 'be judged by the color of their skin, but by the content of their character.' That profiling by race, religion—or species—is anathema, no matter how useful."

If Asil had realized his expression was also wistful, doubtless the old Moor would have found a different smile for Anna.

"Werewolves are a bit more frightening than a black man in an all-white restaurant," said Sage.

Anna pursed her lip. Her father was a high-profile liberal lawyer who'd started his practice defending protestors, which gave her a certain perspective on the subject.

"Not to someone raised in ignorance," she said. "The unknown is a lot more scary than something you understand, no matter how bad that is."

"It isn't the ignorant," said Asil softly, "who fear our kind. And their fear is not baseless. What do you think would happen if Bran chose to take over the government?"

Sage started to speak, then her face went blank except for the narrowing of her eyes.

Asil nodded toward her. "Yes, you see it, don't you? We hear all the time that the fae couldn't do it—they are too few for all of their power. Human weapons have advanced unimaginably far since my birth. Eventually, in any match of strength to strength, they would win an outright battle with any of us on the supernaturally endowed spectrum. The vampires . . . I think the vampires believe that they are in control. That spider in Europe could no more resist allowing the government to run without unwitting slaves in key positions than he could resist . . . poking his fingers into the Nazi pie in the middle of the last century. But if Bran wanted it?"

Anna, her eyes bright, was still mouthing "supernaturally endowed spectrum" at Charles, when Sage murmured, "Bran is more subtle than the vampires. Even Bonarata. Bran is . . . like everyone's favorite big brother. He's charming. He looks so harmless until he doesn't. And you know that he really does care."

"My da," said Charles dryly, "Dictator at Large."

"Well, yes," said Anna, recovering from her amusement. "Of course, he could make a fine stab at it. But since he really *doesn't* care about anyone who doesn't turn furry in the full moon, I'd rather he leave the government to the humans."

"And so would Da," agreed Charles.

"But if he wanted to . . ." said Sage, her voice soft.

"No," said Charles firmly. "It wouldn't be as easy as Asil makes it sound."

"I'd help," said Asil.

But the seriousness had gone out of the moment. Anna made a pithy sound.

"Seduce the women," she said, her accent a flawless copy of Asil's. "It is the women who run everything, anyway. If a man's wife says, 'do this,' he does. Simple. If you want a government to do thus and such, get their wives and mistresses on board."

It sounded like a quote. Charles gave Asil an interested look.

"I was teaching Kara about your Revolutionary War," Asil said with dignity.

Sage grinned—she was a beautiful woman, but her grin transformed her face. Made her less beautiful and more approachable. "Or how Benjamin Franklin's skill between the sheets managed to win the war."

"Which is true," said Asil.

"True-ish," admonished Sage. "And, in current times, incredibly sexist. A lot of the people in power are women. What are you going to do, seduce their husbands?"

Asil smiled slowly, his eyes bright. "Want to watch?"

"Getting back to your question, *children*," said Charles, deliberately using the word Asil liked so much, "assuming we can put world domination, sexual politics of the eighteenth century, and flirting aside for the moment, I don't think this is a government operation. Too much money in some areas and not enough in others. That doesn't mean there isn't some glory hound watching for a chance to change the game. I don't want to give anyone something they can hold over us."

He dumped his overfull backpack on the bed of the nearest convenient truck, and Anna did the same with hers. Laid out in the open, it made an interesting pile in several ways.

Tag pursed his lips. "Helicopter. Trained men and werewolves. Twenty thousand dollars of equipment. You're right: too much money to be casual but not enough for official government."

Anna sorted out the tech by nose until she had three piles. "Tech guy the first," she said, pointing at one pile. "Tech girl" was the second pile. "Tech guy the second" was the third pile. "Just guessing, but from the wear and tear and the scent of tech gurus, this was set up in three waves."

Tag nodded his agreement. "That first group was out here last fall—you can see the effects of winter—maybe eight months ago. The second was put out this spring. The third batch looks new. Two weeks, maybe a month. Each set of equipment is topflight, bleeding-edge stuff. I was off by maybe ten thousand on the cost." He tapped his finger on the first group. "Prices on this have gone down since last winter. Someone spent thirty grand on tech to keep watch on Hester and Jonesy—who mostly didn't do anything interesting."

"I bet they wanted to know what they were going to be dealing with," Sage said thoughtfully. "I mean, they came here specifically for Hester—that damned cage was meant to hold a werewolf. Maybe they were being careful, trying to make sure they knew what they were getting into."

Tag grinned suddenly, showing his teeth. "Jonesy. I didn't catch it until it was all laid out." He looked at Charles. "Do you see the pattern?"

He did.

"Jonesy found all of the tech when it went up—probably right away," Charles said, thinking of the forest spirits. The fae probably had some other name for them, interacted with them in some other fashion than Charles did, but they had been much too in tune with

Jonesy and with his death for them not to have had some kind of contact with him. "The oldest set were simply disabled, the power destroyed with a surgical blow."

"Zap," said Tag, popping his lips.

"The second bunch were damaged a little more severely," Charles said.

"Double-zap," said Tag.

"That is not a technical term, I hope," murmured Asil.

"Only the most technically advanced people can use 'double-zap' correctly," Anna told Asil sotto voce. "You and I shouldn't try it."

"By the third wave," Tag said, "Jonesy was insulted. He was a chess player—and these idiots had used the same strategy three times in a row and expected different results. Thus this third wave of tech is not just zap or double-zap but truly borked."

"So why didn't he tell Hester about them?" Anna asked. "Or did he? Did she know they were being watched? Why didn't she tell Bran?"

Somberly, Sage said, "The only people who know the answer to that are dead."

Charles found himself considering that last question. Tag said Hester was faking her troubles so that she could protect Jonesy. He said, and Charles agreed with him, that probably Bran had known that.

So why hadn't she called his father about the planes that had been flying over them? Had she known they had people trying to spy on them?

But as Sage said, the only people who knew that were dead. Unless, he thought, Hester had called his da. He considered that for a moment—and decided that, while certainly possible, the idea that his da had known about someone's flying over Hester's cabin and not alerted the pack carried some uncomfortable possibilities with it.

THE GROUND AROUND the wooden building was raw where the backhoe Tag brought up had done its work. After careful consideration, the chain saws that had cut the ATVs free had been employed again to cut down a tree that stood midway between the house and the rest of the forest. Better to lose one centuries-old tree than thousands of them.

They laid Hester on the bed next to the remains of her mate. The room was too small to hold the pack, so they entered the cabin in twos and threes while the wind played background music, with the trees as its instrument.

Charles let Leah and Anna sort the shuffle of pack and sought out Asil, who stood a little distance from all the hustle.

"Fire," Charles said, "may be a purifying force. But it is not one of the usual methods of destroying fae magic."

Asil made a considering noise. "Do you think there are fae artifacts in that cabin?"

"I didn't feel anything when Anna and I were in there earlier," he told the old Moor honestly. "But according to Tag and to Brother Wolf's independent assessment, Jonesy was a Power. I think he could hide his toys well enough that they would not attract my casual attention."

Asil said nothing for a moment. "You think I could find them?"

Charles chose his words carefully because flattery was not something he did. Anna had (often) suggested it as a good way to get cooperation from Asil—and pointed out that the most effective flattery had only truth.

Charles decided that now was as good a time as ever to test out her advice.

"I think that any wolf who has survived as long as you have has at least as much a nose for fae magic as I do. I would appreciate it if you would come down there with me and help look. I've asked Anna and Tag to keep the crowd occupied with stories about Hester while we go in."

The Moor snorted. "You just want help searching the field for land mines and are looking for cannon fodder."

But despite his words, he came with Charles and slipped into the cabin with him under the guise of paying last respects. It shouldn't take them too long, Charles thought. Tag could tell stories all night, though, so they had time.

They began in the basement.

Asil paused beside the bed and touched the surface of the blanket between the remains that had been people just this morning. Then he raised both hands, palms flat, and said, "*Allāhu akbar.*"

Charles, recognizing the sacred when he heard it, in whatever language or religion, fell still, folding his arms and saying his own prayer, as Asil folded his hands in front of his chest.

Asil's prayer was soft for the most part, punctuated by several calls of "*Allāhu akbar.*" When he was finished, the Moor touched his hand to Hester's hip, and said, "Good-bye, formidable lady."

"I thought that the funeral prayer was only for Muslim people," said Charles.

Asil's face lit with a smile that he was using to hide some emotion he didn't want Charles to see. "But I am a very bad Muslim—and Hester was old. One believes many things in a very long life. Who knows if she was not Muslim in her heart of hearts?"

"You knew her?" Charles asked.

Asil shrugged. "I knew of her—the stubborn woman who would belong to no pack. She killed a dozen wolves—some of them Alphas—before they let her alone. I did not meet her. Bran said that she and her mate wished to be isolated, or I would have paid my respects. It saddens my heart when the great ones die. This world is the less for her passing."

He glanced where the earth lay on the bedding. "The fae?" he said, as if Charles had asked a question. "Him I am less saddened by. I never met him, either, but I have seen too much of what their kind have wrought in carelessness. He was certainly not Muslim, so the *Salatul Janazah* was not for him."

"And yet," said Charles, whose silent prayer had been for both the dead, "Hester loved him."

Asil shrugged. "It is impossible to account for the taste of women." But his eyes were sober.

The first thing they looked at was the sword. It was obviously old and well used and of fae making—the blade was something other than steel. Charles had felt nothing from it when he picked it up earlier. He picked it up again, paying attention—and still felt nothing.

"It is magic," Charles told Asil. "But I can't sense it."

He handed it to Asil, who raised his eyebrows. He took it in a two-handed grip and brought it up and around in a quick practice swing.

"Remarkable," Asil said, dropping his left hand away and making a second, more complex swing with just one hand. "A great weapon," he pronounced when he had finished. "I am sure it has killed almost as many as I have." He didn't say, "I, too, am a great weapon," though Charles had no trouble hearing it.

Asil looked at the blade closely, then let it drop to a less ready position. "It doesn't feel magical to me in any way," he said. "But it most certainly is."

"How do you know?"

"How did you?" Asil countered.

"The blade isn't steel. It is some sort of silver alloy." Charles knew silver. "Or an alloy with silver in it—a metallurgist would tell you the silver content was not high. The fae like to use silver in their magical weapons. It holds the power better than other metals."

"A metallurgist would have to despoil this blade to tell anything," Asil said distastefully. "But that is an interesting answer. I expected that you might have made that assumption because Jonesy used it to kill himself. Such a one would never die by an ordinary blade. But there is a more sure way to know that this blade is *A Blade*."

Charles could hear the capitals in Asil's voice.

Asil turned the blade to the light and moved it until Charles could see three runes set into the blade, all three of them together no larger than a thumbprint.

"This is the mark of the Dark Smith of Drontheim," said Asil, indicating the runes without touching the blade. "That one did not bother with magicless blades."

Charles looked around the room and sighed. "We're going to have to come back after we burn this place and look for anything that emerges unscathed." Maybe his da would be back by then.

"Probably," Asil agreed. "But do not despair, this is difficult magic, even for the fae. I do not believe that there are a dozen such objects of power here."

An hour later, Asil was not so sanguine.

"At least we know it isn't the Gray Lords we're facing," Charles said, holding a broken, decorative hair clip he'd found in Hester's dresser drawer.

"How so?" Asil was emptying out a blanket chest so they could use it to store what they were finding.

"If the fae had any idea of what a hoarder Jonesy was, they wouldn't have bothered with cameras. They'd have broken down the walls and taken everything as soon as they knew it was here."

There were amulets, cups, gems, knives, a spear, four arrows from three different regions, three rugs—two simple rag rugs and a small Persian rug. There was a bone bowl and a handful of coin-like items.

Most of the items held fae magic, or fae-like magic. But the bone bowl was witchcrafted and stank of blood magic as soon as Charles touched it. There was an arrowhead that looked neolithic to Charles—and *something* slept within it. Brother Wolf warned him not to wake it up, whatever it was, because it smelled bad.

There were powerful items, but most of them, as far as Charles could tell, were just junk that happened to contain a spark of something. A bronze knife burned clear and bright with magic, like an artesian well. There was a blue-and-purple pottery jar that made him want to wash his hands after he touched it.

A lot of the magically charged things they found were broken pieces of larger items. Sometimes Charles could tell what it was part of—like the bowl of a clay pipe or the tongue of a buckle. Jonesy, he thought, was not very picky about what he collected. "Hoarded" was probably the right word for it.

The search took Asil and Charles too long to keep what they were doing a secret. If there was any doubt, it was dispelled when Leah opened the door, and said, "Everyone knows what you are doing in there—I didn't tell them, Tag did. Is there any way you can hurry this up?"

Charles hadn't told Tag what they were doing, but he couldn't remember where Tag had been when he approached Asil. Tag, for all of his orange hair and size, could avoid being noticed if he wanted to.

"No," Asil said shortly. "We will be done when we are finished."

Asil liked Leah considerably less than he liked Charles—and he only tolerated Charles for Anna's sake.

On their third search of the basement, Charles noticed an oddity in the soil on the bed—a straight line where there shouldn't be one. With a grimace, he freed a folded piece of paper from Jonesy's remains—a page ripped from a book.

"What do you have?" Asil asked from the other side of the bed.

"A page from *The Silmarillion*," Charles said, opening it. Across the typeset letters of Christopher Tolkien's foreword, someone had written in a jerky hand without punctuation:

Hester Hester says they were asking about the wildlings
there is a traitor and it is one of us Hester Hester

Hester's name, repeated on either end of the message, was written in noticeably smoother strokes of the pen than the rest of it.

Of course there was a traitor, Charles thought. How would anyone know about Hester's isolated cabin if there wasn't a traitor?

"Well," said Asil, who had approached so he could read over Charles's shoulder. "He could have been more helpful. Is the traitor one of the wildlings? One of the fae? One of the pack? At least we know they were looking for one of the wildlings." He paused. "Or all of the wildlings."

A hunt, said Brother Wolf with grim satisfaction. *Hester has given us a hunt.*

IN THE END, most of their finds fit in the blanket chest. The sword they wrapped in one of the discarded blankets. There was no disguising what it was, really, but at least no one would have details. Magical swords tended to have histories and be identifiable to someone with enough motivation. This way, all an observer would see would be him and Asil with random stuff—no details to attract someone (or something) out there looking for the silver shoe buckle of Asmodeus or some such nonsense.

Charles refolded the paper and stuck it in the back pocket of his jeans. They had agreed that it would be best not to talk to anyone except Anna about that note. If there was a traitor, the less said to anyone about it the better.

Charles was reasonably certain that Asil was incapable of betraying his da. It helped that Asil had vowed his loyalty to the Marrok and Bran (as if they were two different people) as soon as he had read the note through.

Asil closed the lid of the blanket chest and turned the latch so it wouldn't fall open when they carried it out. "You know we did not find everything."

"I do," agreed Charles. "I also believe we have found everything we are going to."

Asil smiled. "I do not miss being Alpha," he said. "Especially at times like these I do not mind that you are more dominant in this pack than I. It means that I am not responsible for that which we have found—and more importantly, that which we have not found."

Brother Wolf did not find Asil funny.

"Good for you," Charles said.

Asil's smile broadened, though he did not show his teeth. "Jonesy was a hoarder of the sort who make appearances on TV reality shows. Who knows how long he had been collecting? You and I will be out here as soon as the fire burns itself out—assuming Bran isn't back, and probably even if he is. And we will still not find everything. And there is this, too. Jonesy, whoever he was when the world was young, could make the earth listen to his desires. If I had this ability, I would hide the prizes of my collection deep in the earth. You need to be very careful, or what you'll have is a bunch of treasure-hunting fae invading the mountain, digging for treasure."

He didn't, Charles thought, have to sound so happy about it.

The flat area of the valley resembled a parking lot, but one filled with an unusually high percentage of trucks and SUVs—even for Montana. The three tractors and the backhoe completed the picture.

Maybe, Anna thought, approaching Charles's truck (and though they'd been married for a while now, it was still Charles's truck), *a parking lot of a feed store.*

Her orders were to bring the truck as close to the front door of the cabin as she could so that Asil and Charles could load it with whatever they found in the cabin. Either there was a lot of it, or it had been difficult to secure, because it had taken them a long time to finish.

The truck had been pulled close to a trail to reduce the distance the bodies had to be carried. She almost just hopped in and drove, but as she stepped into the cab, she noticed that whoever had thrown the bodies into Charles's truck hadn't shut the tailgate. Even though they had gone to a great deal of trouble to secure the concealing tarp down. Fat lot of good that would have done to hide the load, with a leg sticking out the back.

Anna had to partially unhook the tarp in order to get at the macabre cargo and move the bodies around until she could close the tailgate.

Dear Dad. She composed a mental letter as she unhooked bungee cords. *Life in Montana is pretty interesting. Killed a man today—it was justified. Really. But just in case, you should talk to your buddies and see if there's a good criminal attorney in Missoula or Kalispell who wouldn't mind representing a werewolf.*

She considered whether or not she should explain exactly what she was up to just now—moving dead bodies around so she could shut the tailgate—to her father, even in an *imaginary* letter. She decided that there were some things he did not need to know.

She pulled the tarp aside—and a horribly familiar scent caught her off guard. She stopped everything and took a deep breath, knowing she must be mistaken. And for a moment after that, she couldn't breathe at all. Once she could breathe again, she unhooked the tarp a little more so she could get a good look at the faces of the dead.

"Hello, hello," said Sage—and Anna jumped.

It said something about Anna's state that she hadn't even noticed Sage approaching.

"What did you do to your hand?" Sage asked in a much more serious voice before Anna could say anything to her greeting.

Anna looked down blankly at the bright purple vet wrap that wound around her right hand. Charles had utilized the time between when he'd used Jonesy's phone to call for help and when help started arriving, about fifteen minutes later (some members of the pack lived almost as remotely as the wildlings), to do a little first aid.

"They shot Hester with a silver bullet," she managed to get out reasonably smoothly. "I held on to it too long when I recovered it. It's fine."

"I got sent over to see what was taking you so long," Sage said briskly, sensing, with her usual perceptiveness, Anna's volatile emotional state and that Anna would rather not expound upon it. Sage was very good at knowing exactly what to say and when to leave things alone. "Her royal highness is getting restless." Though Sage got along with Leah just fine, it didn't spare Leah (or anyone else for that matter) from Sage's pointed comments. "I think she just wants to know what Charles and Asil have found, like all the rest of us."

Sage's voice was beautiful. Born in the Deep South, it flowed out like honey on a sore throat, soothing and sweet. The rest of Sage was beautiful, too. She was tall, though not as tall as Leah, and slender as a runway model. Sage was funny, sharp, and warm at the same time, a combination that let her get away with saying things that a lot of people were thinking—and not getting in trouble for it.

Before Anna could decide to tell her that she knew one of the dead people, Sage rounded the end of the truck and saw Anna's initial problem.

"Ha," she said. "Did the idiots who loaded the bodies forget that you'd have to shut the tailgate or risk dropping dead people all the way home?" She hopped up without a fuss and started shifting the bodies around.

"Some people have no sense at all," Sage said. "And I include Charles in that. Sending you, of all people, out to deal with all the dead bodies."

Anna found herself at a loss for words. Still reeling from . . . PTSD, she supposed, it took her a moment to realize that Sage seemed to be ascribing any oddity in her manner to all the dead bodies in the back of the truck.

Well, she was right in that, if not for quite the reason she thought. Sage hopped out and shut the tailgate. Anna stirred herself and began reapplying bungee cords, ignoring the pain in her burnt hand.

"Oh, I wouldn't do that, honey," Sage said. "They'll probably just have to undo the tarp all over again when they load whatever they found in Hester's cabin."

Anna let her hands drop, and Sage muttered to herself, "Leave it alone. Leave it . . ." She snorted, shook her head, and asked, "Are you all right, Anna? Is there anything I can do?"

Anna made a helpless gesture because, while Sage had been moving bodies, Anna had decided that the first person who needed to hear that she knew one of the dead men was her mate. And because she couldn't tell Sage she was fine. Sometimes living with werewolves sucked—like when it made little social lies impossible.

When she didn't answer, Sage gave her a sympathetic smile. "Sometimes it hits me, too." She looked at the truck bed, at Hester's cabin, then a sweeping glance that took in the pack altogether. Sage closed her eyes and took a deep breath. When she opened them, she said, "What I wouldn't give to live an ordinary life, you know? No monsters. No dead bodies. The kind of life where I could get outraged that some guy is getting paid more than me for doing the same job. That a speeding ticket is enough to ruin my whole day."

Anna started to agree but then stopped and shook her head. "No. Then I wouldn't have Charles. He's worth all the rest."

"Charlie?" said Sage. She started to say something else, but she shook her head and gave Anna a rueful smile. "Charlie sure thinks the sun rises and sets on *you*, that's for sure."

Even without telling Sage everything, the other woman had helped Anna find balance. Just having someone else there helped, someone who reminded Anna by her very presence that she wasn't in Chicago and that there were people here she could trust to have her back.

So Anna had recognized one of the dead men. That was no excuse to break into a cold sweat of memory. He was dead, after all, and memories couldn't hurt her unless she chose to let them. And she was no one's victim these days.

Taking emotion out of the discovery, there were some interesting implications about her knowing one of the men, weren't there? Especially given the ammunition that had killed Hester.

"Are you okay?" Sage asked again. "Is there anything I can do to help?"

Anna gave her what she hoped was a reassuring smile. She did want to talk things out but not with Sage. At least not with Sage first. "You already have, thank you. I was just having a moment—it's been a long day. Let's get the truck over before Leah has an aneurysm."

"Do you think she would?" asked Sage, with interest. "That she could?" She made a happy noise. "It probably wouldn't kill her, but it might get her to cool her jets a little. We could wait here for a while longer, don't you think?"

"Leah's a werewolf," Anna said dryly. "I think she'll survive a little frustration. Do you want to ride over with me?"

"No," said Sage. "I'm also on my way to find Tag and 'make sure the *enfant terrible* has not forgotten where he put the fuel for the fire.'" The last was said in Asil's unmistakable accent.

"I thought Tag was up at the cabin telling stories about Hester," Anna said.

Sage nodded. "So did Asil. But he wasn't. So I'm to fetch him—" The sound of a great diesel engine engaging rumbled through the air.

Sage threw up her hands. "What does he think he's doing with that backhoe?" She hopped on the edge of the truck bed and balanced on it for a moment and looked, presumably, over the cars to where the backhoe had been parked. She shook her head. "I have no idea. None. That man. But I guess I'd better find out."

She leaped, cleared the bed of the truck, and took off running, presumably for the backhoe with Tag in it.

ANNA DROVE THE truck right up to the front door of the cabin and hopped out. By the time she had the tailgate down, Asil and Charles had come out of the cabin with their discoveries.

Between them they carried a small cedar chest, each holding on to one of the handles on either end. Impossible to see how heavy the box was—two werewolves could probably stroll around carrying a VW Bug from the bumpers and not show much strain. Balanced diagonally across the top of the chest and overhanging the sides was something—Anna was pretty sure it was the sword Jonesy had killed himself with—wrapped in a blanket.

They gently set the box down on the tailgate. Sage had rearranged the bodies so there would be some room, but neither she nor Anna had envisioned an entire cedar chest. Charles and Asil unhooked the tarp the rest of the way and rolled it back, working together as a silent team, one on either side of the truck. They were *so* apparently unconcerned with all the attention they were getting that Anna knew they were very conscious of the eyes on them.

They must have found the mother lode of fae magic. Anna glanced at the pack and saw that same realization on the faces around her: excitement, greed, and—on the smartest of them—worry. Only an idiot would get excited about having something the lords of Faery might want.

Charles hopped up on the truck bed and redistributed the dead men again so there was room for the cedar chest. He set the wrapped sword down on the bed and hopped back out. Anna shut the tailgate, and he and Asil rolled the tarp back and secured it.

Charles looked up. "I need not tell you how dangerous the cargo in the back of the truck is," he said to the pack at large. "Neither Asil nor I know exactly what we found here. We're taking it back and putting it in my da's safe room, where it will stay until he gets back. The Marrok will dispose of it as he sees fit."

After he spoke, he slowly panned his gaze over the gathering, meeting the eyes of each pack member until they looked away.

Silence hung powerfully in the air as the pack waited for Charles to say something else. But apparently, he'd said all he felt necessary, because he held his peace.

Asil frowned at him, cleared his throat, and said, in a clear, cold voice that was missing his usual accent, "We do not need to remind any of you what would happen if the Gray Lords discovered that we found fae artifacts in Hester's home. We lost two of our own here, and if I read the signs aright—and I always read the signs aright—we are about to find ourselves engaged in war with an unknown enemy. We do not need to add a battle with the Gray Lords on top of it."

From the back of the crowd, Tag growled, "What he means is, shut our mouths or someone will come pay a visit."

He bristled—and Anna was pretty sure that it was Asil's implied threat that Tag was bristling at. Charles, she thought, hadn't been wrong in his assessment that he'd said enough.

This was the kind of spark that caused wolves to fight within their packs—and could leave them with more bodies. Anna's job was to prevent fights. On the other hand, she was her father's daughter, and any civil-rights lawyer in the country would be on Tag's side of this.

"No," Leah said clearly. It felt as though everyone was holding their breaths. Even Tag paused, his mouth partially open—doubtless to say something that would increase the ugly energy in the clearing.

Into the silence, Leah said, with soft promise, "Asil will not be paying anyone any visits on this matter."

Okay, thought Anna. Give the woman points for courage—if not for brains—in directly giving Asil such a shutdown. Especially since Anna knew, the pack knew, that Leah was scared spitless of the Moor.

"I won't allow it," Leah continued—not looking at Asil. "It isn't necessary. No one here will make a move that would harm our pack. We all know the dangers of letting word of what Charles found in that cabin escape before Bran chooses. There is no need for threats. In protecting the pack, protecting what is ours, we are one. Asil was merely warning us of the danger—but I am certain"—she raised an eyebrow and looked at Asil, in that moment as cool and controlled as the Moor had been—"I am certain that he would not issue a threat, especially as it is not necessary."

There was a long, pregnant pause.

Then Asil bowed formally to her. "As you say," he said silkily.

Leah was lucky, Anna thought, that Asil's anger was a cold thing, so he heard Leah's argument and agreed with it. Only a fool would think that any of Bran's pack would betray them, and Asil was no fool. He had just been too long an Alpha before coming here, and his ruling style differed a great deal from Bran's.

And still there was tension in the air. Leah wasn't the only wolf afraid of Asil. Because the pack might be filled with all the crazies Bran didn't trust with any other Alpha, but it wasn't filled with stupid people with death wishes—those ended up with the wildlings. Even Tag was afraid of Asil—if he hadn't been, he wouldn't have reacted to Asil's threat so hotly.

"Can you—" Charles murmured to Anna without taking his eyes off the dramatis personae, "pull the truck far enough from the house that it won't burn when we light Hester's cabin but close enough that if anyone tries to get into it, we'll see it?"

"Sure," she said. *Later,* she thought. *There will be time to tell him about the identity of the dead man later, when the pack isn't ready to ignite along with Hester's house.*

There must have been something in her voice, though, because he gave her a sharp look. She pretended she didn't see it and headed to the front of the truck.

The pack opened a path for her as she slowly drove away in a truck full of dead bodies, fae artifacts, and that weird, witchcrafted gun, which she had pulled out of her jeans and set on the bench seat of the truck. She tried to figure out just how far was close enough to make people think they would be spotted and too far for something from a burning house to explode and crash through the windshield. It was good to have something to focus on instead of the cold fingers of her past that were trying to unravel the core of the woman she'd become since coming to Aspen Creek, to this pack, to Charles.

In the end, she decided to pull the old truck next to Asil's very expensive, brand-new Mercedes SUV, reasoning that no one would risk the double whammy of both Charles and Asil—and that "no one" probably included the fire they were going to set.

Once she was parked, she stayed in the cab, though. She watched Charles say something to Leah, watched the pack start moving in an organized fashion. Asil and Tag working together, their former antagonism . . . not so much forgotten as pushed behind them. The wolves could do that, she'd noticed. They were so much creatures of the present that as long as their human halves stayed out of the picture, quarrels that were over and done with stayed that way.

From the driver's seat of Charles's truck, Anna saw Tag step into the cabin with one of the long-nosed lighters more commonly used for lighting barbecues than setting house fires (she fervently hoped). A moment later, orange light flared in the window—more brilliant because the dusk was quickly fading into darkness. Tag came out of the front door as the flames licked hungrily up the old wood of the cabin.

Anna should be out there, she knew, instead of huddled in the truck where she could draw comfort from the scent of her mate without any of the inconveniences of his actual presence. He saw too much, her Charles did.

She really didn't want to tell him she knew one of the dead.

BEFORE ASIL GAVE in to the impulse to make Leah pay for being right, Charles said, "We should light the cabin." He paused. "Did anyone think to call the Forest Service?"

"*I* made the call before we came here," Leah said. "I told them that the Aspen Creek volunteer fire department had decided to burn an old cabin that posed a fire hazard. They weren't happy, but it's on private property, and there isn't a ban on open fires"—someone said "yet," and she nodded at the speaker to acknowledge their accuracy— "so there wasn't much they could do."

That had been smart, Charles thought. And not entirely a lie: if they had a fire department in Aspen Creek, it would consist of the pack. He would just have told them he was burning a cabin on purpose.

"Good," Charles said.

Asil added, "Even if someone from the Forest Service decides to come all the way up here, they'll be checking on a controlled burn and not bodies." He didn't say "good girl"; that would have been too much. He didn't look at Leah, but he let her hear the approval in his voice. Leah's shoulders softened—the only sign of her pleasure at the compliment paid to her by the Moor.

That, said Brother Wolf, *was diplomacy.*

Asil kept talking, "Tag—you're the only one who knew Hester well, the only one here, anyway. Do you want to be the torchbearer?"

Asil's question sparked the pack into action. Hester and her mate were not the first bodies the pack had burned, though they generally used a proper cremation process. The place of torchbearer was usually a place of honor only—a wolf who witnessed the cremation of the body.

But wolves who died as wolves couldn't be buried where someone might dig them up believing they were going to find a human.

Fire was good at destroying evidence. Because of that, Charles had supervised the burning of a number of houses over the years but never in the Marrok's own territory before. Never a formal funeral— though he knew the protocols.

Asil seemed to have taken it upon himself to take charge of the burning, and Charles was content to let him work off steam by taking over the organization of the fire itself.

Charles wished the fire would do as good of a job destroying the magical artifacts he and Asil hadn't been able to find as it would turning Hester's body to ash.

He had himself never seen so many things imbued with magic in one place before. The mishmash of magics made the hair on the back of his neck stand up worse than waiting in the middle of a busy airport did. The thought of that chest sitting in his truck left an itch he couldn't scratch right between his shoulder blades. So did the note in his pocket.

Anna should be back by now.

He started to turn to look for his mate, but he was distracted by the flash of fire out of the corner of his eyes. He hadn't expected, with Asil in charge, for them to light the cabin so quickly.

Tag, smelling of smoke and diesel and gasoline, took his place next to Charles, and Asil joined them.

"I liked her," said Tag, without any of his usual drama.

Charles thought of the way Hester had chided him without a word from her cage, and said, "As did I. Though I did not know her well."

As fires do sometimes, this one roared up in a sudden burst of light and sound. It seemed exactly right, a fitting tribute to a tough woman and her mate—hot and wild and powerful. Leah shouted, and the pack called back, answering both Leah and the roar of the fire. Charles threw his head back and howled—and the call of the pack changed as the other wolves replied in kind. Then they fell silent and stood witness.

Tag had said that her people burned their dead, and Charles wondered who her people had been. Hester was an ancient name. It might even have been her birth name, though old creatures tended to change their names now and then.

His da said that names had power. Names that had belonged to you for a long time had more power. Like many of Da's sayings, it was true on different levels. Both witchcraft and fae magic could use a name in working evil magic upon someone. But the magic of names went further than that. Charles had found that his own name, Charles Cornick, the Marrok's son, had often saved him trouble. The fear of his name caused people to give up the fight before it started.

Hester was a name like that—a name of power. She had been a legend among the wolves, hers a quieter legend than the Moor's or the Marrok's because she herself preferred it that way. But her name had served admirably to distract people from the troubled man who had been her mate.

Charles hoped that Jonesy had enjoyed the peace that she had bought him with her name.

"Godspeed, Hester," Charles whispered. "Sweet dreams, Jonesy. Good journey."

On the tail end of his last word, there was a cracking noise inside the cabin and the fire leaped upward, and Charles felt the increase in heat on his face and his skin roughened with the breath of . . . something.

Correlation not being causation, it hadn't been Charles's wish that had caused the sudden flare-up. Asil met his gaze (briefly) and shrugged. That explosion had been something they'd missed in their search. Fae magic was elemental magic, based in aspects of earth, air, fire, or water, and those same elements could have unpredictable effects on fae artifacts. He did not except the fire to destroy everything they hadn't found. He only hoped they hadn't missed something that was going to kill everyone in the clearing.

Charles sensed Anna approach just about the time that he was ready to go look for her. Anna set her cheek against Charles's arm. "I think the fire was a good send-off for them both."

Yes, agreed Brother Wolf. But Charles thought it was more a statement of support for Anna than any real opinion about what they should do with the bodies of their fallen. Once someone was dead, Brother Wolf was usually pretty unsentimental about the remains.

Anna gave him a little smile of agreement. She knew Brother Wolf, too.

Her face beneath the smile was pale, the small muscles of her jaw tense.

"What's wrong?" Charles asked—because it was obvious to him, once he paid attention, that something was.

She tucked her arm in his and led him away from the others. Then, in a very quiet, not-to-be-overheard voice, she said, "I know one of the dead men in the back of the truck." She let go of him and stepped back—and he didn't think she knew she did it. Her voice shook a little, and she spoke faster. "I don't know his name, but I saw him at Leo's. We should get a photo of him to the Chicago Alphas as soon as we get somewhere with cell reception."

Leo had been the Alpha who had ruled his Anna's first pack. Charles had killed him for his crimes. Anna's expression meant he didn't have to ask her if the dead man had been one of those who'd abused her at Leo's behest.

Charles didn't reach out to touch Anna, not when she had just stepped away from him—and not when there were such ghosts in her eyes. He couldn't say anything for fear that the thing he would say would be the wrong thing. She didn't need his rage. He waited for her to do something that would tell him what she needed from him.

After a moment, she let out her breath and shook her head. She stepped into him and twined her right arm around his left, gripping his arm hard briefly before her whole body softened against him.

He took that moment to glance around, but no one was watching them—and if they'd overheard what Anna had said, they were being circumspect. Anna was being quiet—but they were surrounded by werewolves. It was unlikely that they had been entirely unobserved or unheard.

Anna stared at the fire, though he didn't think she was really seeing it. But after a while, she said, "Fire is a powerful thing. It cleanses as it destroys—and it brings light to darkness."

"Yes," he agreed.

"I think I understand why some cultures burn their dead," she said. "It feels like a celebration, doesn't it? The final conflagration." She paused. "Burn bright, Hester. Drive away the shadows, Jonesy. Sleep with the heroes and the saints."

With the cabin and all the other things burning, the scent of burning flesh was very faint. Charles rested his chin on the top of her head and reflected that it was for the best that, as young as she was, she probably couldn't distinguish the scent of the fire devouring Hester's body from the scent of the rest of the burning things.

He'd have burned Anna's past for her if he could have—but memories are not so easily set alight as a cabin.

ANNA AND CHARLES left after most of the others. There were still flames, so five of the wolves stayed—and would stay until the last ember was out.

Charles got into the passenger seat, but before Anna started the car, he put a hand on her arm.

"Wait," he said, then pulled a folded paper out of his pocket. "Asil and I found this in the bedroom while we were looking for things that might blow up the mountain if they caught fire."

She spread it on the seat, but it was too dark to read. Before she could turn on the cab light, Charles illuminated the page with the much dimmer light of his cell phone. Kara had brought both of their cell phones with her. Hiding Hester's home was no longer a directive; if they couldn't find a blazing house fire, the feds were welcome to track their phones. It would be a long time before anyone lived near this clearing again.

She read it and absorbed the implications. Hadn't she just been thinking that there was no way any member of the pack would betray the others? It looked like maybe she'd been wrong.

"Traitor," she said slowly. "Do you know how we have been betrayed?"

"For a start," Charles said, "someone told our enemy where Hester lived. And probably the timing of the attack means that they knew Da was not here. I've been thinking about other things, too, since I found this note. Maybe Gerry Wallace didn't go out looking for someone to finance his weirdly complex assassination plot against Da. Maybe someone recruited him. Last winter, someone fed a lot of information about Adam's pack to the rogue Cantrip agents."

"Right," said Anna after a moment. "Jonesy left this for you?"

Charles nodded. "It looks like it. After Hester died."

"She could talk to him, mind to mind, the way Brother Wolf and I do?" Anna asked.

Charles shrugged. "Yes. Though not exactly—I don't know if Hester's wolf could speak like Brother Wolf does."

Anna nodded slowly. "She told him some of it before they managed to kill her. He tried to tell us what she'd want us to know."

She started the truck up, and he turned off the light.

Still thinking about the implications, she said, "Can you keep an eye out on the phone reception? I want to send that photo of the dead man to both the Chicago Alphas. Maybe they can give us a name."

"All right," he agreed.

They drove awhile in silence. The track was not made better by being negotiated at night. "Hester knew," said Anna. "She knew who it was—or they thought she knew. That's why they killed her. So she couldn't tell us."

"That's what I think," agreed Charles.

"Is it someone in the pack?" Anna's stomach was tight at the thought. These were her family as much as her birth family had been. Some of them might be difficult or horrifying—but they were still family. "Or is it one of the wildlings?"

"Jonesy was notably unhelpful in that," said Charles apologetically. "I suppose that 'us' could mean the fae, but in this context, that is unlikely bordering on ridiculous."

"Okay," said Anna. "How many wildlings are there? I know three, and I've heard of a couple more."

Bran kept the wildlings away from the pack. Part of it was they were dangerous and needed to be isolated—and part of it was that a lot of them were very old. Very old werewolves tended to collect enemies. As far as she knew, only Bran himself, Leah, and maybe Charles knew all of them. They weren't kept completely isolated, and some of them sometimes joined in the hunt—but no one spoke about them when they did.

"Eighteen," Charles said. "Now that Hester and Jonesy are dead."

She made an involuntary noise of surprise. "That's a lot more than I thought. But it's still a reasonable suspect pool." She did not want to think about it being someone she knew.

He nodded. "Asil knows—he was there when I found the note. But I don't want to tell anyone else until we understand more. Here."

"What?"

"There's reception here."

She stopped the truck and uploaded the photo and an explanatory note. Her phone had a contact list that included all of the Alphas under Bran's rule, so she didn't have to ask Charles for the number.

"Jonesy said that they asked her about the wildlings," Anna said, once they were moving again. "If their agent was one of the wildlings, why would they have questions about them?"

Charles grunted. It was his "I'm puzzled, too" grunt. But then he said, "The wildlings don't all know each other. Some of them do, but a lot of them are very isolated because they want to be. Or they need to be. Most of our wildlings change their name when they come here—Hester was an exception. Collectively, I expect that there is a lot of knowledge that our wildlings have that exists nowhere else on the planet. I can think of four things, just offhand, that would start a frenzied hunt if anyone knew about them."

"Or maybe it's an item—like all the things you brought out of Jonesy's house."

Charles nodded. "Of what we found, only the sword would really attract interest by itself." He made an unhappy noise. "There were a couple of other things, too, I guess. But even without those, the whole collection represents a fair battery of power for someone who knows how to release or use it."

"Maybe Hester knew who or what they were looking for," Anna said soberly. "But she can't tell us now."

"Yes," said Charles, very softly. "We know they were asking for information that was important enough to step up what has previously been a long game. We know they were asking about the wildlings, and they don't know that. We'll find out who their agent is, then we'll use that person to hunt them all down."

Anna inhaled and nodded. "Yes," she said. "Okay. Yes."

BOYD HAMILTON CALLED as they were pulling into Bran's house. More specifically, he called Charles's phone. Anna had texted him the photo from *her* phone.

Anna looked at Charles's phone and gave an exasperated sigh. She turned off the truck and turned to the man who held her heart.

"I survived," she told him firmly. "I don't need to be coddled as though I'm some fragile doll. I can talk to Boyd—who never did me any harm anyway—and not dissolve into a spineless puddle."

Charles gave her a look. If he were anyone else, she'd have been sure he had practiced those looks in the mirror: they were too effective to be naturally occurring. But he didn't worry about things like that—he didn't need to. Scary was easy—it was not-scary that was sometimes a problem for him.

She raised her eyebrow to show that she wasn't impressed.

He almost smiled but caught it before it was more than a softening at the corner of his eyes.

"Maybe it's not about you," he told her. "Maybe it's about a man who failed to protect you from Leo when he should have. If you want to punish him, you could answer my phone and make him tell you all about this dead man who he also did not protect you from."

"He couldn't do anything," she said hotly, unable to let the attack on Boyd go on without defending him. Boyd had been the key to her getting out of Chicago, to her finding Charles. "Leo was his Alpha—and he kept everyone under his control. Boyd was not dominant enough to challenge him or disobey a direct order. Boyd protected people when he could. Without him, more bad things would have happened to people who couldn't protect themselves."

"You really believe that," Charles said, as if he didn't. "Good for you." He sighed, his gaze focused somewhere in the darkness outside. Another car pulled into the Marrok's driveway, pack members coming to gather with the others. That they were coming here instead of going home spoke to the unease that Hester's death had caused.

The wolves who got out looked away from Charles's truck with studious care.

Charles spoke after they were alone in the darkness again. "I sometimes think that you could be right. But mostly I believe that any dominant worth his hide protects those who cannot protect themselves. I expect that's how Boyd looks at things, too."

She, personally, had quit thinking about her first pack a long time ago. From the sound of it, she had been the only one. She used one of Charles's grunts to express herself.

"A dominant wolf protects his own with his life, Anna," Charles told her. "That means from everyone. If he felt Leo was too much for him, Boyd had Da's number. He could have called it at any time."

"He couldn't disobey Leo," she said doggedly—she'd watched him try. "Leo forbade it."

"His wolf couldn't disobey a direct order," agreed Charles, so mildly that Anna flinched even though it wasn't directed at her. She knew that mild tone.

He closed his eyes and took a deep breath. When he spoke again, the killing quiet was further away, and his eyes had returned to their usual almost-black.

"We are more than our wolves, Anna," he said. "Boyd is also a man—and the man is in charge. He could have disobeyed by shutting down his wolf. It would have been difficult, but he is not a newly Changed wolf. He has the control to do it. He just didn't try."

She bit her lip. Did that change things? Knowing that Boyd could have stepped in earlier? *No,* she thought, with something approaching relief. There had been things that she could have done, too—if only she had known. One of the things she'd learned from being a wolf in Bran's pack was that all the ability in the world did her no good if she didn't know how to use it.

"He knows better now," her mate continued in a low growl, as if he'd been following her thought path.

"Charles?" she asked, honestly unhappy. Charles wasn't exactly tactful. Being in Leo's pack had scarred her, no doubt, but it hadn't been a picnic for anyone else, either. Boyd had been as close to broken as she had been, though she hadn't seen it at the time. Boyd didn't need her forceful mate telling him how he'd failed his pack—he already believed it.

"Not me," Charles said. "It was Da. He educated him—then he put Boyd in charge of the pack. Boyd wasn't strong enough to control the territory, not in his condition, especially when that pack was so broken. But Da thought that Boyd would heal better if he were put in charge for a while, so Da made it happen." His phone had long since quit ringing. "As it turns out, Boyd rose to the occasion, and Da left him in charge."

"That sounds . . . odd," said Anna, feeling off balance. "Bran is all about the good of the many outweighing the good of the one."

Charles smiled grimly. "We failed that pack, too. Failed you. Da or I should have noticed the situation sooner. In retrospect, both of us noticed oddities that we should have looked into and did not. Rather than let Boyd break under the weight of his inability to protect his subordinates from his Alpha, Da left him in a position where he could work out his guilt with action. Boyd needed to know he could take care of his pack, that what he had been and who he was now could be different, better." He pursed his lips, and said thoughtfully, "I have no doubt at all that Boyd Hamilton will never again stand aside while someone is being hurt."

Clearly, Anna noted, that didn't keep Charles from being very angry with him anyway.

"So," he asked Anna, in a suddenly brisk tone, "are you going to punish him by making him talk to you about how much he failed you? Or are you going to let him talk to me about it?"

She gave him a shrewd look. "Which one is better for him?"

"You'll make him feel guilty. I'll only make him mad," Charles assured her.

She laughed—and it was only a little strained. She should insist, but she didn't really want to have that conversation, either.

"Okay," she said. "Go for it."

And she left him alone in the truck to make the call where she wouldn't overhear it.

* * *

BOYD ANSWERED AS soon as Charles called him back.

"Hamilton," he said, his voice wary.

"You know who our dead body is?" Charles asked, watching Anna until she closed the front door behind her.

"Yes." Boyd's tone was brisk—and relieved. He wasn't stupid—he'd probably been expecting Anna to call him back even though he'd used Charles's phone. "His name was Ryan Cable. Before . . . very early on, in the dawn of Leo's troubles, Leo brought in five military men to be Changed in secret. It was highly implied, though never spoken outright, that they were special forces. Only the old second—Harvey Adler—plus me, Jason, and a couple of others knew . . ." There was a pause. "I think out of all the pack members there that night, I'm the only one who is still alive."

Charles thought that it might be a good time to get the conversation back on track. There was something in Boyd's tone that indicated Boyd would have been happier to be among the dead. "Ryan Cable."

"Sorry," Boyd said, his voice unapologetic. "I'm trying to get the details right. It was a long time ago. I think it must have been in the early nineties. The Gulf War had just broken out, and patriotism was strong in all of us. Leo told us that there were people in the military who knew about werewolves and that one of those men had asked him for help. Leo had agreed, and his contact sent us these five men to Change. This was hush-hush stuff, both on our side and theirs."

Brother Wolf grumbled. This was exactly the kind of thing that had driven Bran to bring the werewolves out to the public. Blackmail was less useful now—either as an incentive or as an excuse.

Boyd made a pained sound back. "Believe me, I know. But Leo had been a good Alpha up until that point. It's only looking back that I can see that he was starting to change, and that was probably the turning point. We all have done things against the rules now and then. All of us." Boyd included, that meant. "Leo said it was for the war effort, and we could tell he was telling the truth."

"Not all of the five made it," Charles said.

His father might have been able to Change five humans and make them survive, though he'd told Charles he wouldn't ever do that. Forcing someone to Change was not ethical. Most of the time, a person who couldn't fight hard enough to survive the Change wouldn't survive long being a werewolf, either.

"I warned them," Boyd said, "but Harvey took it further. He told them, in graphic detail, exactly what Changing a human to a werewolf meant. A couple of them looked pretty spooked, but they all chose to go forward." He paused. "I wonder now what would have happened if they'd objected. If it was hush-hush, maybe they'd have been killed if they tried to get out of it. In any case, Cable was the only one who Changed. Leo and Harvey handed the dead men and Cable over to the people who came for them. Harvey didn't like the looks of those people. I remember that. He didn't think they were military. Leo told Harvey something that made him happier—though I couldn't tell you what it was."

"You think Leo took a payout for it?"

"I more than think it," said Boyd. "We've spent the last few years going through the old books. Bran asked us to look for the names of people who paid Leo for things that we couldn't verify were legitimate expenses. Leo took fifty thousand up front and another twenty after we delivered Cable. In his notes, he complained because he'd expected to get another eighty K. Thirty thousand per werewolf we successfully Changed, with one-third up front that we'd keep either way. I sent the financial files and the pack interviews—everything we've gathered about what Leo was doing—to Bran when he asked me for them, about a month ago."

There was a little silence as Charles absorbed something more than just Boyd's words. His father had asked the Chicago pack to send him their files, and that information had never made it to Charles, who handled all the pack finances and always had—except for a six-month period last year when Leah had taken over.

Leah had lost them a lot of money. Almost 20 percent of their net worth. It had taken him two weeks to replace it. Not that he was competitive or anything.

"When your father asked us to send the information to him," Boyd said, reading Charles's silence pretty accurately, "he said he was putting together a puzzle and would bring you in as soon as he had a target to aim you at. I gathered that he thought you were still angry about Leo and what he did to Anna. Bran didn't want you to go on a search-and-destroy mission until he was certain he had the whole setup."

"I see," said Charles. If his da hadn't given Boyd actual facts, just enough for Boyd to draw his own conclusion, Charles was pretty sure that it was the wrong conclusion. He wondered why his da hadn't wanted to show him the books.

"I tried Bran's phone before I called you," Boyd said in a neutral tone. "He'll have those files."

"The Marrok is away," Charles allowed. "That is need-to-know information that shouldn't go past you."

"Got it." He made a thoughtful sound. "How about I e-mail you the file on this transaction and all the banking information we have on it?" There was a pause. "Then I'll compile the whole mess that we've been amassing and overnight it to you on disk. If you have Cable dead in your territory, Bran has run out of time to organize everything to his pleasure."

"I'd appreciate that," Charles said, because Boyd was right. He'd hunt down whoever his father had given those files to anyway, because then he wouldn't have to spend all his time redoing work someone else had already done. But that might take time and he wanted that information now.

Somewhere in those files was a trail to the man who had paid for Ryan Cable's Change. Tough to follow a financial trail that old, but if one of the account numbers matched an account Charles had in his "to watch" files, he'd have a name. Someone had been running Cable and his dead friends, and there was a good chance that it was the same person who'd paid for his Change—or some close associate.

"After Cable was Changed," Boyd continued, "whoever ran him used him as a messenger. He'd show up, meet with Leo, and be gone the next day. Three or four times a year. Often enough that I didn't have to search my memory for his name but not so often that I knew him more than to nod at. If we had a real conversation, I don't remember it. I can brainstorm with a few of the other old pack members who survived Leo and see if we can get some sort of general feel for when he came—and maybe someone will remember a bit more about him. At the end, Leo pretty well ignored the more submissive wolves. They witnessed a lot he should probably have kept hidden from them."

"I'd be grateful for anything you can turn up," Charles said.

"I didn't know Hester," Boyd said. "But I've heard stories of her. For her to die like this . . . I'll do what I can."

Charles picked up the witchcraft-laden weapon that had dropped him unconscious in the midst of his enemies.

"Did Leo ever work with a witch?"

"Not while I was in the pack," Boyd answered without hesitation.

"Did he have weapons that were especially effective against other werewolves?"

"No," Boyd said, though this time his response was slower, his voice raw. "Other than Justin. But I know about the drug someone developed using the wolves Leo had made and sold as guinea pigs."

Charles took a deep breath and forced Brother Wolf to really examine the situation Boyd had found himself in—a gradual wearing away of all the rules until all anyone in that pack could do was cling to their Alpha because there was nowhere else to go. And Brother Wolf still thought that Boyd should have done more. So did Boyd, obviously.

Charles gave him what comfort he could. "You learned what not to do," he said. "Teach the others. Move forward. Backward does no one any good."

"How is Anna?" Boyd asked, and there was hunger in his voice. Not sexual hunger, but the need to know that he had, at the very least, helped Anna out of that mess.

"She wanted to take this call," Charles said with amusement.

"Shit," said Boyd. But then he laughed. "Next time maybe I'll call her on her phone."

"She'd be glad to hear from you," Charles said. He looked at the witchcrafted weapon again. "I'm going to send you a photo of a witchcrafted gun that was effective enough on me." He explained something about how he'd come to have it. "Maybe one of your submissive wolves saw something that you didn't." It was possible if, as Boyd said, Leo had not viewed submissive wolves as a threat and did not pay attention to what they witnessed.

"I'll check," said Boyd, sounding more like himself. "If they don't know, they might have some ideas where to look." There was a pause. "I don't recall anything about witches in this business, though. But Harvey—he could smell a witch at a hundred yards." Boyd paused again, then said slowly, "Harvey's reaction that night—that might be about right if one of them was a witch."

"Keep the weapon as pack-only information. I don't want all the witches on the planet trying to figure out how to take out werewolves for fun and profit."

"What about Hester's death and the attack on the Marrok's pack?"

Charles gave an involuntary laugh. "I'd have kept it quiet if I could have, but I suspect that people in your pack are getting calls from friends and acquaintances right now. It's harder to keep things quiet than it was fifty years ago."

"I hear you," agreed Boyd with feeling. "Talk to you if I hear anything interesting."

"Sounds good." Charles disconnected. He started to get out of the truck, stopped, and picked up the phone.

"Da," he said, as soon as the message program picked up. "I don't know what your game is, but let me lay out for you what happened today with all the important pieces that I know."

CHAPTER

6

Anna let herself into Bran's house. She felt jittery and unsettled. She'd much rather have been walking into her own house so she could deal with the stir of old memories without witnesses. Despite the lateness of the hour, the whole house was abuzz with the chatter of voices and the smell of woodsmoke. She'd known by the cars outside that everyone had apparently decided to congregate at the Marrok's house instead of going home to sleep, like sensible people.

Even with a fair warning, she almost turned around and walked back out. Only the knowledge that Charles would think something was wrong kept her moving forward.

She wondered how often Bran wanted to turn around and walk away from it all. Wondered if that's what he'd done.

The thought of Bran's not coming back, of his leaving this pack and the wildlings—and, well, all the werewolves in North America—in Charles's hands was almost enough to spark a panic attack. *Of course* he was coming back. He was a control freak. There was no way that he would stay away very long.

Her quiet house would await her until he returned.

Bran's home was always teeming with people and noise; only the bedroom suites and Bran's office were private. She knew that in most packs, the house of the Alpha's second was nearly as busy. But most of the pack, dangerous as they were, were afraid of Charles. Having a house that was a haven rather than the pack clubhouse was a blessing she hadn't fully appreciated until this week.

She entered the large gathering space filled with pack members—who all quit talking and looked at her as she walked in. They knew. Someone must have overheard her when she told Charles about the dead werewolf she'd once known. They had added two and two and gotten four somehow—she could see it in their faces.

There wasn't a wolf here, not excluding Leah, who wouldn't throw themselves between her and anyone who would harm her. Some of that was because she was Omega, but some of it was that they were her friends and family. There were compensations for living elbow to elbow with other wolves.

The problem was that she didn't need rescuing, except maybe from them. The force of their concern, of their knowing that she had been a victim made her feel like a victim again.

"Hey, Anna," said Kara cheerfully. Her rescuer appeared from the direction of the kitchen with a plate filled with peanut-butter cookies. "Leah and I made cookies."

The teenager's face was nearly expressionless except for the wry laughter in her eyes. As the youngest werewolf in the pack, Kara had dealt with her share of overprotectiveness. "There was some dough in the fridge, but Leah said she'd rather have peanut-butter cookies."

Anna rolled her eyes. "Passive-aggressive" did not even approach describing Leah's usual modus operandi. She regretted the gesture instantly—partially because she'd sworn to herself that she wouldn't let Leah bring her down to her level. But mostly because, mid-eyeroll, Leah walked around the corner into the far side of the living room and caught Anna.

Leah raised a superior eyebrow.

Anna shook her head at Leah and took one of the cookies off the plate because they smelled good, she was hungry, and Kara had started to look uncertain. Kara liked Leah, but she wasn't unaware of Leah's games. She also knew that usually Anna was more inclined to laugh about them than be offended.

There was no chocolate in the cookie, but it was good anyway. Especially since the whole cookie thing had broken up the way every wolf in the room had been focused on Anna's history as a victim.

"Yum. Thank you," Anna said—and Kara gave her a relieved grin.

Tag came up and picked a cookie off Kara's plate. "Thanks, *a leanbh*, I'll take another. Your cookies are always worth a second visit." He was, Anna thought, deliberately unclear about whether his endearment was aimed at Leah or Kara.

He took a big bite and looked down at Anna. He was taller than Charles, who was very tall, and outweighed her mate by fifty pounds of muscle—and still the most impressive thing about him was his hair. Bright orange, it covered his head and hung nearly to his waist in strands of dreadlocks. His beard was a shade darker and exploded exuberantly down his chest in a mass that the members of ZZ Top could only envy.

"For the record," he told her gently, in the light tenor that always seemed wrong for such a beast of a man. "We'll not stand for any to hurt you."

And so he undid all the good distracting the peanut-butter cookies had achieved.

Tag gave a nod to the rest of the room, and there was one of those low growls that, until she'd become a werewolf, Anna associated with groups of men watching their favorite football team when the official makes a bad call. Sage, perched on the back of the couch next to the fireplace, paused in eating her cookie to give her a grimace.

Sage's silent support allowed Anna to swallow the lump of cookie in her mouth, and say, with innocent earnestness, "For the record, Tag, *I* wouldn't let anything happen to *you*, either."

For a moment, the tension held. Tag's eyes widened for an instant, lightening as his wolf considered if she'd insulted him. Then he threw his head back and laughed like a coyote.

When the room broke out in scattered snickers that had more to do with the break in tension than anything Anna had said, she considered them thoughtfully.

Hester and Jonesy were dead. All the attackers who had set foot on pack territory were dead, but those men had been backed up by real money. Someone who could acquire a helicopter.

And all that this bunch had to talk about was Anna, and what had happened to her in Leo's hands—something that was over and done. She wasn't sure what that said about them, but she was sure she wanted to redirect that focus.

"This is not about me," she told them. "This is about someone's coming into our territory and killing Hester—which directly led to the death of her mate. We may have killed those who put foot on our land, but they went to a lot of trouble to try to take Hester. We didn't kill them all. We don't know that they won't be back."

"Do we need to send a warning out?" asked Asil. "To the pack in general, but also to the wildlings—it seems like they may have targeted Hester because she was isolated."

Asil knew about that note. He was finding a reason to go out and talk to the wildlings. He skirted the truth of what he knew with the wussy words "may" and "seems." Anna made a note to pay attention when Asil used those kinds of words.

"I think warning the wildlings is a good idea," Anna said before Leah could quash the idea. "If we're being alarmist, there's no harm done. If there is a second attack, being prepared would be useful. Leah? You know all the old wolves hunkered down in the mountains—how do you think we should do this?"

Leah glanced around the room and frowned. "You know Bran doesn't like to broadcast where they live and who they are. Too many of them still have enemies who would love to know where to find them when they are . . . less capable."

"Charles and I can do it," said Anna. "He knows them."

Leah frowned. "That will take several days. They are scattered all over our territory. I think we need to break this job down."

"I know most of them," Asil said. "One way or another. And none of them is likely to want to attack *me*. Anna and Charles can take one group, and you and I the other."

That wasn't going to work, thought Anna. Leah was scared of Asil. There was no way she was going to go with Asil. Or Charles.

"Three groups," said Leah briskly. "Even if some of them answer their phones, we'll cover them faster." She frowned, looked at Anna and Asil, then she smiled.

Whoops, thought Anna.

"They know me, and they know Charles. If they don't know Anna, they will understand who and what she is when they meet her. Each of us will take a group. Anna, you take Asil with you, so I don't have to explain to Bran how I let you go off and get yourself killed." Leah gave Anna a smile to show she knew Anna could take care of herself. And because she was pleased with herself.

That Leah would take great glee in sending Anna off with Asil, who would not stop flirting with Anna because it annoyed Charles, did not mean that her stated reason wasn't also truthful.

"Juste?" Leah looked around until she found the quiet man sitting in a chair in the corner of the room.

Juste had been born four or five hundred years ago in France and tended to be reserved. He'd joined the pack after Anna, taking advantage of Bran's offer to provide places for European wolves who wanted to move. Anna didn't know much about him because he didn't talk much—but he'd survived centuries of living in France without falling to the Beast of Gévaudan, so he must be tough.

"I can go with Charles," Sage said—and Leah just lit right up.

Anna could see the thoughts rush through Leah as clearly as if she were speaking them aloud. Sage and Asil had something going on—something they'd been pretty private about. And if Leah could send her off with Charles while she sent Asil with Anna . . . well. If some sparks flew, it wouldn't be her fault, now would it?

Anna opened her mouth to say something, anything—though she didn't know whether it would have been an objection or just an agreement. But Tag spoke before she could put her foot in her mouth—because anything would have been the wrong thing.

"I'll initiate the phone tree," Tag said. "Because we don't know what our enemy wants, we should make sure that all the humans in town know to be careful and to watch for strangers."

From Leah's nonreaction, Anna was pretty sure that Leah hadn't been going to do that. Leah shared Bran's indifference to humans, and she did not make the exception he did for those who lived in his town. All of Aspen Creek was precious to Bran.

"We should keep a pack member at the gas station round the clock," suggested Asil. "If our enemies are running around the woods, they have to find fuel somewhere. I know that Troy and Eureka are both within a reasonable travel distance, but even so, it would be stupid of us not to keep watch."

"I can do first shift," said Peggy.

The whole pack turned to look at the dark-haired cheery little person who'd spoken. Peggy had a female human mate, the safety of whom was the reason she'd petitioned the Marrok to move to his pack. Female werewolves were relatively rare, and they were more or less (depending upon their pack) expected to find a male werewolf to mate with. Peggy's former Alpha had begun harassing her and her mate—so she packed them both up and moved to Aspen Creek. Picking up and moving had been no big thing for them employment-wise—Peggy could carve beautifully and sold her art online, and her wife was a long-distance truck driver.

"I live across the road from the gas station," she said. "I know all the cars that stop there—and I'm a night owl anyway. When Carrie is out, I usually sleep during the day. She won't be back until next week. The kids who work night shift know me, so I won't scare them the way some of you might."

And the time for Anna to do anything about Leah's plans passed without anyone's noticing except her.

* * *

CHARLES STOOD BEFORE the door to his da's house, the witch gun in one hand and the basket of fruit that had been meant as a gift for Hester in the other. He centered himself, promising Brother Wolf that they would take care of business, then retreat—

Retreat? Brother Wolf did not retreat.

There were whole weeks when Brother Wolf was just a silent presence. Hester's death had brought him very close to the surface. Which meant that Charles needed to guard his thoughts and keep control of his temper.

Escort Anna into the peace and quiet of the guest suite, he amended.

Brother Wolf knew Charles's initial word was the one he meant, but he allowed himself to be pacified. Probably because Charles included Anna in the second version of his intentions.

Anna was watching for him as he walked by the biggest of the three gathering places in his da's home, now filled with restless wolves. She ducked out and followed him into the kitchen, which was unoccupied.

The whole kitchen smelled of peanut butter, and there were plates of cookies sitting on the countertop.

"We are going out tomorrow to warn all the wildlings," Anna told him, taking the basket with a grimace. She stared at it a moment, looked around, then set it down on the nearest flat surface.

A good idea, he thought. So why was Anna acting as if there was something he wasn't going to like about the situation?

She continued without pause, explaining plans to tighten defenses, to make sure the rest of those under their care were as safe as possible. She finished by saying, "Tag says he'll try to contact the wildlings, but it's unlikely that we'll be able to get more than one or two of them to pick up their phone."

Charles nodded at this. He sympathized with the general resistance that the older wolves had to modern technology. Da had insisted that everyone had to have phones in case of emergencies. Unless he was present, though, he could not insist that they answer their phones.

And since the point was for Anna and him to meet with them all, the fewer wildlings who answered their phones the better.

"A week is a long time to maintain high alert," he said.

"Shutting barn doors after the cows are already out," agreed Tag, rounding the corner. "But it would be stupider not to shut 'em if we still have a few cows inside."

"Sometimes I'm glad I don't know how your mind works," Sage said, trailing behind Tag.

If he were the opposition team, Charles thought, he'd wait two weeks—two months, assuming time wasn't a factor—before moving again. Maybe Charles would get lucky, and their enemy was impatient, or time *was* a factor.

Hopefully, in a week, Da would be back, and this would be his problem. The traitor would be his da's problem. And the artifacts currently in the back of Charles's truck would be Bran's problem.

But the dead bodies, also in the truck, were probably still going to end up on Charles's plate.

Figuratively speaking, he told Brother Wolf before that one could get any ideas.

"Is that the witch gun?" asked Tag.

Charles held it up—and when Tag reached for it, he handed it over.

"Is that wise?" asked Sage.

Tag aimed it at the fruit basket and pulled the trigger.

"Possibly not," admitted Charles ruefully. Though nothing had happened to the fruit basket.

Tag pulled his hand off the grip, holding the gun by the barrel, and he shook the hand that had held the trigger. "Bites," he said. "That's how it's powered? It doesn't seem to do much."

"Don't you think that setting off a weapon you know nothing about in the house is a little stupid?" asked Sage.

At those words, there was a sharp exclamation, and Leah bustled into the kitchen carrying an empty plate. Tag abruptly set the weapon on the counter and tried to look as though he had nothing to do with it.

Leah snorted, but instead of berating Tag, she asked Charles, "Are you going to stay in here until the whole pack follows you?"

Without answering her, Charles picked the gun back up, frowning at it. He took the basket outside and set it on the porch, aware that Tag, Sage, Leah, and Anna trailed behind him. He aimed at the basket of fruit.

He pulled the trigger. Nausea rose in his stomach, a tingling ran through his body, and the fruit and basket dissolved into a revolting, stinking mass of grayish mud, leaving the cement it sat upon unharmed.

They all stared at the result a moment. Charles rubbed his trigger finger, paying attention to the numbness that faded slowly.

"Witch blood is apparently necessary," said Leah coolly after a moment. "Thank you for experimenting in my kitchen with that thing, Tag. Oh, and I'm not cleaning that up. Come into the living room when you're finished."

She left, pausing to collect the remaining two plates full of cookies. Sage and a grinning, unrepentant Tag followed behind her.

Anna grabbed a garbage bag while Charles got a dustpan and a roll of paper towels.

"So why didn't it do that to you?" she asked, her voice tight as she snapped the bag out and opened it.

"I'm tougher than a basket of fruit?" suggested Charles, going back outside to work on the mess.

"Very funny," she said in a broken voice that told him humor might not have been the best idea he'd had today. She put her hand out and touched the muck that smelled of fruit, rot, and blood magic. Her hand shook.

Oh my love, he thought. Quietly, he said, "I don't know, Anna." He ripped off a paper towel and watched as she used it to clean her hand. "Maybe adding my mother's magic alters the effect of the gun, my blood makes it more powerful than his did. My mother's magic is close to witchcraft—but more attuned to the turning of the earth. Maybe her blood offered some protection. I don't know why. But I am alive and unharmed."

She sucked in a deep breath. Nodded. She stuffed the wadded-up paper towel in the bag, then bent and held it open next to the step, so he could just push the mess into the bag.

"What did Boyd have to say?" she asked.

"We want to know, too," called Leah's voice clearly. "Wait to answer that until you are in here."

"She meant to say 'please,'" said Sage cheerily when Brother Wolf let out a growl of annoyance.

Anna muttered something unhappily under her breath. Charles

didn't hear it all, but he knew it had to do with the lack of privacy at his da's house.

"Exactly," he told her.

"**WHAT DID BOYD** have to say?" asked Leah as soon as he and Anna came into the living room.

Charles glanced around the room and saw that a good two-thirds of the pack was here. From their attentive eyes and the hyperprotective glints of wolf eyes he caught here and there, he realized that they all knew about the dead man's connection to Anna. He couldn't see her telling them, so someone must have overheard them. Hard to stay quiet enough that any werewolf in sight couldn't overhear you without trying.

So he told them what Boyd had said to him. When he finished, he looked around the room, and asked, "Do any of you know what Da did with the electronic files, financial and otherwise, that Boyd gave him?"

"Bran still has them," said Leah. "He got them about a month back. He's been working on them himself. He told me that you had enough on your shoulders, and he'd give them to you when the time was right."

"Okay," he said quietly.

Da had taken the files to work on them himself? What did that mean? "When the time was right"? His da could run a spreadsheet or conduct an Internet search, but he wasn't in Charles's league. Had his da just forgotten about it? That didn't sound like the Marrok at all.

Had Da found something in the books that he didn't want Charles to know about? Was that something the reason Bran wasn't here?

He wasn't in Africa. The last call Charles had made, before coming into the house, was to his brother. Samuel had not heard from their da since he'd gotten a call that all was well with Mercy. He had not heard that Da was headed to Africa—and he'd not seen him.

That meant Bran had lied. Over the phone, Charles reflected, lying would have been easy enough.

Good that Boyd was sending the files to Charles, then. He'd told his father's message app about that, so his da would know that Charles was about to receive whatever information that data held. If he really didn't want Charles to see something, he could come home and take care of this matter himself.

Anna brought a plate with crumbs and two peanut-butter cookies on it. "Have a peanut-butter cookie," she told him. "They're good."

He looked at the cookies, still lost in trying to follow his da's Byzantine thought process with half the information he needed to come to any kind of accurate conclusion.

"I thought you were making brownies," he said.

"Brownies?" said Tag, distracted from his quiet conversation with a couple of other pack members. "I like brownies."

"They have orange peel in them," Leah told Tag, and Charles could tell that she thought that was a bad thing.

"Mercy's recipe?" Tag said happily. "Awesome. You should get those baked before you go, Anna. One of your brownies, and those recluses will be happy to come out of their hidey-holes to have a few more."

"The brownies can wait," said Leah firmly. There was something in her voice that told Charles that the brownie dough would be in the garbage before it ever saw an oven.

If a dog made the sound Tag made then, Charles would have called it whining. But Tag's eyes were shrewd and focused on Leah.

It was, Charles thought, very easy to make the mistake of buying Tag's cheery-barbarian appearance and miss the sharp man inside who knew very well whose brownies he was praising—over the peanut-butter cookies that Leah had evidently made. And, once recognizing that sharp man, it would be easy to make the mistake of thinking that the barbarian berserker was a disguise. Tag was both— and that was *before* his wolf entered into consideration.

"**TELL ME HOW**," Charles said, "you managed to get stuck going out to warn the wildlings with Asil?"

Anna couldn't see his face because he was in the process of stripping out of his soot-stained shirt, and she couldn't read his neutral tone.

"It wasn't me," she said. "Asil spoke up at just the wrong moment and sparked Leah's desire to stir up trouble. It's a talent he has. To her credit, she's right, we need to get them all warned as soon as possible. Three teams will do that better than one."

Charles emerged, his face as neutral as his voice had been. "All right." Anna winced in sympathy when he jerked at the band at the end of his braid, and it snapped.

"I know," she said with a grimace. "I know you would be happier pairing me with a different wolf. Maybe Sage should come with me and Asil go with you?"

Charles considered her suggestion that they switch partners but finally shook his head. "No. Brother Wolf doesn't like it, but it is better this way. Some of these wolves wouldn't listen to a messenger they see as lower-ranking." He snorted. "Some of them won't listen to any of us, either. But if one of them decides to cause trouble . . . Asil is a better deterrent than Sage or you. No one sane would attack the Moor."

"Do we tell Leah about the traitor? So she can keep watch for oddities, too?" Anna asked. "Or work it so Asil is her partner, so one of us in each group knows to keep an eye out?"

He unbraided his hair, something Anna never got tired of watching. It wasn't just that his hair was beautiful—though it was. It was the intimacy of the moment. No one else got to see what he looked like with his hair down.

"No," he said finally. "Asil and you and I know. That is enough. I'm not convinced any of the wildlings is our traitor—you'll see what I mean when you meet some more of them. Not only would they have trouble accumulating information—because most of them never see the main pack—but only a few of them are stable enough to hide lies this big without betraying themselves."

"Okay," Anna said. "Hester could have. How many Hesters are there among your father's wildlings?"

He paused, raised an eyebrow, and nodded at her. "Score for you," he said. "How about I warn Leah that we have reason to believe that these people were asking about the wildlings?"

"You don't want to tell her that there is a traitor?" Anna asked.

He shook his head. "I don't trust her to be subtle."

Anna laughed despite herself. No, subtle was not something Leah was particularly good at.

"Who is Leah going with?" he asked.

"Juste," Anna told him.

Charles grunted in what sounded to her like approval.

"She gave you and Sage the ones she thought would be the worst to deal with," Anna said. "She gave Asil and me the most broken. She was careful, she told me, to make sure that ours have trouble controlling their wolves, not the other way around. That way, hopefully, Asil won't have to kill any of them."

"She took the easiest," Charles said, taking off his boots.

"That's not how she put it—but I think that's how she sees it," Anna agreed. "Should I have objected when she paired me with Asil?" She hadn't planned on asking him, but the words came out anyway. "I probably could have made her send Asil with Sage if I had wanted to push it."

Charles's eyes brightened for an instant, and though no word came out of his mouth, she heard Brother Wolf's *Yes* as clearly as if he'd spoken into her ear.

"No," Charles said firmly. "She might enjoy stirring up trouble, but she came to the right conclusions. You'll be safe with Asil. Sage will be safe with me. Leah will be safe because of Da—but Juste will be a good reminder."

He pulled out clean clothes. "From the standpoint of getting a look at all the wildlings, it might have worked out better if you and Leah had been paired up. As it is, we'll have to find a way to see all the wolves that Leah and Juste have on their list. Logistically speaking, the wildlings most likely to have betrayed the pack are in Leah's group—because they are the most stable of the bunch."

Anna thought about it. "I could probably get her to change it up that much."

Charles shook his head. "I don't think that Leah is dominant enough to get the wildlings to back down on her own, and your effect is too unpredictable." He gave her a laughing glance over his shoulder. "And if Juste and Asil are in a car for a full day, we might be pulling out bodies. Juste has a problem with Asil."

"Why?" Anna thought about it just a second, and said, "You mean he blames Asil for not killing the Beast of Gévaudan?" The Beast, Jean Chastel, had controlled most of Central Europe for centuries. The Moor had kept Chastel out of the Iberian Peninsula.

Charles grunted agreement. Evidently finished with the subject of tomorrow's task, he said, "I tried calling Da before I came in. He's still not answering his phone. I left a voice message filling him in on what's been happening. He'd have felt Hester's death. If he's not getting back to me, it's because he doesn't want to. He's not with Samuel, I checked. So he's got some other game going on."

Anna had come to the same conclusion.

"Bastard," she said with feeling.

It made him laugh. He touched her cheek and pulled back his finger to show her the dirt on it. "Wanna shower with me?" he asked. The laughter hadn't left his eyes, though his face was serious.

This house, she thought, was a prison in which everyone knew what everyone else was doing. Too many sharp ears and sharper noses to keep their private life private. She understood that Charles didn't care who knew when they made love—the opposite, in fact.

But he'd taken Anna's desires into consideration. At the Marrok's home, they slept side by side in the guest bedroom, and all they did was sleep. Most days they stopped in to check on their own house. The horses were being fed by someone else, but they needed to be worked. Usually, they managed to sneak in an hour of privacy for lovemaking—and just being alone together.

Today hadn't been most days.

His eyes were tired, she thought, beneath the laughter. Through their bond, she could feel his lingering sadness.

She leaned forward and took his smudged finger into her mouth, feeling his whole body jolt with surprise . . . and something else. Heat flared, brightening his eyes to gold. His breath caught, but except for that single stiffening, he didn't move at all—a cat waiting for his prey. She let him feel her teeth while she thought about that.

No. Not prey. Playmate. Lover. But never prey.

His stillness wasn't a predatory thing; he was waiting for a proper invitation to play. And enjoying the beginning of the game.

She sat back, satisfaction at his response sliding through her skin. She still depended upon her wolf to teach her how to play in intimate circumstances, but she no longer let that bother her—she and her wolf were one in this. She licked her lips, and said, in a voice that came out husky because a good seduction seduces both parties, "Are you, by any chance, implying I might be *dirty*?"

The smile that only belonged to her slid across his face and did interesting things to her insides. "Who, me?" he said in a thoughtful voice. "Maybe. But in case you thought it was a complaint . . ." He leaned forward and kissed her, touching her only with his lips because that was all he needed.

Unlike her initial move into foreplay, his kiss was as soft as a cello played *pianissimo*, hinting at the power of the song but lulling the unwary with its sweetness.

Her body went soft, her lips felt heavy and oversensitive as she closed her eyes to concentrate on her senses, on him. He smelled of smoke, the musk and mint that was werewolf, and the underlying scent that was his alone. *Mine. All mine.* All of his beauty of body and spirit was hers.

He was worth facing a little embarrassment for. *Get brave, Anna,* she admonished herself.

He pulled away, his lips hotter than they'd been when they first touched hers. He gave her another smile, this one full of love and kindness. People didn't always notice how kind her mate was because he was sneaky that way.

"I need to get cleaned up," he said. "And I need to stop this before we're both grumpy. When we get done running around tomorrow, we should stop at home." *Where it is private, and you won't be uncomfortable* was what he didn't say.

"Cherish" was a word often used in traditional wedding ceremonies that Anna didn't think many people understood. They should observe Charles for a few days; they might learn something. Charles was a man who knew how to cherish the ones he loved.

Anna had always been a good student.

She said, "Are you taking back your invitation?"

He'd already turned to go into the bathroom, but her words froze him in his tracks. He looked back at her—and she could see Brother Wolf lurking in his eyes.

"No?" he said tentatively. Then he looked pointedly at the door to the suite, through which it was possible for anyone with werewolf ears to hear the chatter of a few die-hard pack members who were still up talking. "But I don't . . ."

She pulled off her shirt. Before she'd freed her head, warm hands, *his* warm hands, were undoing her bra strap.

"I am," he said, meeting her eyes as she tossed her shirt on the floor, "all out of chivalry."

She smiled at him as he dropped her bra on top of her shirt.

"Funny," she said. "So am—" *I* she would have said except that his mouth at her breast distracted her.

For a moment she let him take the lead and do as he pleased because she'd learned that pleased him, too. She gave him her stuttering breath, her hums of approval. She was very careful not to squeak because squeaking would attract the attention of the people on the other side of that door. Attract their attention sooner, anyway.

But she was simply not comfortable just taking and not giving back. Besides, his body was lovely, and she enjoyed touching him as much as she did being touched. More. So she wriggled on top of him and proceeded to give as good as she got. A small part of her was aware of when the chatter outside paused, rippled with happy laughter, then returned to chattering. That part of her writhed with embarrassment—but it was a very small part of her and easily subsumed in the emotional and physical sensations of making love with her mate.

A rather long while later, limp and breathless, Anna said, "I'm still dirty. More dirty. Because . . . sweat and stuff."

He gave a low laugh that vibrated through her happy body. "Good to know. Me, too." There was a short pause, and he said, "We can shower later. When I can move."

She put her head back down on his sweaty and smoky skin, breathed him in contentedly, and said, "Okay. I can go with that."

ASIL DROVE AS if he were a human, with human reflexes. It was nice, Anna decided, to not have to choose between driving herself or living with Charles's sometimes-sudden decisions to drive as though a wreck could not possibly injure anyone in the car. Anna could relax while Asil navigated the almost-roads they traveled.

Since they'd taken Asil's new Mercedes SUV instead of Charles's truck, she could also not wince when the scrape of tree branches or rocks against the sides and undercarriage of his pristine vehicle made

Asil growl. The growl was just noise, without any passion behind it. Unlike her husband, Asil didn't love his cars. He appreciated them and took meticulous care of them, but they were just vehicles to get him from one place to the next. He enjoyed them more if they did it with style and power, but they weren't anything he was attached to.

Not that she wouldn't rather be driving in Hell itself if she could do it with Charles, but she'd take the good where she found it.

They were going to see Wellesley first, and Anna couldn't help a frisson of fan-girl excitement. Wellesley was an artist, *their* artist.

His oil paintings held places of honor in the homes of the pack—and she'd seen them cherished by other packs when she and Charles traveled. There were two in her living room that would be less out of place hanging in the National Gallery of Art in Washington or maybe the Met than on the walls of a modest home in the wilds of Montana.

He was an artist who should have been world famous instead of werewolf famous. She considered that a moment. Maybe he was famous, but if so, it was under a different name—because she'd looked before, to see if she could find his work in the real world.

"What's he like?" she asked Asil, because she knew that Bran used Asil to deal with Wellesley most of the time. They got on together, and she gathered that Wellesley could be difficult.

He glanced at her as if he couldn't fathom who she was talking about.

"Wellesley," she said impatiently.

His eyebrows shot up. "He's one of Bran's wildlings. That means he's broken."

She growled at him, and he grinned—and the expression made his normally austere face look friendly and approachable. "I am sorry, *querida*, but I don't know how to answer that. He is troubled in a way that is very like schizophrenia but is more likely a damaged interaction with his wolf. He is very shy, but I think that is a product of his condition rather than a natural tendency." He paused. "I can tell you that you aren't his only fan. People keep trying to get me to ask him about commissioning a piece." He laughed. "Just this morning, Sage petitioned Leah to switch with me so she could come and meet him."

When she'd first come to the pack, she'd thought that Sage and Leah didn't like each other. But she'd grown to understand that they were possibly as close to friends as two very dominant women (werewolves or not) could be. Leah actively liked Sage and usually behaved herself in front of her. Sage snipped and snarked at her and about her but ultimately had Leah's back.

"So why are you and I together instead of Sage and I?" Anna asked.

"Because there is the distinct possibility that putting Charles and me in the same car together might make the universe implode," said Asil. "I might have said that to Leah when she looked like she might make the switch." He paused, and said slyly, "I waited until Charles could hear me, then I told her that I'd been looking forward to a whole day traveling with you."

Anna's first thought was surprise that Charles hadn't put his foot down and paired Sage and Asil together instead. Her second thought was that Asil had made that suggestive comment in front of Sage, too.

"Aren't you and Sage dating?" she asked.

"Sometimes," Asil said. "Currently, she is playing hard to get."

Anna took a good look at his face to see if it was okay if she asked for more details.

"She believes I am arrogant and treat her as though she cannot take care of herself," he clarified.

"She's right," Anna said.

"Yes." He gave her a graceful bow of his head. "She is." He took a deep breath and gave Anna a humorless smile that told her he was more upset about it than he let on. "I am too old to change who I am—a man a hair less arrogant would be lost to the beast that lives inside me. You cannot look at a person, and say, 'If I could change this or that, if I could pick what I want and discard other things, I could love this one.' Such a love is pale and weak—and doomed to failure."

She thought about that. "I tried to change Charles," she said in a small voice. "I told Bran to quit sending him out on killing missions."

Asil sighed. "You are so sensible most of the time, I forget how young you are. That was not changing Charles; that was trying to change the world so Charles could survive. That is protecting your mate from the things he cannot protect himself from."

"Maybe Sage is trying to save you, too," Anna said thoughtfully. "Saving you from death, really. If you keep trying to protect her when she doesn't need it, she might have to shoot you." Sage was a pretty good shot.

Asil fell silent; he didn't smile at her attempt at humor. After a moment, he said, "I will consider this. It will not change how I act, but perhaps it will make her argument less aggravating."

She couldn't tell if he was joking. She was sort of afraid he wasn't.

"I can tell you a few things about Wellesley," Asil said after they'd traveled far enough to leave the subject of Sage behind them, along with several miles of twisty dirt track. "He can use magic—and not always on purpose. He isn't a witch—his magic is closer to Charles's magic, I think. But it makes him especially good at pack magic. He comes on pack hunts sometimes, but no one except Bran and I know it. And probably Charles. If Wellesley doesn't want you to notice him, he is difficult to perceive, and you'll have trouble remembering details about him, like exactly what he looks like."

He paused. "I am old and powerful, so I have no such trouble. It is for this reason Bran started sending me to deal with him."

"So he could come on pack hunts, or go into Aspen Springs, and no one would notice?" Anna asked. Because that was what Asil was avoiding saying. "He could gather information without anyone the wiser."

"Yes," Asil said. "I've known a few other wolves who could do this." He paused. "I'm fairly certain that Bran can do a bit more."

Anna nodded solemnly. She thought there was a reason that visiting wolves sometimes seemed not to notice Bran until he drew attention to himself. Part of it was his ability to hide the force of his personality, but on several occasions, she would swear that people just didn't notice him at all.

"He likes to sing," Asil said.

"Wellesley?" she asked. They'd just been talking about Bran, but she was fairly sure that Asil wouldn't feel impelled to tell her something everyone knew.

Asil nodded. "He is a bass and usually slightly flat. Like Johnny Cash."

"Johnny Cash wasn't flat," Anna objected, having newly become a fan, much to the amusement of certain members of the pack. "He just sang melodies in unexpected ways—choosing other notes in the chords than the note our ear thinks the melody should probably carry."

"Or the songwriter intended," said Asil.

"It reduced the range of the songs," Anna continued doggedly. "But made them sound like Johnny Cash songs."

"Yes," agreed Asil. "But you say this as if it is a good thing."

"Lots and lots of people agreed with me," she said.

"Philistines," Asil proclaimed grandly.

"Charles likes Johnny Cash," she told him. Charles had been her gateway to a lot of music she'd once dismissed as old or hokey. Before Charles, her usual listening favorites were either truly classical—preferably with lots of cello—or whatever was current on the radio. Life with Charles had opened up her musical library considerably—and she had once thought herself thoroughly educated on the subject.

"Barbarian Philistines," Asil corrected himself. "Johnny Cash was an uneducated, backwoods man with a deep voice. You are wasted on Charles."

"Cash was a national treasure," she said, starting to feel a little hot. "He took folk music, church music, and rock, and fused them into something that spoke to a lot of people. And I'm so lucky I found Charles that I must have been blessed by leprechauns in a former life."

"You've never met a leprechaun, or you wouldn't say that." Asil gave her a superior smile before turning his attention to keeping the heavy SUV from sliding off the track when its right wheel hit a patch of soft dirt.

"I don't want the traitor to be Wellesley," Anna told him.

"Nor do I, *chiquita*."

After a while, during which she went over their conversation in her head, Anna asked suspiciously, "Do you like to listen to Johnny Cash?"

"I enjoy Dolly Parton," he said. "Now, there is a unique voice."

"That's not what I asked," Anna said. "Do you like to listen to Johnny Cash?"

Asil sighed and gave in with such overt embarrassment that she knew it wasn't an important issue for him—not that liking Johnny

Cash was something to be embarrassed about anyway. "Only the good songs." He glanced at her. "If you tell Charles, I'll deny it."

She raised her eyebrows. "Only if Charles asks me."

Asil's sigh, this time, was full to dripping with dramatic sorrow. "You shall be the death of me, Anna. The very death of me."

And at that moment he made a sudden right-hand turn off the cliff. Anna grabbed the oh-hell handle, reminded herself that she was a werewolf and unlikely to die in most motor-vehicle accidents— especially since Asil's Mercedes was less than a year old and came equipped with all sorts of airbags.

But the Mercedes didn't fall, just continued down a very steep track for twenty yards and twisted sharply to the right.

"Looks like that erosion control Bran had put in here held for another year," Asil said, as if he hadn't noticed her panicked reaction. "Until five years ago, every summer Wellesley had to rebuild that road because the edge where we just turned kept rolling off down the cliff every spring."

"You did that on purpose," Anna accused him.

He grinned whitely. "Maybe. But it was fun, no?"

She huffed at him and wouldn't give him a grin in return no matter how much she wanted to.

The big SUV rocked slowly down the rough track that ended . . . continued into a natural crack in the side of the mountain that was just big enough to swallow the Mercedes. Asil paused at the opening and blasted his horn twice. He paused for a count of five (because he counted out loud) and turned his lights on bright and continued down the track and into the heart of the mountain.

The darkness was so profound that the lights of Asil's Mercedes barely penetrated—or else there was just nothing to see. Anna saw a flash of reflective tape, and Asil's slow progress drew to a halt.

When Anna started to open her door, Asil shook his head as he turned the engine off. "Wait up a moment."

They sat in silence for a while, the lights of the car fading to off. Anna had gotten used to being able to see in the dark, and the stygian lack of light started to make her feel claustrophobic. And other kinds of phobic, too.

Finally, Anna couldn't stand the silence anymore.

"So why are we sitting here waiting?" she asked him.

"Because if we get out before Wellesley acknowledges our presence, bad things will happen. Wellesley was once an ordnance sergeant."

"A what?" Anna asked.

He snorted softly. "I keep forgetting how young you are. 'Ordnance sergeant' means that he blew up a lot of things with chemicals found around battlefields, farmyards, and nineteenth-century factories. He has this whole place—maybe the whole side of the mountain—wired to blow. Or so Bran told me once."

"Okay," Anna said thoughtfully. "Does it worry you that Leah sent you and me here together? She'd happily see us both dead. You more than I, generally, but not at the moment."

"Not in the slightest," Asil told her. "I am not destined to be blown to bits by a mad and talented artist. No artist would willingly destroy such a work of art as I am."

There was a clicking sound, then lights turned on around them.

"Now we can get out," Asil said. Which would have been more reassuring if he hadn't murmured softly, "I think."

Anna hesitated, but remaining in the car was unlikely to protect her if Wellesley did decide to blow them to kingdom come, so she got out. As she closed the door, she took her time looking around.

The entrance had been natural, but the track they'd followed in looked more like a mine shaft complete with hand-scraped timbers holding up the dirt ceiling and railroad track unmoored and piled up along the wall.

The place where they'd stopped had been widened so it could accommodate three cars. Presently it held Asil's Mercedes, an elderly Jeep, a motorcycle, and a snowmobile—the last two occupying one space. The ceiling directly over the parking area was ten feet high, if it was lucky, and I beams supported giant concrete blocks that (hopefully) endeavored to hold the mountain off their heads.

A narrow and irregular opening just in front of the motorcycle drew attention to itself by being more brightly lit than anywhere else.

Anna followed Asil past the motorcycle and into the opening, noticing that Asil seemed completely relaxed. If she were with anyone else, she'd have been reassured. But Asil had spent over a decade waiting for Bran to kill him—he didn't care as much about safety as she did.

There was a small landing just inside the opening followed by a sort of winding stairway. This wasn't a hand-carved work of art like she'd seen at Hester's home. This was a round, mostly vertical tunnel with dirt sides and chunks of two-by-fours stuck into the earth at irregular intervals, more like a ladder than a stairway, really.

Climbing up proved to be interesting. Sometimes the boards worked as treads for her feet—and sometimes she had to duck the boards above her in order to climb. About twenty feet up, there were far fewer boards. She had to jump and grab the one above her, chin-up until she could throw a leg over it, then stand on it and do it all over again.

The boards were pitted with claw marks, and it occurred to her that this would have been a much easier climb in her wolf form. She also noted that there were holes in the dirt wall where boards used to be. A thirty-foot fall was unlikely to kill her—but all the boards she could hit on the way down might just do the job.

At the top, there was a gap with no helpful two-by-fours for a distance about twice as high as she was tall. Asil had led the way, and he made the jump easily. He stood at the edge at the top for a moment, blocking her way. Then he stepped to the side and bent, giving her an arm to grab at the top. She had a moment to visualize herself jumping high enough to make it but then having no way to move sideways at the top of the leap. A childhood of Bugs Bunny cartoons allowed her to picture it all quite clearly.

As it was, she managed the business with about half of Asil's grace, even with his arm. But at least she didn't end up back at the bottom.

The hole through which they'd emerged was centered in a small, plain room without windows, which was illuminated by a single electric bulb. The flooring was simple, packed dirt except for the rim of metal around the edge of the hole. The walls of the room were rough-finished concrete. The only door was flat metal without visible hinges or any way to open it from their side.

"If this is what it takes to reach the people on our list," Anna told Asil, "we're going to be at it all night and then some."

"Wellesley will be the most difficult," Asil told her. "His trouble makes him a little paranoid. I thought that we should start with him and work down to the one where the only thing we can do is put a note in a mailbox and hope he checks it sometime this month."

"List?" said a gravelly bass as the door opened.

Asil was right. His voice did sound like Johnny Cash's, if Johnny had been born in the Carribbean instead of Arkansas.

He was a black man of about average height, with a barrel-chested build and thick, stubby fingers. For a werewolf, his face was weathered and his mouth soft.

He looked like he should make candy for a living, or stuffed toys, or some other blameless occupation. He didn't look like an artist, and he didn't look like someone who could harm a fly. But as much as she loved his art, he was still one of Bran's wildlings—he was plenty dangerous.

Asil said, "List of wildlings we are visiting today."

Wellesley was looking at Asil's knees, but he abruptly shook his head—a decidedly canid movement that involved his shoulders. His nostrils flared, and he inhaled noisily twice. He jerked his head, rocking back on his heels, then looked at Anna with widened eyes.

Almost immediately, he ducked his head so his gaze hit somewhere near Asil's boots. She got the impression that he wanted to look anywhere but at her.

"Sorry," he mumbled. "I've forgotten my manners. I don't usually get guests. Would you like to come into my house and have some . . . oh, tea, I suppose. I also have a little cocoa and some orange juice."

He stood back from the door and opened it a little wider in invitation, though he was still staring mostly anywhere except for Anna. It was the *mostly* that was disconcerting—because when he *was* looking at her, his gaze was yellow and desperate.

Anna could see that the living space beyond the door was the opposite of the tight little room they were in. There was lots of light, polished woods, and open spaces. She couldn't see any paintings within the narrow visual window that the door gave her, but she smelled oil paint and turpentine.

"Not necessary," said Asil politely. He didn't exactly step between her and Wellesley but near enough for everyone to understand that he considered Wellesley a threat to guard Anna from. "Wellesley, we're here to bring a warning." He told Wellesley about the attack on Hester and Jonesy.

As soon as Asil told him Hester and her mate were both dead, Wellesley jerked the door to his house closed—as if to protect it from damage from the words Asil was speaking. The artist leaned against the closed door and heard Asil out, a hand to his mouth, his eyes closed, and his whole body twitching.

Anna hoped that there was some way to open the door from this side that she wasn't seeing. Maybe he had another entrance?

When Asil was finished, Wellesley waited in the silence for a while. When his body was finally still, he said, in a hushed voice, "We are betrayed."

"Yes," Asil said simply.

Anna blinked at him a moment. And then at Wellesley. It had taken Jonesy's note for Anna to come to that conclusion. Maybe she was stupid, and everyone else would have seen it without the note.

"It was not I," Wellesley stated clearly. He raised his head and stared into Asil's eyes. "I told no one by any means that Bran was gone. I have never to my knowledge spoken to a living soul other than Bran about Hester or Jonesy—though I knew them both quite well at one time."

He dropped his eyes away from the more dominant wolf as soon as he'd finished speaking.

Anna's ability to suss out lies was much better than it had been when she was human, but she wasn't like Charles, who could feel them almost before they were spoken. If she didn't know that Charles could lie to Bran . . . she'd have seen Wellesley's declaration in front of Asil as proof positive that he had not betrayed them. It complicated matters that Wellesley's reactions had been so all over the place in the few minutes since they'd arrived. His words felt like the truth, but she'd let Asil make that determination.

Asil bowed his head at the other male, accepting his statement. And that simply, Wellesley was clear. Anna felt a wave of relief— which was ridiculous. She didn't know the man, just loved his work.

She wondered if they could just have all of the wildlings deny their culpability. It would make their job a lot easier. She was pretty sure that Bran could make them do that, but she wasn't sure that Charles could. Kill them, yes. Force them to answer insulting questions? Maybe not. If Charles couldn't, then she and Asil stood no chance.

Wellesley tapped his toe on the floor and cleared his throat. *Not-staring* at Asil with such intent that he might as well have his eyes locked on the other wolf. Asil's lips curled into a smile.

"It was not I," Asil told Wellesley clearly, catching his reluctant eye and holding him in his gaze by a willpower that Anna could feel even though she was not its focus.

"I would never willingly betray a trust given to me," Asil said. "I told no one outside of the pack that Bran was gone."

He hesitated thoughtfully, still holding Wellesley, made a soft sound, then continued, "I did not know Hester or Jonesy except through the stories of others. I never met either of them, though I knew they were here and approximately where they lived. I cannot recall what I have said about either of them or to whom, only that I would not speak of them in name or in any detail to anyone not in this pack.

"I would not willingly take part in any attack upon Bran's people or upon this pack, which I now call my own. This attack was underhanded—and clumsily done. If I were to do something like this, it would have been much better handled. Five years from now, Bran would still be scratching his head and wondering what happened to Hester and her mate."

Wellesley grimaced at Asil, then looked away from them both.

"Really," said Anna, amused despite herself. "That's your defense? 'If it had been me, I'd have done it right'?"

Asil smiled at her. "And what did you hear, wolf child? Was I lying?"

Anna hesitated, then shrugged. "You could probably tell me you had four aces in your poker hand, and I'd believe you even if the ace of spades was in *my* hand. Sadly, I think your last statement is more persuasive to me than whether or not I could tell if you were lying."

"Agreed," said Wellesley.

He was being very careful to keep his gaze away from Asil, staring mostly at the wall as he spoke, but there was a confident amusement in his voice totally at odds with his body posture. "I dare you to tell that to Bran."

"Bran would tell that to him," Anna said with a put-upon sigh. "Bran knows Asil."

Asil looked at her. It was a look with weight to it. She'd seen it on Charles before but not on Asil.

She raised her eyebrows in disbelief. "Really? You think I could be married to Charles and betray this pack? Charles?" *And I'm not a wildling,* she didn't say, but she thought it very hard. If she thought it was just a show for Wellesley, she wouldn't have been so annoyed. Hurt.

"I raised a witch who killed my mate," he told her, deadly serious. "I have learned not to trust my instincts about such things."

There was that, wasn't there?

"Okay," said Anna to Asil. "Here goes." She held his eye—not that eye contact was important to a wolf who was evaluating statements for truth, most of that was their nose and hearing. But it seemed to be how they were doing this, so she could play along.

"I did not betray this pack." She thought about the factors that spoke of betrayal, and said, "The enemy probably knows that Bran is not here. I discussed Bran's absence with no one outside the pack. I told no one in the pack or out of it about Hester because until yester-day I had no idea who she was or where she lived." She was getting mad, having to spell things out, so she brought it back to something simple. "I have never knowingly betrayed the pack, *would* never betray the pack."

"No one not in the pack knew of Hester," said Asil, an arrested look on his face.

"Samuel?" asked Anna.

"Oh, probably Samuel knew," Asil said dismissively. "But to imagine Samuel betraying his father or this pack, which was once his own? I cannot conceive of Samuel's doing such a thing."

Anna knew Samuel, of course, but he had left the pack long before she'd joined. She'd met him now and again, but she didn't know him well enough to say anything about him. But she trusted Asil's judgment.

"She could not do this," said Wellesley, waving his hand at Anna without looking at her. "She doesn't know enough to have planned it. And no mate of Charles could be untrustworthy—Brother Wolf sees more clearly than most."

"Agreed," said Asil with a sigh. "Truly, it would have been too easy if it had been any of the three of us."

"Whoever it is, they could teach the fae about deception," Wellesley said. "Whoever it is has lived with Bran—and not betrayed the fact that they are a traitor. Never lied and yet betrayed the Marrok just the same." He turned his head suddenly and whispered something she didn't catch.

Anna started to ask him to repeat it, but Asil caught her eye and shook his head.

"I cannot conceive of such a thing," Asil said.

"Gerry Wallace," said Anna dryly, "betrayed Bran and all his kin and kind." She might never have knowingly met him, but his betrayal still rang through the pack at odd moments. "Let's not turn our enemy into someone who is superhuman."

Asil gave her a sharp look.

"You know what I mean," she said, harassed. "Of course we are, all of us, superhuman—but giving our enemy more power in our imaginations is not useful."

"Still, it would be hard to keep an act like that going," said Asil. Apparently, even though Wellesley had cleared himself, they weren't going to let him in on the note Jonesy had left.

It would be a lot easier to keep a secret from Bran if you were one of the wildlings and weren't living under his thumb on a daily basis.

As Asil had indicated as they drove here, Wellesley, with his ability to go unnoticed, would have been a reasonable candidate for their spy. Except now that she'd met him, she was pretty sure he didn't have the focus.

"Sorry," said Wellesley. "I'm pretty isolated. I'm not much help. Sorry."

"Maybe, Anna," suggested Asil, his attention on their host, "you and I should go warn the other people on the list."

Anna, who'd been lost in her thoughts, glanced at Asil, then at Wellesley. The artist was shaking a little, and sweat had broken out on his forehead.

"Oh, stay," said Wellesley, in a low, clipped tone that was nothing at all like the voice he had been using a moment ago. "This is more interesting than anything that has happened in a while."

Anna looked at Asil, but he didn't see her. He was watching Wellesley like a cat watches a mouse—but more wary and less hungry.

"Let us look at the newest members," said Wellesley, sounding more like himself. Or at least, more like he'd sounded at first. He opened his hands and closed them a couple of times as he contin-ued, "They would have had to deceive Bran the shortest length of time."

In another person, Anna would have taken that as a threat. But it didn't track with what they were talking about or with the rest of his body language, which had been submissive to Asil the whole of this encounter.

"It's not Kara," said Anna positively.

"No," agreed Asil. Anna noticed that Asil had seen those hands, too. He paced a little as if he were thinking, but the movement in the small room left him directly between Wellesley and Anna. "She is a baby—and we know her background. She could not lie to me, let alone Bran." He paused. "And I'm pretty sure that she didn't know anything about Hester. It's not like anyone talks about the wildlings other than as a general warning."

What was Asil's game here? To see if Wellesley could finger one of the other wildlings?

"She could have heard something," Wellesley said, but this time it was a soft whisper, apologetic and tentative. "Children do." He was still bent low, staring hard at the corner of the room away from both Asil and Anna.

Wellesley shook his head violently. "That's stupid," he growled. "Stupid. Stupid. We have seen her when she didn't know we were watching, haven't we? She is weak, she is prey. We should eat her. She would taste like the girl in Tennessee. Better maybe."

Anna looked at Asil again, her eyes wide. She expected to see the same alarm or confusion that she felt. Or more probably anger—Kara was a particular favorite of Asil's. He was angry enough, she saw, but there was compassion on the Moor's face, too.

"Wellesley," said Asil, with cool command in his voice. "You will not speak of my little friend in that way. I don't like it."

Wellesley growled, and Asil growled back. The artist glanced over his shoulder with wolf-yellow eyes. He was taller and more muscled than the Moor, but he backed down as soon as his eyes met Asil's. He dropped to one knee, almost like a man proposing, his face turned again to the far corner of the room, though his body still faced Asil.

In a soft voice, he said, "It might be that someone spoke in front of her. That she told someone she shouldn't."

In her head, Anna heard again the voice of Wellesley's monster saying "like the girl in Tennessee," and wondered what Wellesley had done.

"It isn't Kara," Asil said again.

"If it were Kara, you could give her to me," said Wellesley in a singsong voice.

"You go too far," warned Asil, his lip beginning to curl.

Anna decided that if someone didn't step in, there would be trouble. And there was no one else but her. She couldn't risk soothing them with her Omega abilities—there was too great a chance that it would be more effective on Asil than Wellesley. Then she'd really be up a creek without a paddle.

She decided to try to distract them with words instead. Or even just Asil. There was something really wrong with Wellesley.

She had visions of Jack Nicholson in *The Shining* in her head. Leah had said that she had given them the most broken of the wildlings, and Asil said he'd picked the worst one first. Asil had told her Wellesley's condition most closely resembled schizophrenia. She'd known a girl in college who coped with schizophrenia, but that girl had never been creepy.

She hadn't been a werewolf, either, but still . . .

She didn't know how to distract Wellesley, but Asil was easy.

"Kara talks to Asil," she said firmly, as if she weren't stepping figuratively between two angry werewolves. "She talks to Leah and a little to me. But with the rest of the wolves, she is really wary—and I don't think she talks to any of the kids at school. Bran keeps getting letters from her teachers: 'Kara is hardworking and intelligent. I am concerned that she has no friends among her peers. She doesn't participate in group work or in any outside sports activities'—and variations of that. Leah makes her write a letter every week to her parents, most of which are four sentences long because Bran imposed that rule after her first letter was 'Dear Dad, I'm alive. Kara.'"

Sometime during her monologue, Asil pulled himself together. *More or less,* Anna thought.

"It's not Kara," said Asil definitively—and then he put some power in his voice, and said, "Stand down, Wellesley. Leave Kara alone." He paused. "And I better not catch your scent anywhere near her or where she has been."

Wellesley abruptly sat on the floor, turning until his back was toward them. He nodded, showing he was paying attention to the conversation.

"Okay," he agreed, his voice a lot more normal than his posture. Almost conversationally, he asked, "What about Sherwood? He would know about the wildlings—he was one for a while. He would know about Bran's absence because he is in Adam's pack now."

"Sherwood Post?" said Asil. "No."

Wellesley looked at Asil then, an exasperated look over his shoulder. "Well, it has got to be someone. And Sherwood is next newest after Kara and Anna."

For a wildling, Wellesley seemed to be pretty well versed on who was who in the pack. No wonder Asil had put him at the top of their suspect pool.

The artist's eyes narrowed thoughtfully at Asil. "You *did* know him before the witches got to him and took his leg and his memory. Who was he?"

Asil frowned, then shook his head. "It doesn't matter now. It is highly unlikely that he'll remember who he once was. No matter what Bran thinks. But the core of him is the same: he was the champion of underdogs. He would never facilitate an attack on someone vulnerable. No. It is not Sherwood. Besides, he only knew that Bran was gone while they were out rescuing Mercy. As far as I know, no one who is not pack knows Bran is still gone."

This conversation was pretty weird even by werewolf standards. She wished she'd grabbed Asil and left when he had suggested it. The echo of "that girl in Tennessee" kept the hair on the back of her neck up and her wolf restless.

"It has to be someone," said Wellesley. Then he paused. "Maybe not. What about some sort of electronic spyware? It could be something planted in the Marrok's house—or even on a person who didn't know about it. I've read about things that people swallow, and they listen to everything." The artist had his face pointed back toward the corner of the room, so he didn't see Asil's thoughtful look. "Maybe I read about it," Wellesley muttered. "Or maybe someone did that to me. I forget. Stupid."

"Not stupid," Asil disagreed. "There is still a bill out in Congress suggesting that all werewolves should be implanted with a tracking device, but it's stalled because they can't come up with one that survives a shift," said Asil.

And part of the weirdness of this whole conversation had to be the way Asil mostly ignored Wellesley's strange actions and talked to him as if they were having a normal interchange. Well, she could do that, too, if it was useful.

"As Charles demonstrated how technology explodes during a change," said Anna.

Asil gave her an interested look.

"When we were working with Cantrip and the FBI in Boston," she clarified. "Charles said he didn't think it would work, and he was happy to demonstrate."

"Charles is witchborn," said Wellesley dismissively. "He could blow up any technology he chose." Then in that odd voice, the one that had spoken of killing young women, he said, "Witches are evil."

Anna chose to continue to follow Asil's lead and react only to the normal things Wellesley said. "If it helps anyone be less paranoid," she said, "Charles told me that he was pretty sure that their device wouldn't have worked even if he hadn't helped it along. As for electronic spyware at the Marrok's house—Charles does a sweep for them a couple times a week."

She left the witchborn comment where it was. It was true. In this company, there was no profit in dwelling on it.

"Paranoid bastard," said Asil, with something that sounded oddly like affection.

"He finds listening devices and cameras once in a while," she told them. "Usually during the Changing moon in October, when we have so many strangers."

"Werewolves bring spying devices?" asked Asil with soft interest.

Anna shook her head. "Not on purpose, we don't think. So far it's all been on werewolves who admit what they are to the world. The kinds of things Charles has found have been bugs on cars, clothing, or luggage."

"Then why doesn't the human world know about Aspen Creek?" asked Wellesley.

"They do," Anna told him. "They don't know about the Marrok, we don't think. But they have known about Aspen Creek since the 1970s at least, probably earlier than that. A select group of 'they.' That was one of the things that drove Bran to bring the werewolves out into the open. Secrets are only useful as leverage as long as they are secrets." That last sentence was an almost-direct quote from Bran.

"Then why doesn't everyone know about Aspen Creek?" Wellesley asked again.

"Bran doesn't want the tourist trade," Asil said. "And he's managed to convince the people who do know that it would be a bad thing to bring out into the open."

"The monsters need somewhere to run," Anna said.

Wellesley rose easily to his feet. "Indeed," he agreed.

"You made a valid point, Asil," Anna said firmly. She wasn't sure that Wellesley's rising to his feet was anything good. Her wolf was beginning to get agitated. Which valid point had she been talking about? She grabbed one at random, jumping back twenty minutes of conversation to do it. "I mean, when you noted that you'd have done a better job of the mess at Hester's. *If* the intent was to abduct Hester."

"Interesting," said Asil. "What other intent could they have had?"

"They could have wanted her dead—and muddied the waters of motivation by implying that it was a bigger operation than a simple assassination," Wellesley offered. "Or they could have wanted Jonesy dead."

"Or they could have wanted to know where all our lone wolves, our powerful and vulnerable damaged wolves are," said Anna slowly. *They were asking about the wildlings,* Jonesy's note had said. Charles had told her that there were wolves out here that had dangerous knowledge—things other people would kill to know. "Surmising that we would have to go out and warn them." It only made logical sense, as long as you knew enough about how the pack worked, how the wildlings worked to know that a phone call was probably not going to do the job.

"We weren't followed," said Asil.

"On *NCIS*, they use satellites and can pick out individuals in guerrilla-troop ground movements," Anna told him.

"What is this NCIS?" asked Asil.

"They also have a mass spec that can look at a clump of mud off a shoe and tell Abby the cross street it came from with no error. And it only takes five minutes," said Wellesley dryly. "Mass specs don't work like that."

Apparently, Wellesley watched TV. And knew what a mass spec was and how it worked. This conversation could not get more surreal.

Asil growled.

"It's a TV show," Anna told him. "About the Naval Criminal Investigative Service. It's a mix of mystery and military thriller."

"A TV show," Asil said disdainfully.

Wellesley grinned, ducked his head, and raised a hand to high-five Anna.

There was a crystalline moment when she understood that this wasn't a good idea. Wellesley clearly had some issues. All of the werewolves had a bit of multiple personality disorder—the human half and the wolf half sometimes existed in a state of conflict. Charles and Brother Wolf were a functional demonstration of how separate the wolf spirit and the human could be. But her mate and his wolf existed in harmony.

Wellesley and his wolf were not functional at all. Getting close enough to touch him when he had spent the last half hour switching back and forth between normal and creepy was stupid.

And still, she was the mate of Charles Cornick, who was second in the Marrok's pack. If she let that friendly gesture hang, that would be quite a statement—one she did not want to make.

She stepped around Asil and slapped Wellesley's upraised hand with her own.

Anna was a werewolf. She had been working out with Charles virtually since he'd brought her to Montana. Her reaction time was good; she was quicker than a lot of the wolves.

And she had no time to respond as Wellesley's hand closed over her wrist, and he plowed into her like a grizzly bear, sending them both to the floor. She hit the hard-packed dirt floor underneath his not-inconsiderable weight. He wrapped himself around her, his body shaking. Her stomach lurched with memories that she thought were long behind her.

Something hit the ground right next to her ear, startling her out of her panic. She turned to see that Asil had buried a knife . . . a sword . . . something with a beautifully crafted hilt in the dirt. The blade was only visible for about a quarter of an inch.

Asil had been going to kill to defend her, she realized. But he'd apparently understood much faster than she exactly what had happened—and more importantly, what hadn't.

Wellesley hadn't attacked her . . . hadn't meant to attack her, anyway. He was trying to get as close as he could while sobbing wildly and muttering something in a language she couldn't understand.

"Omega," said Asil quietly. He crouched beside her, his face only a few feet away from hers. "I should have stopped you from touching him. My wife, she had better control of what she was. No one would have understood what she was, or been affected by her by a casual touch unless she wanted them to."

"What do I do?" she whispered, partly so that she wouldn't startle Wellesley into anything more violent. But mostly because her throat was so dry with fear and remembered horror that she couldn't have made a louder sound if she tried.

"Stay still," he said. "Hopefully, his reaction will ease after a few minutes."

She looked at him. She wasn't going to be able to lie here, with a stranger on top of her, for a few minutes.

He saw it. "If I try to pull him off," he told her, "it's not going to help anything."

She nodded. She understood that Wellesley was getting some sort of relief from her, and he would react badly if someone tried to take it away from him. Asil didn't think Wellesley was rational enough to let her go.

"Okay," she said, trying not to sound panicked. Hoping that Charles wasn't picking up on this. He wouldn't if she managed to keep herself from blind terror. "Okay."

"What can I do to help?" Asil asked.

"Talk," she said. "Distract me."

"How about a story?" He reached out and put a hand on Wellesley's shoulder. "His mate died, and his wolf wanted to die with her. It happens that way sometimes. As far as I know, they've been at war ever since, he and his wolf. A hundred years more or less, I think. Like a split personality disorder, but your other half is a killing machine, and you can never let it take over."

"The girl in Tennessee?" Anna murmured, fairly certain that Wellesley wasn't attending the conversation between her and Asil. He was crying noisily, and it was a horrible thing to hear from a grown man. But it reassured her, because he didn't sound like . . .

Anyone else.

Asil nodded to her almost-question. "After Tennessee is when Bran brought him here. Back in the 1930s, I think. He'd been a well-known artist under a different name when his wife died." The old werewolf, whose mate had also died while he survived, made a sympathetic sound. He patted Wellesley again, and this time left his right hand on the other werewolf's shoulder.

"He tried to keep up his life, but one day he just left. Left his pack. Left his house with everything in it. A wolf who was there, a member of his pack, told me it was eerie. As if one morning, just after breakfast was ready to eat, he decided he was done with it. No one heard of him for a while. It was the Depression, and traveling on trains was a way of life for a lot of people. There was no easy way to find him."

"Not like now," Anna said. It was hard to get the words out of her throat, but at least she didn't have to whisper.

"Not like now," agreed Asil. "Technology has made a lot of things easier—but also Wellesley's case in particular made Bran decide that it was important not to lose track of any werewolf if he could help it."

"You were in Spain during the 1930s," Anna said. Her voice was shaky. She didn't like sounding like that—fear was dangerous around werewolves. But even knowing that there was nothing sexual about what Wellesley was experiencing, she couldn't help the cold sweat that trickled down her back.

Asil made an assenting sound.

"You know a lot about this for a man who was on another continent at the time."

Asil's smile flashed. "I know everything worth knowing," he told her. But his face grew pensive. "I asked after I started to visit with him. I wanted to know as much as I could in hopes I could help him. I knew a little before, of course. His story was widely published at the time. I think part of what has made Bran so harsh on the wolves, now that the public knows about us, is that he is afraid that someone will remember the old story of Wellesley."

"Tell me?" she asked.

"As you said," Asil told her, "it was easier to be lost and wander back in those days. Lots of men without families or pasts wandered the railroad and the highways in the Depression era. Wellesley was just another one of them until he finally lost control of the wolf in a little town with a population of about four hundred people. It's not around anymore, that little town, or maybe more people would remember this story. Wellesley is sometimes certain that there was a black witch—or something like a black witch—involved. But in the aftermath, there was only Wellesley and some bodies: a black man in a mostly white town."

Asil patted Wellesley again, but the other werewolf didn't appear to notice him. After a moment, Asil started talking again.

"That's when Bran became aware of him. He sent Charles to break Wellesley out." There was a pause, and Asil said sourly because he didn't want to respect Charles, "I understand he broke into that jail where Wellesley was under heavy guard and left with him. But if you can get that closemouthed wolf to tell you how he did it in plain sight of two guards, leaving an empty and locked cell behind them with no one the wiser, there would be a lot of people who'd love to hear that story."

"Can't you ask Wellesley?" Anna asked.

Asil shook his head. "He doesn't remember anything except bits and pieces—mostly that's his wolf, anyway. Wellesley doesn't have enough memories to defend himself from anything someone wants to claim about that day if someone goes digging up old newspaper records or someone's diary about the matter."

"You think he is innocent?"

Asil sighed. "I think that truth is complicated—and speculating on things without adequate facts is useless. You can ask your mate if you are curious. His orders were to kill or rescue, depending upon what his judgment told him was best—and here is our Wellesley, safe if not sound."

Wellesley's sobs had been quieting, but Anna was deliberately focusing on Asil, so she didn't notice the difference in him soon enough.

Asil, though? *Asil* was on Wellesley before his sharpening teeth could do more than scrape against her collarbone. Then they were both rolling around the room while Anna scrambled to her feet. Before she could jump in and add her weight to the game, Asil had Wellesley pinned to the floor in some complex wrestling move that didn't allow the werewolf to use his great strength to break free.

And Wellesley—or the wolf spirit that lived in Wellesley—was trying. His eyes, those brilliant gold wolf's eyes so startling in his dark face, saw nothing but enemies. His face, changing slowly to wolf, was wild. His jaws snapped and snapped at the air as if there were some way that he could climb out of the bones of his body to get at Asil—but would be satisfied with anyone.

Asil crooned to him in Spanish as if the mad creature were a child. There was power in his voice, the werewolf magic of a very dominant wolf trying to settle Wellesley.

She could feel the other man trying to come back, but the wolf spirit was dominant, too. Asil, she thought, could have subdued the other wolf, but he was hoping that Wellesley could control it himself. A wolf this old who couldn't control himself better than this would need to be killed.

The impulse to soothe Wellesley, to bring him the relief that her Omega nature brought to troubled wolves, was instinctive and felt desperately necessary. But she gathered herself together and thought before she gave in to that desire.

She was in control when she reached out with her power to do what she could. She wouldn't have tried it if it had been Charles holding Wellesley, but it was Asil, who had been mated to an Omega wolf. He'd had a long time to learn how to guard himself, to stay alert, no matter what his wolf felt from her.

She took a deep breath, centering herself, and crouched, staying on her feet in case she had to move fast. She put her hand on Wellesley's cheek with enough pressure that he'd have trouble turning his head to bite her.

The trapped wolf shuddered at her touch.

Asil turned his croon to English, speaking to her in the same voice he was using for Wellesley. "Be careful what you do, Anna. Your abilities allow you to bring a wolf terrific relief—but it comes at a cost. When you pull away, he has to take up the burden of controlling the beast again—and that requires a lot more courage and fortitude than doing it in the first place."

"I know," she said simply. "I'm not likely to forget the disaster of Bran's experiments with me. But my read on this is that we don't have a choice."

Asil closed his eyes, opened them again, and nodded. "If you can't fix him, I will send him to a final rest, where this burden will no longer trouble him."

"Will you be all right when I soothe him?" she asked, half expecting him to take offense, but she had recognized that he had been speaking of himself, too, not just Wellesley, when he warned her of the possible results of her meddling.

Asil smiled grimly. "I do not want to kill this one, who has fought so hard for such a long time. One who creates such beauty as he does is worthy of anything we can do to help him."

It wasn't a yes. But she thought she might have a fix for that.

She'd been practicing using what she was ever since she came to Aspen Creek. It was sometimes hard to find victims . . . subjects. As Asil said, most of the wolves didn't object to the initial effect—it was afterward that made it difficult. Kara was her most consistent volunteer.

Before she learned to handle it better, what her Omega aura did was flood an area with a wave of peace that sent the beast spirit of unprepared werewolves into sleep. She and the only other Omega she knew about had consulted over the Internet (because he lived in Italy) and pulled in Asil, who knew more about Omegas than either of them did. They had been working on other ways to utilize their effect without dropping their friends in their tracks. One of the things they had come up with was something that was more . . . invitation than hammer.

She closed her eyes and visualized a quiet little hollow under an old tree next to a fast-running creek that was a favorite spot of hers. The sound of the creek rushing by, the smell of growing things, the peace of the place took hold of her heart.

For a long time, this method had only worked with Charles because she could use their mating bond as a conduit. She'd gotten practiced enough that she could use the pack bonds as well, and lately she'd been experimenting using only touch. Unexpectedly, that had proved more powerful—or at least differently powerful—than using the mate or pack bonds.

With skin contact, Anna gained an insight she had never received with her mating bond or the pack bonds: empathy. Or empathy of a sort, anyway. It wasn't so much that she felt the other wolf's emotions; what she got was a sort of pressure reading. She could gauge how *much* emotion they were holding. She'd learned to work with that, to soften the full force of whatever they were feeling, then back away.

It worked better with some wolves than others, of course. She couldn't get a read, most times, on Bran or Asil, let alone affect the amount of emotion they were feeling. Kara was her best subject. Between them they had fine-tuned the effect so Anna could help Kara just take the edge off—or coax Kara's inner wolf into a willing sound sleep without affecting any of the wolves nearby. Or at least allowing the nearby wolves to resist the rest she offered them. She planned on trying that now, so that she was less likely to affect Asil.

She didn't know if her touch would allow her to influence Wellesley's wolf at all. But if not, she always had her big hammer to whomp him to sleep with. The whomp would hit Asil, too, though.

"I'm going to try asking him to let his wolf sleep—like I do with

Kara. I don't know if this will affect you," she told Asil. "I've never tried it when someone else was touching my experimental subject."

He laughed, just a little, as if he were not wrestling with another werewolf. "I am prepared, *mija*. Do what you need to."

She used her touch on Wellesley's cheek to extend her invitation of peace. He reached for it immediately—and then yanked her out of her forest glade into Hell.

There was a moment when she could have broken free, then that moment was gone, and Wellesley was in charge. Sort of.

Pain swamped her, pain and weariness so deep that it felt bottomless, and it hurt to breathe. She was lost in Wellesley's emotions for a long, horrible, endless time.

"Anna? *Chiquita*? Talk to me." Asil's quiet voice grounded her, reminded her that there was a reality besides Wellesley's pain and brought her back out to where she could have dropped the connection between herself and the other wolf again.

He had let her go.

She took a breath, but she didn't take her hand off Wellesley.

"I'm all right," she told Asil. "But this is a little strange. Bear with me—and do not let him up."

She put her other hand on Wellesley's face, drew in another deep breath, and let him suck her back into his prison. She didn't pull away from his pain, and in accepting it, she discovered that she could separate herself a bit—and she understood what had happened.

Wellesley had invited her in. And his invitation had power. His power wasn't like Bran's; nor was it witchcraft . . . not quite. But it wasn't not witchcraft, either. Asil said that Wellesley had magic more akin to Charles's—and the magic Charles usually used belonged to his mother, a healer and a shaman's daughter. The power felt more like Charles's than like Bran's. But it was not the same as her mate's.

The space—it wasn't quite a place—that she found herself in was dark and felt hollow to her ears, as if it were somehow enclosed. But she didn't know how far to trust her perceptions.

When all else fails, the memory of Charles's voice rang in her ears, *follow your instincts. Werewolves have pretty good instincts.*

This felt like the kind of place where instincts would be more useful than intellect.

She moved through the darkness and came upon Wellesley. It wasn't as if she found him where he had always been. One moment he was not anywhere, and the next he came into being, quite near. Near enough that she took a step backward, becoming aware in that moment that she *could* step, that she had something that felt like a physical body.

She could perceive Wellesley, the man, quite clearly. But she could also feel the struggle he was carrying on, feel his great weariness and his pain, as if those things were part of what she was seeing, just as easily as she could perceive his outer form.

He fought so hard, and he had been fighting a very, very long time. Nearly a century of battle had worn him down to his essentials. She could see places where he was worn thin, his body fading to gray in patches.

That's where you can see me, something whispered in her ear. *There, in those bare spots.*

And *that* wasn't scary. Not at all.

But she followed her instincts and didn't look behind her, though the hairs on the back of her neck were raised as if they were her wolf's hackles. Whatever was back there smelled evil, rank, and rotting. In a place like this, sometimes noticing things too hard gave them more reality. And that wasn't instincts talking, it was something Charles had taught her.

She concentrated on Wellesley. What was he fighting? Because she couldn't perceive his wolf at all. That thing that had whispered in her ear, that wasn't a wolf. She knew that as instinctively as she saw his fight—though he wasn't moving at all.

If he wasn't fighting his wolf spirit, despite Asil's story, maybe he was fighting *for* his wolf. That felt right. As soon as she accepted that idea, her connection to Wellesley increased appreciatively until she could feel the echoes of his emotions. It was a terribly intimate connection to have with someone who was basically a stranger—someone not her mate.

She didn't find the kind of heartbreaking sadness that Asil had led her to expect. There were oodles of despair. But despair was not a synonym for sorrow or regret. Despair was the loss of hope.

Please, he asked her, his voice coming, as that evil thing's voice had, from just behind her left ear. *Please help us,* Namwign Bea. *We are dying, healer.*

What can I do? she asked him, but he just repeated the same request, over and over again, as if he could not hear her.

She reached out and touched his cheek, as she had in the real world. He did not react to her touch, nor did touching him change her perception of him or this place. He had, she thought, told her as much as he could; it was up to her to find out more.

She set out to do that very thing, leaving the human seeming of Wellesley behind her. She couldn't hear or smell his wolf, but the scent of the evil that had whispered behind her back—that was sharp in her nose. At first she tried to avoid it, but when nothing else drew her attention, she followed her senses.

Eventually or immediately (it was frustratingly difficult to tell), she found a forest of thick green vines that were so tangled she could not go through them. When she turned, to see if she might go around them, they had encircled her.

Trapping her.

She swallowed down fear. Asil was in the real world, watching over her. And her ties to her mate were strong, stronger here than in the real world, as if they had more substance here. She was not alone, no matter what her fears tried to tell her.

She reached out and touched the fibrous growth. As Wellesley himself had, the plants felt real under her touch. She couldn't see any structure that was holding the vines up; they seemed to be holding themselves in place. Out of the corner of her eye she could see them move, but the ones directly in front of her were motionless.

She closed her fingers around one of the vines. It was nearly as big around as her wrist. Experimentally, she gave it a tug. It gave a little and was answered by motion farther in the tangle, the sound of rustling plant matter filling the emptiness.

She gave it a sharp jerk, calling upon her wolf to help and putting her shoulders and hips into the effort. Reluctantly, the vines shifted until she caught a glimpse of golden fur.

She tried to reach through, to touch the fur—and impaled her hand, the one still hurting from the silver bullet that had kill Hester, upon a thorn as long as her pinkie. The vines, she saw, were covered with long, sharp thorns, though they hadn't been a moment before.

She growled and redoubled her efforts to pull the vines away. Her hands bled until they were slick, and she left bright trails of blood on the skin of the plants. Wherever her blood stained the vines, they loosened until she could, at last, see the sickened and enraged creature trapped within.

The wolf, presumably Wellesley's other half, looked plague-ridden. His coat, damaged as if by mange, revealed oozing sores where the thorns had dug in. There were places in which the wolf's flesh had grown over the vines that trapped him so that he was part of the structure that held him prisoner.

Rationally, she was pretty sure that she was using constructs to try to organize what she felt through the magic: her magic and Wellesley's magic. That what she saw was more symbolic than actual. But maybe not.

Anna was her father's daughter, and her father believed in science and rational thinking. She'd been a werewolf for years now, and she still tended to think about it from a scientific viewpoint, as though lycanthropy were a virus.

Faced with a wall of briar-thorned vines straight out of a Grimms' fairy tale, she'd never had it brought home so clearly that what she was and what she did was magic. Not Arthur C. Clarke magic, where sufficient understanding could turn it into a new science that could be labeled and understood. But a "there's another form of power in the universe" magic. Something alien, almost sentient, that ran by its own rules—or none. Real magic, something that could be studied, maybe, but would never rest in neatly explainable categories.

With that in mind, she tried visualizing a knife, or something she could cut through the vines with. But apparently that wasn't something her magic could do. In frustration, she called upon her wolf.

But found that she couldn't change to her wolf, not here in Welles-ley's . . . what? Imagination? Soul? Prison.

But she managed to give her hand claws. She dug into the vines, sinking her claws into the surface of the vine.

Querida, said Asil, *are you sure you want to bleed him?*

For a bare instant she got a flash of the real world, where her real claws had sunk into Wellesley's skin.

Horrified, she pulled her claws out of the vines. Almost inadver-tently, her gaze met the determined eyes of the trapped golden wolf. A gray, viscous substance leaked down the green exterior of the plant from the holes she had dug in it. And the substance smelled nox-iously awful.

And it whispered in her ears. It whispered terrible things, the kinds of things that sounded just like those vines smelled.

There was magic in those vines, which she had known. But what she had not been sure of was whose magic it was. Now she knew that Asil had been very wrong—this was absolutely not a case of Wellesley's human half and wolf half at odds because their mate had died.

This was a curse, something done to them by someone else. The blood of the vines smelled horribly familiar—Anna knew what blood magic smelled like. In Asil's story, there had been a mention of a black witch. She could now inform him that the rumor was true. There had definitely been a black witch involved, someone powerful enough to set a binding spell on a werewolf that lasted . . . however long this had lasted.

She didn't know how to help him.

She could soothe the wolf spirit of any werewolf. She'd learned to send them to sleep, too, for a while. With her help, they had reduced the number of newly turned wolves who died because they could not control their wolf within the first year after their Change.

But if she sent this wolf to sleep, no matter how much he needed the rest—and she could tell that he was as exhausted as his human counterpart, if not more so—he would lose the fight against the thorns.

This was witchcraft, and she knew nothing about how to break a cage wrought by witchcraft. But she knew someone who knew more than she did—and who had his own kind of magic.

Charles, she thought, reaching for him without letting go of the carnivorous vines. *Charles, I need you.*

"She put us together just to be annoying," Sage told Charles, sounding not in the least annoyed.

They had taken her SUV because she refused to drive his truck. Her SUV was pretty upscale for the rough roads—she was a Realtor, selling high-priced Montana dreams to very rich people who wanted to get away from the city. When he'd told her that the road was too rough for her overly civilized SUV, she'd laughed and told him she'd rather replace her vehicle than put those scratches on his beloved truck.

He'd rather she not scratch his truck up, either. If she was planning on doing that, then taking her car made good sense.

"Leah?" asked Charles, though he knew quite well which "she" Sage was talking about.

She nodded. She gave him a glance out of the corner of her eye. "Why didn't you put a stop to it? Everyone knows that she can't order you around. No one would have been surprised—not even Leah, I don't think. So why did you let her do it?"

Charles eyed Sage, evaluating what answer to give.

Like his stepmother, she liked to wear nice clothes. Part of the reason for that was her job, and part of it was she wore them like armor. She didn't wear soft things, colors and fabrics to make her look sweet. The clothes she wore gave her visual power. Here, they declared to the world, is a strong woman.

To him, they said something a little different. Here, they said, is a woman who needs armor, a shield to hide behind. Here is a woman who is afraid but puts her chin up and whistles in the dark.

He remembered what she'd looked like when Bran had brought her here, the look in her eyes the same as Anna's eyes when they'd first met.

"Leah is my father's mate," he told Sage. "As long as she does nothing that will harm the pack, it is not my place to object."

Sage raised an eyebrow at him in disbelief before returning her attention to the road. Sage didn't look at him with fear in her eyes anymore. He liked her. She was smart, funny, and wise. Someone he could trust to have his back.

He relaxed into the too-cushiony seat and gave her all of his truth instead of bits and pieces as he might have another of his pack mates.

"Though Asil and I are not friends, he likes Anna. He will give his life to make her safe. She likes him, too, and is comfortable in his company."

"You left your mate with Asil because she likes him?" Sage asked archly. "Charlie, I'd never have thought it of you."

She was the only one who ever got to call him that. Because the first time she'd said it, she'd been bruised and scared. When his father had introduced him to her, she'd raised her face to look him in the eyes, terror making her shake. Then she'd said, with hopeless defiance, "Hello, hello, Charlie."

He took a better hold on the door as she turned her tame car off the road as he directed. The track they traveled on had tall grass that brushed the underside of her car. He half expected that they were going to be running back on four feet.

"I left my mate with Asil because neither of them is capable of betraying a trust," Charles told her. "And, as much as she dislikes me, no one could ever say that Leah works against the pack's best interest. As long as that is true, I will follow her as I follow my father."

Sage laughed when he said that. "Yes. We've all heard the battleground of your obedience to Bran." She laughed harder. "Or Leah. The funniest part of that statement, though, is that you actually believe it."

It was the truth, he thought, a little indignantly. But he seldom argued with people other than his da or Anna, so he let it go. She'd slowed down, so he released his hold on her car and folded his arms impassively. He stood by his word: he'd follow Leah exactly as well as he followed his da.

She glanced at him. "Okay," she said. "Here's another question, then. Why did you bring that thing along?"

"That thing" was the witch gun.

"Some of the wildlings we are going to visit have interesting backgrounds," he told her. "All of them are old. I want to know if any of them have heard of something like this."

She pulled into a flat meadow and stopped in front of a ranch-style house that would have looked more appropriate on a city street than in the middle of the woods. His home was a ranch-style, too.

But in this setting, the little gray house looked like a house cat in a tiger's den.

He knew these wildlings well enough to have put the probability of their being his traitor pretty low. Long-term deception wasn't so much beyond them as beneath them. Cowardly.

He got out of the car, and as soon as he did so, he felt eyes on the back of his neck. He let Brother Wolf do the work of finding their watchers.

Long-term deception was cowardly, but ambushing your allies was just fine.

"Behind us," Sage said, having walked around the front of the car—and then returned to his side.

She wasn't afraid, not exactly. She smelled of stress, worry even. She probably should have been afraid. She was also wrong.

They weren't behind them—though that was an interesting ploy. He wondered if they actually were able to use the pack magic to manipulate the wind, as Bran could, or if it was a trick of the geography that they'd learned to take advantage of. With wildlings—especially with these wildlings—it could be either one.

"We bring a word and a warning," Charles said, without raising his voice. "Hester and Jonesy are dead at the enemy's hands. An enemy that included a helicopter and teams with werewolves willing to attack the Marrok's wolves. They hit Hester's place with the intention of taking her captive. They had her caged. When we freed her, they killed her on purpose."

He turned, as if to get back into the SUV, and a man dropped out of a tree twenty feet in front of the car.

He was, like Bran, the kind of person who would fade into a crowd even without using pack magic. He wasn't tall or short, good-looking or ugly. There was nothing particularly memorable about his face at all. Except for his eyes. His eyes were white, wolf's eyes, and they were predatory.

"Bran's gone," the man said, his English very British. "Now Hester is dead because you aren't capable, Charles Marroksson, of protecting the pack."

He had already known about the attack on Hester. It wasn't surprising. These wolves had closer contact with others in the pack than most of his da's wildlings because one of them regularly participated in pack hunts and had a few friends in the regular pack. If it weren't for his brothers, he'd probably be out in the world, a safe-ish, sane-ish member of a normal pack.

There were three of them, brothers all, a set of twins and their younger sibling. If the stable twin hadn't been with them, Charles suspected Bran would have had the other two executed for reasons of public safety.

"You think you could do better?" Charles said very softly. The wind didn't favor him. He couldn't tell which of the brothers he was talking to other than it was one of the twins.

The other twin dropped down to the ground from a higher branch in a different tree. His landing was loud—louder than it needed to be to cover for their third, as yet unseen, brother.

"We could hardly do worse," he said. And, confident that his twin had an eye on Charles, he looked at Sage and smiled. "Hey, pretty lady. You'll make a fine prize."

Despite herself, despite the years between Sage as she was now and the beaten woman she'd been when she came to them, when she said, "Try me," her voice was tense, and she took a step closer to Charles.

The second twin laughed, a full-throated, merry sound. "Oh, I intend to, yes. Don't we, Geir?"

The other twin smiled. "Yes."

Geir was the sanest of the three.

Charles had no intention of believing them about which of them was which, of course, not when they were being so careful to stay downwind, where his nose couldn't make the distinction. He took a slow step away from Sage, putting her between him and the twins.

She stiffened at the unexpected move. She'd asked for his protection by stepping into his personal space. His movement was a denial. But he couldn't help her perception—or worry about it too much.

He was too busy spinning to catch hold of the axe that Ofaeti, the third of the Viking brothers, tried to stick in his back. He grabbed it by the haft, one hand on top, the other at the end, Ofaeti's hands caught between his. The Viking wasn't expecting it, so Charles was able to swing the big man around, off balance. Charles snapped a quick kick into his knee, which gave with a crack.

And right then, right at that moment, Charles felt Anna call him.

"Sage," he said. "Get in the car and stay out of this."

Strictly speaking, a fight for dominance was supposed to be one-on-one. For that reason, he wanted Sage completely out of it. And maybe he'd seen that look of betrayal on her face and wanted to remove any doubt in her mind that he had kept her safety at the forefront of his decisions.

Unlike his Anna, Sage would follow orders. He put her out of his considerations—except as a noncombatant to be protected.

Ofaeti had released his hold on the axe when his knee broke. Charles tossed it up and caught it in a proper grip. It was a good axe, heavy and weighted for fighting rather than cutting down trees.

The twins, Geir and Fenrir (Charles was pretty sure that wasn't the name he was born with but a name he'd earned), had sprinted forward when Ofaeti attacked, but seeing Charles with the axe in his hand and Ofaeti out of the fight (more or less), they slowed to a more cautious pace.

Charles? If you aren't busy, I could use some advice.

Charles heard a soft sound behind him and, without looking, swept the flat side of the axe to his right about hip height like a backward swing of a baseball bat.

Now, said Brother Wolf in satisfaction as behind them the ground accepted a probably-not-dead body with a hollow thump, *Ofaeti is no longer a factor.*

Charles smiled in amusement—and the simple joy of battle. The Viking brothers had been fighting for longer than Charles had been alive, but they did not have Brother Wolf as a partner nor had they had Bran Cornick and Charles's uncle Buffalo Singer as teachers.

The twins separated, trying to make him defend both of his sides at the same time. He let them do it because it would make no difference to his game. He was only a little hampered because he'd prefer not to kill either of them. His da had put them in his hands to protect, and they had not done anything (yet) that would force his hand.

Fenrir closed first, aiming a kick at Charles's thigh. Charles stepped into it, and Fenrir's kick slid up his thigh and into his hip, its force spent before it did any harm. Charles grabbed that leg under the knee and hit Fenrir in the belly with his other hand. The force of it bent the other wolf over, and Charles tucked Fenrir's head under his free arm, then pulled them both over backward in a suplex.

Fenrir's fall was outside of his control, and his spine came down across the stump Charles had been aiming him at. It broke with a loud snap, and Fenrir let out a whine.

Charles was free of Fenrir and rolling to his feet before Geir's sword struck and missed. The second strike Charles caught on the axe.

Charles? Anna's voice was small. *I really need your help, or I'm pretty sure that some of us aren't going to make it out of this.*

A moment, he told her. And he quit playing because his wife needed him. He broke the sword with a swing of his axe and caught Geir's eyes—only then realizing it was Fenrir, not Geir. He'd rather it really had been Fenrir lying with a broken back.

Hopefully, Geir would survive.

"Enough," Charles said. "I do not have time for this. We are *done*. Submit."

The old wolf fought the compulsion, sweat dripping down his face and dampening his shirt. But his fist opened and the blade dropped to the ground as he dropped to his knees, tilting his chin for Charles's pleasure.

Brother Wolf was tempted to give him the coup de grâce. This one had kept him preoccupied when he needed to be attending his mate. Charles hit him on the side of the head with the blunt end of the axe instead. Enough to keep him out for a few minutes, not hard enough to kill him.

If it had been Geir, he could have counted on him to honor the submission as a cease-fire. But Fenrir wasn't the kind of wolf he could trust that far.

Anna? he sent along the bond between them. *What can I—*

And he was sucked into a cartoon. He recognized it vaguely as the rendition of a fairy tale. The sky was dark, and the colors were bruise-like: purple, deep blues, deep grays, and black. The ground was squishy under his feet, which made him vaguely uneasy, but not as uneasy as the reek of black witchcraft. He looked around but didn't see anything except the towering forest of thorn-encrusted vines.

"Anna?" He couldn't see her, but he could feel that she was near and that she was worried.

"Charles!" she called. "I'm here, trapped in the stupid plants. I can't get out."

He waded through the sticky, sloggy ground, and when he reached the forest of vines, it opened reluctantly before him. It would have kept him from Anna if it could have, but their bond and his magic was too strong here, where such things had more meaning. But the vines closed behind with a wash of malice and dark whispers.

In a very small clearing, his mate stood contemplating the vines with her arms crossed over her chest, her back to him.

"What are you doing?" he asked.

"It's witchcraft," she said, without looking away from the vines. "I don't know what to do with witchcraft."

He approached her and became aware that her clothing was ragged and there were bloody scratches up and down her arms and on her cheek. She was frowning fiercely.

"Is the cartoon yours?" he asked.

She looked up at him then. "Oh good, you're here," she said, as if she only now saw him, though she'd answered his question. It was that kind of place. "Cartoon?"

She turned around slowly, looking around. She shook her head and laughed. "I think I've built this as a metaphor. But I'm not sure who is really in charge here. This"—she waved her arms to indicate the whole scene—"is a conglomeration of my powers, Wellesley's magic, and that." On the last word, she pointed at the briar-vine hedge. "That is black magic, witchcraft. And I don't know how it got here or how to break it."

He surveyed the hedge a little more thoroughly. The first thing he noticed was that the plants bore only a vague resemblance to any plant he'd ever seen—but this wasn't reality. He'd had some experience with this kind of magical dreaming, though his adventures usually looked a little more like the real world and less like a Disneyland adventure.

"So is there a sleeping princess trapped behind the thorns?" he asked.

"No," she said. "It's Wellesley's wolf."

Interesting, said Brother Wolf. *We never sensed any witchcraft about him. Is it new?*

"I don't think so," Anna said. "I think it's been here a long time. Asil said there might have been a witch involved in the business in Tennessee."

"Rhea Springs?" Charles asked, frowning. "I didn't find any signs of witches there."

Anna raised both eyebrows and flung her arm out toward the thorn hedge and its distinctive scent of the blood and wrongness that was witchcraft.

"Point made," he said.

"So how do I take down the hedge?" she asked him.

Blood, Brother Wolf said.

Anna held out her hands. "I bled here and—" She flushed. "I accidentally dug claws into Wellesley in the real world. The more real world, anyway. And he bled. Nothing happened to the witchcrafting."

"This is a fairy tale," Charles said thoughtfully.

"Yes?"

"If not blood, then maybe a kiss," he told her.

A lot of pack magic worked with blood—but there were a few very select offerings that were symbolized by a kiss. He had an idea about how that could work for this.

He reached out and took her hand—the one still bandaged, so he was gentle about it. "I kiss you. You kiss Wellesley in the real world."

She pulled her head back in instinctive rejection, though her hand tightened on his. *"Love's first kiss?"* It sounded like a quote. "I don't love him."

He put his chin on the top of her head and pulled her against him. Even in the Dreamtime, it felt good. She made him smile.

"No love necessary between you and him," he told her. "But Bran holds him as pack as he holds you and me. If I kiss you here, and you kiss him in the real world, maybe we can work a little magic, you and I."

Then he bent down and kissed her.

ANNA DIDN'T UNDERSTAND exactly what Charles intended, but she was willing to trust him.

She blinked uncertainly, trying to be aware both in the real world and in the inner vision. It felt awkward and distinctly uncomfortable.

Asil still had Wellesley pinned to the ground but not without a great deal of effort. He saw her focus on him and smiled grimly. "Whatever it is you are trying to do, it is working. I can tell by how much easier it has become to hold him down."

She couldn't tell if he was being sarcastic or not. And she didn't have enough brainpower to puzzle it out right now. The angle Asil held him in was wrong to kiss Wellesley on the mouth. She could kiss his cheek, she thought, and felt a wave of relief.

On the mouth, love, said Brother Wolf, because in the not-real world Charles was kissing her and so could not speak. *It is symbolic. We give our word, we communicate, we eat, we intake food through our mouths. Through his mouth, we can feed him power. Charles says that Wellesley has some abilities of his own. If we can feed him enough, he should be able to free himself.*

"Can you move him around?" she asked Asil. "I have to kiss him on the mouth." Even to herself, she sounded grumpy. She wasn't sure that feeding him power with a kiss felt less intimate or more.

Asil paused with his whole body—and Wellesley struggled fiercely. He snapped at her hands—which she managed to keep on his face only by throwing herself forward on top of both Asil and Wellesley. She had a feeling that losing that touch right now would be bad.

Asil swore in Spanish, moved his grip a little, and jerked. Wellesley's struggles became instantly less effective, though no less passionate.

"He's under a spell," she told Asil before he could say anything. "Witchcraft. Charles says I have to kiss him on the mouth."

Incredibly, irritatingly, Asil's own mouth, which had been tight with anger, suddenly blossomed into a grin. "Did he, now? Told you that you needed to kiss the handsome prince. All right, let me think. You can't break your hold, right?"

Anna nodded uncertainly. "I have no idea what I'm doing here, Asil. But if it's working, I'm wary about screwing with it."

Wellesley snapped his teeth together again, and Asil gave her a look. "You are certain about this?"

"Brother Wolf is."

Asil rolled his eyes—Anna was afraid that she was teaching everyone in the pack bad habits. "And Brother Wolf could never be wrong," he muttered. "Fine. Your job is to keep your hands on him, then, while I position him for kissing. For your kissing him." He muttered something to himself and grunted.

She couldn't tell exactly what he did, only that Wellesley moved, Asil moved—and she did her best to keep up with them. Eventually, Asil was underneath Wellesley, and Wellesley was faceup with his mouth accessible.

"Do it quickly," said Asil. "This is not a secure hold."

Anna leaned over, concentrating on the feel of Charles's mouth on hers in that other place. She pressed her lips to Wellesley's. It felt like she'd kissed an electric fence.

Wellesley's eyes opened, bright gold laced with chocolate, and he drank down her power until she was empty.

SHE SWAYED IN his arms, and Charles growled. Stupid Wellesley, he thought. He could tell that Wellesley had a power akin to the gifts Charles's mother had passed to him. The other wolf should have been able to use Anna as a conduit to the power that Charles held—the power of the Marrok's pack.

Charles opened his mating bond as wide as he could, then opened the pack bond and drew upon it—shoving all of that power into his mate and through her. He wished he were physically with her, so he could explain, could tell Wellesley what to do instead of hoping that he saw . . .

ANNA'S SKIN WAS suddenly hot with energy that felt like Charles, felt like pack. She fed it into Wellesley as he writhed in Asil's grip. He bit her lip, and blood welled.

Okay, she thought. *Let's see if Brother Wolf is right.*

In that other place, where she was still kissing Charles, Anna reached out and grabbed a vine with her sore hand. It writhed and wriggled and struggled—but she was a werewolf, and she knew how to hold on. It burned her hand and whipped her wrist with thorns, and still she kept her grip.

She opened her eyes and saw the briarwood explode into flowers that reminded her of the flowers that had covered the valley when Jonesy died. For two breaths, the air smelled fresh and beautiful; and then she and Charles were wrapped in vines.

Thorns dug in, sharp pain followed by a dull ache. The flowers turned from bright yellow to gray, then died away. Around them, the vines tightened until she could barely breathe.

And Charles . . .

Something protected her, maybe it was Charles himself. But her mate's body was stiff against her as the thorns dug in and sent shafts of agony that she could feel through their bond.

Feels like silver, said Brother Wolf.

They weren't going to be strong enough, she thought.

Brother Wolf howled.

IN HIS HOTEL room, Bran paced, fighting his wolf. He'd had every intention of going to Africa. Africa had sounded as though it was far enough. But Spokane was as far as his wolf had allowed.

He picked up his phone and listened, again, to Charles's dry rendition of Hester's death. Of Jonesy's cryptic note. Of the connection between their enemy and the one who had been stalking them for years.

My fault, Bran thought. *It was my fault that she died. She trusted me—and I failed her.*

He set the phone down carefully and started pacing again.

Hester was dead, and he was no closer to knowing who their traitor was—or at least no more certain who their traitor was. He glanced at the computer on the fake cherry desk, but he didn't dare touch it until he calmed down. He'd pulled out the financials on Leo's pack and the much simpler financial data on Gerry Wallace and had been going through them, again, until his wolf had had enough.

Follow the money. The enemy had a lot of funding from somewhere. That much money should leave a trace, but he couldn't find it. Nor had the much more capable accountants that the Chicago Alpha had turned the records over to. He should have given those records to Charles instead. Charles might have been able to find something . . . which was why Bran hadn't turned them over to him. Because he was afraid of what Charles would turn up.

"Treachery is dirty business," he told the beast inside of him. That was his mother's gift, the monster who lived within. She hadn't infected him, true. But he had absolved his father of that responsibility a long time ago. Not even the Lords of Faery had been able to get the best of his mother. His father, who had been a simple farmer, had no chance once she had set her eyes upon him.

The beast roiled inside of him. Angry. Afraid.

Well enough, so was he, and worried on top of that.

Something yanked hard at the pack bonds that he'd tightened down to threads after Hester's death. He loosened them, just a hair, ready to be angry at being so rudely disturbed—and found Brother Wolf.

* * *

ASIL HELD ON to the mad wolf as best he could, though he was pretty sure that the best thing that he could do for all of them was to break Wellesley's neck and save everyone trouble. Yes, Wellesley was an artist of the sort to make Asil's soul soar. Yes, Wellesley was insightful and witty—even as he struggled with the beast inside him.

But Anna was an Omega. A treasure. Asil had lost his mate, but Allah, who knew men's hearts and how to heal them, had given Asil a second Omega to guard. He loved her—though he was not *in* love with her. He loved her as a man must love the well that brings water to his people in the desert. For her sake, he would give his life. For her sake, he should simply eliminate Wellesley.

For her sake, he could not do so.

He felt it when Charles opened the pack bonds and asked for power. He gave all that he could and not lose his hold on Wellesley. Attuned through the bonds, he could sense the surge of pack-and-Charles-flavored energy sweep through Anna and into Wellesley, felt the other wolf's body shake under the onslaught of so much magic.

The scent of witchcraft, of black magic, seeped out of Wellesley's pores. Asil wrinkled his nose. It smelled of power, of age, of death.

"Yes, yes," he muttered irritably to himself. "And pain and misery and suffering, too, no doubt."

He waited for the scent to ebb, for the power of the pack to sweep it away. But it wasn't the scent that ebbed, it was the power . . .

He flung his bonds open and pushed everything he had into the tide of pack magic that was slowing to a trickle. The pack magic began to feel like the reek of witchcraft on Wellesley's skin. He felt Charles launch a desperate appeal to the Marrok, who had abandoned them.

Asil knew that wasn't fair. He, of all people, understood the burden of Alpha. He'd given that position up because it was such a burden. But they needed Bran, and he was not there.

Until he was.

Power, raw and huge and flavored with the magic of a hundred packs (or a thousand, Asil wasn't in the frame of mind to count), burst through the bonds. Above him, Anna's eyes widened, turned ice blue, and her whole body glowed with the Marrok's magic.

ANNA SCREAMED WITH the fire that flooded her veins, the sound she made muffled by Charles's lips. The fire slid down her arm and into her burnt hand, turning her flesh into agony.

But she held on to the vine. She held on when the whole briar-wood caught fire and burned with a fury that started from her hand and met another power from within. She closed her eyes against the brightness, plastered her body against her mate's, and held on until the vine disintegrated into gray dust.

As the last of the dust fell from her hand, Charles broke their kiss. He took a step back, holding her steady until she found her balance. Then he disappeared into the darkness that was falling in the wake of the destruction of the briar hedge. She didn't lose him, though; she could feel his weariness through their bond.

The set from *Sleeping Beauty* faded, as Charles had faded, until she stood in a vast, grayish emptiness. The only thing present besides her was a gaunt golden wolf.

His fur was matted, and there were gouges that leaked blood and yellowish goo. He panted, head low, looking even more tired than she felt.

Go home, Namwign Bea, the wolf told her in Wellesley's voice. *Go home and rest.*

That made very good sense, as she was tired. She took a step and crumpled. The ground rose and caught her in gentle hands. She patted it gently. "Thank you," she murmured, and closed her eyes.

SOMEONE RUDELY WOKE her up.

"Drink this, *mija.* I promise it will help."

She should have known it would be Asil, she thought grumpily. Asil didn't respect anyone's boundaries except his own.

Knowing that there was no use in fighting him, she drank the sweet tea he put to her lips. And she drank the second cup, too. By the third cup, she was sitting up on her own and alert enough to look around.

She was sitting on a love seat in a room made of light. One wall of the room was a great window that looked out onto the forest. The room was huge and mostly unfurnished. One corner of it was a well-appointed modern kitchen, and the love seat she was on was near that corner of the room. There was a great gaping hole in the wall next to the love seat.

Beyond the hole was the dirt-floored room where she'd helped Wellesley fight for his freedom. Wellesley's curled-up body was still on the dirt floor.

She blinked at him a moment. She couldn't tell if he was breathing or not.

"Finish that," Asil said from the kitchen. He had the refrigerator open and was examining the contents. "I will make you some food."

"Is he dead?" she asked.

Asil pulled his head out of the fridge and looked out the gaping hole where the steel door—and the steel doorframe—had been, toward their prone host.

"No," he said. "But I expect it will take him a bit longer to recover than it will for you. Being freed from a powerful curse usually leaves the victim with a terrible hangover." He paused thoughtfully. "Or dead. I expect he'll appreciate the hangover."

Anna had been wrapped in a blanket. Her face had been washed (she vaguely remembered that). She'd been pampered with three cups of sweet tea, and now Asil was stealing food for her. Wellesley had been left on the ground where he'd fallen.

"Asil," she said slowly, "I thought you liked Wellesley."

Asil pulled lunch-meat packets and a block of cheese from the fridge and gave her a politely surprised look. "Of course. Why would I dislike him? He figured out what you were, decided it might help him out of trouble he got himself into. He then grabbed you without leave, and if the Marrok hadn't opened the floodgates, you would be dead. And probably so would the rest of the pack."

"I didn't do it on purpose," said Wellesley without moving. "I have only been partially in control of my actions for the last . . . what is this year, anyway? Ninety years or so."

Asil pointed at him with the knife he'd gotten out to cut the cheddar. "Do not blame your wolf for what you did. Your wolf only understood what she offered. It was you who decided to use her to break your curse."

"That's fair," Wellesley said. "I guess I did." He paused. "I'm not sorry. If I'd killed us both . . . us all? Anyway, if we were dead, I'd be sorry. But since we survived, I am merely very, very grateful. If I could move, I would kiss your hand, Anna."

"You'd better get moving pretty soon," said Asil cheerfully. "Charles is, I am certain, on his way. If you think I'm unhappy with you, you just wait until Charles explains his feelings to you." He chopped up some cheese. "Charles is a man of few words. You are just lucky he quit carrying a club."

"I think he has an axe," Anna said.

Asil looked up at her. "An axe?"

She nodded. "I don't know why, but I think he was carrying an axe when I first nudged him to see if he could help."

Asil smiled. "Good. An axe is exactly what this calls for."

"Asil?" she asked. "Speaking of axes . . . Where is the door? Um, and the doorframe?"

"I threw it down the hole," he said, looking a little embarrassed for the first time. "It was in my way."

"It was supposed to be werewolf-proof," muttered Wellesley.

"I am not just any werewolf," said Asil. "And if it had had a door-knob like any proper door, it would still be where you left it."

WITH ANNA THERE to remind Asil of his manners, Wellesley was eventually helped to a chair in his kitchen and fed sandwiches at a rate that made Asil complain about his new calling as a short-order cook. Anna snagged two or three herself and noticed that Asil had eaten maybe twice that many.

There were a lot of things that she wanted to know about what had just happened, but she found herself nodding off between one swallow and the next. The next thing she knew was her mate's voice.

"Anna?" said Charles.

"Sorry," she murmured, without opening her eyes. "Food coma.

It happens when I get sucked into cartoons and do battle with evil thorn-things."

"I'll keep that in mind," Charles said.

You need to wake up, said Brother Wolf. *So that no one dies.*

And that jump-started her adrenal gland just fine. She sat up and rubbed her face. Asil, Wellesley, and Sage were in the kitchen, none of them looking very happy.

Charles was kneeling beside the couch. One hand on her face. The other hand was holding . . .

"That," Anna said, "is a really big axe that you didn't have this morning when you left." And it had blood on it. Not his blood, she didn't think. It didn't smell like his blood.

Not ours, agreed Brother Wolf happily.

Charles grunted, then when she raised her eyebrows, he answered her implied question.

"When you contacted me the first time, I'd just stolen the axe from the Viking who attacked me and broken his leg with it."

"I see," she said.

"It took me a while to take out his twin brothers, or I'd have gotten back to you sooner."

She considered that statement and decided he wasn't trying to be funny. He looked apologetic.

"I would rather you not get hurt by Viking twins . . ." She had to say it again. "Because Viking twins are apparently a thing here. Anyway, please take care of pressing business before you answer me. If you are dead, you won't be of any use at all."

"I'll keep that in mind the next time," he said.

She didn't think that he looked too scary, but then she looked over Charles's shoulder at the others. Sage was a little pale, but her face was very calm. Wellesley looked almost dead—but he'd looked that way when she nodded off. Asil looked like a ticked-off cat cornered by a big freaking dog.

So probably the not-scary was a relatively new thing. Interesting that Brother Wolf had been the one to wake her up, possibly so she could prevent *Charles* from killing someone?

"Since we are all here now," she said, "maybe Wellesley will tell us exactly what happened in"—she looked at Charles—"Rhea Springs, Tennessee, right? Because I think that's where he picked up that interesting *Sleeping Beauty* curse."

"I don't know that it matters," Wellesley said tiredly. "Most of the principals are dead, except for me. Even the town is gone, drowned by the TVA in the forties."

"Call me curious," Asil said. "I've seen a lot of witchcraft, but I've never seen a witchcraft construct that lasted that long and hid itself so well. Usually, they die once the witch dies."

"It makes me unhappy," said Charles, "to know that something like that existed right under my nose—right under *my da's* nose—and none of us suspected anything."

Wellesley rubbed his face. "I can see that. Where do you want me to start?"

CHAPTER

9

"I don't remember everything." Wellesley closed his eyes wearily. "But you have more than earned whatever I can tell you. Asil, my old friend, if you are through being irritated with me, would you open the cupboard above the fridge and get the bottle you will find there? Then, if you will, pour all of those who wish it, but most especially me, a little? I was saving it, but I think this tale . . . I think I need a little strength to tell this tale. I would do it myself, but I would end up on the floor before I got to the fridge."

Asil folded his arms and stayed where he was. He and Sage had both lost the ready-to-defend-myself body posture they'd had when Anna woke up.

Sage heaved a sigh, opened the cabinet, and made a sound of approval as she pulled out a wine bottle.

"Merlot," she said. "And a very good label. Yum." She opened a cupboard and started to close it when she saw nothing but a plastic bag with cups in it.

"No," said Wellesley. "That is what I have."

She looked at him. "You want to drink good wine out of disposable cups?"

He shrugged. "I tend to . . ." He paused, looked at Anna, and gave her a small smile before returning his attention to Sage. "I *tended* to break glass. The plastic is easier to clean up."

She shook her head, found a corkscrew, and pulled the cork—bringing it to her nose. She breathed in—and a warm, fruity smell wafted through the room even as far as Anna's love seat.

"Very yum," Sage said. "Charles?"

"No," he said.

"Anna?"

Anna hesitated but shook her head. "Not just this moment." Her stomach was unsettled. She assumed it was from the same thing that was making her head ache and her eyes burn—freeing Wellesley had taken a lot of energy.

"Asil?"

Asil shook his head.

"That's right," she said, with a little bite in her tone. "You don't participate in vice."

Anna knew for a fact that Asil liked wine, but she didn't think this conversation was about alcohol. It had the feel of one of those painful battles between lovers that continued past the point where either love or logic could put it right.

He tilted his head, and when he spoke, his voice was gentle and half-apologetic. "I assure you that I am a very bad Muslim. Wine is, for a werewolf, only grape juice—"

"Very expensive grape juice," said Wellesley. "Also very good grape juice."

"Though very expensive and good grape juice, I do not feel the need to consume it just now."

"Okay," Sage said casually, as if she hadn't put more meaning into his rejection of the wine than it required. She filled two red plastic cups and brought them both to Wellesley. "You pick."

"Did you poison one?" he asked with interest.

"You're a werewolf," she said dryly. "We don't need to worry about poisons."

"That's not true," Wellesley countered, taking one of the cups and sipping it with a happy sigh. "Our poisons are just different."

"Alcohol *is* technically a poison," Anna pointed out. "If a human drinks too much, it will kill them."

Sage sipped her cup, raised her eyebrows, and nodded at Wellesley. "May all our poisons taste so good." She tipped her cup toward Wellesley without stepping close enough to actually touch his. "To dead brain cells."

He raised his cup. "To freedom," he said, and as he did, his eyes flashed bright yellow.

"Now that we have that out of the way," Sage said, "before story time, I'd like to catch up. Would someone care to explain matters to us?" She looked around and sighed. "To me? Since I have the feeling I'm the only one who doesn't know what happened."

"What do you know?" asked Wellesley.

"Charlie stared off into space for five minutes and left me to sort out the Viking twins and brother on my own." She flashed a smile at the room. "But I learned a lesson in diplomacy from Charlie today. Funny how a few broken bones make even a bunch of Vikings so much more reasonable. I'll try that if I ever have to deliver a message to them again. Maybe in another twenty years."

"So not much," said Asil. "But Sage also knows that you have been having trouble with your wolf—and it made you dangerous to deal with."

"It was not my wolf that was the problem," Wellesley told Sage. "Or at least my wolf was not the cause of the problem. I was in a battle for my soul, and the evil spirit that was trying to possess me has been, very slowly, winning." He smiled broadly, raised his glass at Anna, and said, "Until today."

"What you tried could have killed my mate," said Charles softly, and everyone in the room who was not Anna stiffened. Funny how the man, even kneeling beside the couch, could cause so much fear. To her knowledge, he'd never killed anyone without just cause or the Marrok's orders.

She leaned forward and caught a glimpse of his face.

"I think," Anna said, touching Charles's skin, just below his ear, so that he'd pay attention to her, "I think it was what *I* tried, actually. No one forced me to do anything."

"Not true," growled Asil sourly, "whatever you believe, *chiquita*. I was here, I saw him, *felt* him pull you into his nightmare. But I, who was supposed to keep you safe, could do nothing because I was occupied holding him so he didn't kill you physically instead of magically."

Under her fingertips, Charles's muscles tightened.

Anna glared at Asil. "So *not* helping," she told him. "Okay, so I got yanked into Wellesley's nightmare—"

"Soul," said Wellesley.

"That isn't quite right, either," Anna said. "Charles?"

There was a little silence, then Charles deliberately relaxed against her, wrapping one of his hands around her knee, which he squeezed. *I'm onto you,* that squeeze said.

"Vision," said Charles, "or the Dreamtime, maybe."

"It was a nightmarish vision, at any rate," said Anna. "But once I was there, I could have left at any time. As long as I was willing to leave Wellesley's wolf spirit bound in that witchcraft construct." She couldn't imagine doing that—not if she had a chance of freeing him. "But it was Wellesley's own magic that turned the key, I think. You called it a spirit—was it a living thing that imprisoned your wolf?"

Wellesley nodded. "Magic is a living thing."

Charles agreed with that assessment because he said, "You saw it as a plant, and that was fairly accurate, I think. Living, but not reasoning except in the most basic of drives."

Wellesley took a sip of his wine, then tipped his cup to Asil. "I think it lasted so long because my own magic fed the spell. It was growing stronger, and I was growing weaker. I thought it was my wolf I was fighting, too, until Anna *saw* it with me. For me."

"Cursed," said Sage thoughtfully. "You were cursed, and Anna and Charles broke it? With a little help from the Marrok, our leader, who is absent?"

"In a nutshell," said Anna.

Sage hummed, rubbed the rim of her glass with one of her well-tended nails. "There were rumors of a witch at Rhea Springs."

"Yes," Wellesley said heavily. "There was a witch. Or two." He set his cup on the table and pushed it a little distance from him. "I don't remember a lot more than before." He glanced at Charles. "Do you still want this story?" When Charles nodded, Wellesley said, "I suppose it began with Chloe . . . with my wife's death."

Charles, who had settled down enough to take a seat on the floor beside the love seat, resting against Anna's legs, raised a hand to stop Wellesley. He pursed his lips, and said, "You should begin this story where your wolf tells you to begin it."

Wellesley reached out, took a gulp of his wine, and set the cup rather firmly on the table. "Where my wolf tells me . . ." He blew air out like a startled horse. "He tells me to begin with my Change. That has nothing to do with Rhea Springs."

Charles grunted. Then he made an amused sound. "Maybe, maybe not. That first story is why, when given the choice, I brought you to my da instead of killing you for the murders of those young women."

Wellesley blinked at Charles in evident dismay. "Hmm. I thought . . . Hmm. I guess I wasn't thinking all too clearly then, anyway. I don't tell that story. Only to your father—who told it to you, I suppose."

"Before he sent me to Rhea Springs," said Charles. "Because he knew what I would do with it. If your wolf tells you to start there, please, begin at the beginning."

Wellesley looked at his cup, at his hands, around the room as if looking for something else to talk about. At last, his gaze settled on Anna. He sighed.

"All right. I was born somewhere in Africa. Probably near the western coast because that's where most of the slaves came from. I suppose if I traveled back there, I might find it again, given a year or two to wander. But my village was destroyed, my parents killed by slavers, so there has never been any reason for me to return. I was around eleven or twelve at that time, preparing for my manhood ceremony, but still a boy."

He closed his mouth, shook his head, then said, "I was taken, and none of the next five or six years are relevant to anyone except for me. I choose not to talk about them."

He let that statement stand, glancing at Charles as if expecting an objection.

When no one said—or did—anything in response, he nodded. "So. In Barbados, I was bought by a man looking for, how did he put it? A strong subject. He bought six or seven of us, about the same age, and took us to an island in the Caribbean. It was not a large island, and he owned it all."

He looked at Anna. "I never learned the name his own people would have called him, and I will not call him Master."

"You could call him Moreau," suggested Charles.

Wellesley gave him a quick, tight smile. "No. In the book, Moreau was a scientist, a doctor. The man who owned me was no mad scientist. He was simply evil, his soul destroyed by his own actions.

"But in the end, he is not important to the tale, this man who was not my master," he said. "What is important is that man was raised, as many people in his class and station were, by servants and slaves. His nurse was an evil woman, a woman of power. She escaped hanging by fleeing aboard a ship headed to Barbados as a bondswoman." Wellesley closed his mouth and shook his head slightly, as if the mere words had conjured up too much emotion to allow him to continue.

"Witch," said Asil darkly into the pause, as if he could not help himself. "She was an Irish witch. It is true that she escaped hanging for the death of a child in her care, but I suspect that she was more

221

frightened of the witches who were pursuing her for what she stole from them."

"Who told you my story?" said Wellesley suspiciously.

"You did," Asil told him. "This part at least. One night after a full moon, shortly after I arrived here."

Wellesley stared at him, then looked down, frowning. At last he nodded. "Yes. Yes. I am sorry. My memory is tangled. I think I remember. You told me of your mate's death. I told you . . . parts of this story."

"You were talking of the nursemaid," Sage said, her body leaning forward on the kitchen chair where she sat. She had a white-knuckled grip on the edge of the table.

Anna wondered what elements of Wellesley's story had tangled with Sage's own to make her engage so strongly with it. Sage wasn't old-old. Older than she looked, maybe, but not old enough to have experienced institutionalized slavery. Maybe it was the witches. Witches tended to send the hairs on the back of Anna's neck up, too.

"Yes," agreed Wellesley. "The nursemaid was a witch. No one paid attention to such women. They were to keep quiet and do the work of raising the children. The children who were the future of the family. Someone, you would think, should have understood just how much power that gave them." He shook his head with sorrowful incredulity. "This man's nursemaid was a witch, Irish, yes, because her accent was still strong. But how she came to the Caribbean and why—this was all based on rumors in the slave pens. Who knows how much of it was true?" He sent a frowning look toward Asil.

"The Irish witch part was," said Asil when it seemed that Wellesley had quit speaking. "Sometime since I first heard your story, I realized that I knew another part of it. I knew the witches who were hunting that one. She stole a small book of family spells from one of the nastier witch clans in Northern Europe, the kind of spellbook witches kill for. As I know what that witch did—and I know the rumors of that family's powers—it was not difficult to connect the two stories."

"You knew the witches whose spells she used?" asked Wellesley in a dangerous voice.

Asil smiled, showing white teeth. "We were not friends, Wellesley."

"Asil doesn't like witches," said Anna firmly, and the tension in the air died down a notch.

"That bloodline has died out," said Asil. "Not *entirely* by my efforts."

"Well and so," said Wellesley. "Well and so. It seems that this will be informative for all of us. This Irish witch was sold as a bondswoman to my . . . to the man's parents when he was eight or nine. She was given the raising of him. Rumor was that his parents were the first people he and his mentor tortured and killed—but I suspect not. The slaves were easier prey, and predators usually begin with easier prey."

"Not always," said Sage into the silence that followed. "But usually."

"No one cared about the slaves, not even the other slaves," Wellesley said abruptly. Then he stopped and gulped down the wine until it was gone. He shook his head. "That's not for this tale, either. This witch could make collars that forced the person wearing one to obedience. She had to torture a lot of people to death for the power to create each one." There was horror in his eyes, but his voice was steady.

Wellesley, thought Anna, had witnessed the making of those collars. She occasionally had nightmares about her encounters with witches. So did Charles.

Wellesley continued speaking quietly. "I understand at first she tried to use them on all the slaves but found that it took power to control the collars, too. She could use no more than six of them at a time or they became less effective." He grimaced. "The power in them had to be renewed twice a year.

"It was a matter of great disappointment to her that instead of an island of willing slaves, who would torture themselves for her pleasure, she had to make do with 'special' slaves who enforced her will on the rest of the people on the island. If one of the collared slaves died or was killed, she replaced him with another. All the time that I knew her, she was trying to find a way to make the collars more permanent, to make them power themselves."

He had to quit talking again. Sage reached out a hand to him—wolves tended to touch each other a lot when they were under stress. But Wellesley wrapped his arms around himself and shook his head. He rocked a little in the chair, and his eyes glittered with shades of gold.

"And then they found themselves a werewolf," Charles said when the silence stretched too long.

Wellesley nodded, but he still didn't speak. Maybe he couldn't.

After a moment, Charles went on. "Probably he was himself a victim. He came to the island because there were stories of a woman who knew magic, who knew how to remove curses."

"Be careful of those," said Asil in a low voice. "The only people who can remove curses can put them on, too."

Wellesley looked at Anna. "Not always," he said in an intense voice. "There are healers in the world as well as killers."

"That was mostly Charles and Bran," Anna said, embarrassed at receiving such a look. "They had the power. I was just a conduit, I think."

"As I said," agreed Asil. "It takes someone who can deliver a curse to break a curse." He and Charles exchanged a look of acknowledgment.

Wellesley grunted. He took up the story, but his voice was rapid and his sentences jerky. His account skipped around ungracefully.

"That part all happened before I came to the island. They frequently went to Barbados and bought slaves at the market there—including me. They herded all of us into a shed and turned the werewolf loose on us. Mostly the wolf just killed the people they threw in with him. Of my group, I was the only survivor. After my Change, it took another four or five years before they had six werewolves at their bidding, including the original wolf.

"We were, all of us, bound by the evil thing that the witch collared us with. We had no free will, no thoughts that were not put in our heads by the witch and her leman."

Anna met Charles's eyes, because she knew another wolf who had been forced to do the will of a witch.

Yes, said Brother Wolf. *The Marrok's story is different in many ways, but Wellesley's origin reflects the creation of our father in the dawn of time. It is one of the reasons our father asked Wellesley not to speak of his origin. We do not want witches to know it is possible.*

At the same time that Brother Wolf was speaking to her, Charles said, "Recently, I have learned that Bonarata, the vampire who rules Europe, had a collar he used to control a werewolf, though it was specific, I believe, to werewolves. It was also old. And it has failed—and he has no witch who can replace it."

Wellesley growled and stiffened in his seat.

"Such things are never completely forgotten," said Asil. "It is the way of the world."

"If Bonarata cannot find a witch to make him a new one, then there is not a witch left in Europe, at least, with that ability," Charles observed.

"Or maybe those witches are not willing to work for the vampire king," Sage speculated.

But Asil shook his head. "No witch in Europe could say no to Bonarata. He is extremely persuasive, and it has been a very long time since the witches were powerful enough that they could do battle with such a one as he."

"What happened, Wellesley?" asked Anna. "How did you get free?" Because obviously he had—and she wanted him to finish this story because the memories hurt him.

"She worked her magic only on those of us of pure African blood," Wellesley said. "Holding the witchborn is more difficult than a normal person, just as holding a werewolf is more difficult. She knew that the native peoples in the Caribbean had their own version of witchborn, though nothing as powerful as the European witches—or so she believed. Myself, I am not convinced. Most of the slaves on that island carried native blood, so they bought 'pure African' slaves to turn into collared wolves. She believed there were no mageborn people among those of us born in Africa."

Charles snorted.

Wellesley nodded. "Ridiculous. All peoples have those born who can feel the pulse of the world. My father came from a family known for producing powerful healers. It is magic that is as different from witchcraft as wood is from steel. Subtle and powerful, perhaps, but also slow. My family's magic brought good harvests, rain in season, and kept the wild predators from the village. Influencing natural tendencies toward beneficial results. It was not helpful in keeping the slavers away."

He paused, as if waiting for questions, but when no one said anything, he continued, "I will tell you the next part as a village storyteller would, because that is how I think of it. Because it makes the most sense that way."

He took a breath, and when he began again, his voice was rich with drama instead of jerky and painful.

"One day, in the late fall, without warning, came a storm the likes of which I had never seen before," he said. "The winds came, powerful spirits of the air. They battered the island for hours upon hours until the buildings became no more than piles of toothpicks, picked up and scattered together in a puzzle not even the gods could sort out. The rains came, too, so much rain that the waters in the river and in the lake welled up. The secret hope rose within me that the island might sink beneath the sea forever, that the great sea would drown the evil."

He paused for dramatic effect.

"But it was only a very small hope, buried deep where I kept the few thoughts that were my own, because I was her creature then. And it seemed that hope was doomed because the witch drove away the spirits of the winds and the spirits of the rain, so that the big house and all the ground around it remained safe from them."

He lifted his cup, found it dry, and set it down. Without a word, Asil filled the cup with the rest of the wine in the bottle and handed it over.

Wellesley took a sip and continued, "The eye of the storm came in the middle of the night. The winds calmed and the rain turned into a drizzle. It was at that time that the greater spirit of the hurricane came to me. Larger and more powerful than the wind or rain spirits, he was close enough to this world that he could speak with me.

"'Brother,' he said, 'why do you serve such a wicked one when you have in you the blood of earth magic? Of a priestess lineage that is a thousand years long?'"

Wellesley shook his head and held out his hands palm up and brought them slowly down. "It was as if the rains washed away clouds, and the wind blew away fog. My mind was my own for the first time since the witch had placed her collar around my neck.

"'Spirit,' I told him, 'it is not of my will, but by this evil thing born of foul death and ugliness that I wear. This is a strange working I cannot fight.'

"'Why, then, do you not take it off?' he said.

"I tried then to do that very thing. Before this time, I could not even conceive of such an action. But alas, my hands could not break it, though I tried with all my strength.

"I cried out in despair, 'It is impossible for me. I am born of a grand heritage, it is true. Some of that power and grace lives inside this body, but great is the corruption that binds me. Too great for a man such as I to break or remove.'

"The spirit of the hurricane looked upon that which I wore around my neck, and said, 'Brother, truly this is evil. I can hear the cries of the tortured souls whose substance was used herein. It is greater than even I might destroy.'

"And truly my heart knew despair then. If the spirit of the greatest storm that I had ever seen could not prevail over the witch's power, then I would serve her until the end of my days or hers.

"The spirit of the hurricane, seeing my sorrow, took pity upon me then. He said, 'Come out to my mother, who is far mightier than I. Surely, she can defeat the dark magic in your binding. I will ask it of her, but you should know that she does not always do as I ask. She may decide that to rid the world of such evil, your life is also forfeit.'

"In the end, what choice had I? I would rather be dead than to wear the witch's collar to the end of my life. So I followed him, and he led me past locked doors and my sleeping comrades. No one heard us, and no doors could stand in our way. He led me to the edge of the island. The beaches were all gone, as were any of the gentle slopes, buried under the fury of the storm. If there was an easy way to the ocean, the spirit chose not to take me there. We stood, at last, at the top of a cliff.

"'My brother,' said the spirit, 'if you would be free of this evil, you must jump.'"

Wellesley drank again. There was a trickle of sweat on his face. It sounded like a fairy tale, this story. But Anna, who'd seen Charles interact with the spirits of the forest, believed him. If she had had any doubts, the ring of honesty in his voice would have disabused her of them.

"I knew," said Wellesley heavily, "that I could no longer swim as I had as a child, that the magic of the wolf does not protect us from water. And had I been as good a swimmer as any mermaid's child, it would have done me no good leaping off a cliff that high. But I commanded my own actions and thoughts for the first time in a very long time, so I jumped, and the spirit jumped with me. I can still hear his laughter in my ears when a storm rises here in the mountains.

"'Mother,' he called as we fell, 'I have found a prisoner of wickedness. A child of nature who should be unbound. Will you free him?'

"And, in answer, the salt water reached up and engulfed me."

Wellesley paused again.

"I thought I was dead," he said at last. "I thought I was dead, and I welcomed it. But I awoke on a beach littered with the detritus of the storm. The sun was high in a clear sky, and my skin was covered with salt."

He smiled, a wolfish smile, and his voice roughened and the irises of his eyes brightened.

"The witch came down to the beach soon thereafter. 'I have found you at last,' she said in triumph. 'All of the other wolves are dead. I was worried that we would not be able to make more of you. Come, let us show my love that the fates have not yet turned against us.' And she turned around and started walking back to the big house.

"I had never changed except under the moon. But the ocean and the moon speak to each other as lovers do, and I have no doubt that it was the sea who gave me power and strength. I have never, before or since, taken wolf form as quickly as I did then. One moment I was human and the next a wolf. I killed the witch while she was still planning how to find more slaves to Change and control. The only regret I have is that it was quick and painless—I was too worried about her power to give her the death she deserved.

"Then I went to the big house and killed the man who had given her free rein. I found every one of those collars, and I threw them into the sea where She could do with them as it pleased her. I hope that She freed the tormented souls who gave their pain and their lives for the witch's spell."

He took a deep, shuddering breath. Then, in a perfectly normal voice, he said, "There were only a few of us left alive on the island—

and all of them were afraid of me, for which I have never blamed them. Eventually, a ship came to see how we had weathered the storm. Upon discovering that we were alone, they claimed us all. But without a witch to hold me, I soon left them, and slavery, behind me.

"Bran asked that this tale not be told lightly, which I have never done—" He paused and looked at Asil. "Except the once. These are Bran's reasons, and they are good ones: First, the manner and matter of the collar's making must lie with the dead if it can be made to do so. Second, which is adjunct to the first, that a witch can control a person's mind and body is something that should not be known if those of us who are not wholly human want to live shoulder to shoulder with the humans in peace. And finally, there is this, my own reason. This is the story of my making, a private thing. I do not wish that it be a matter of common knowledge."

Anna thought of the way the wolves had all watched her last night as she came in from the truck where the body of one of the people who had abused her rested. She understood exactly why he didn't want people talking about it.

"You said 'manner and matter,'" said Sage thoughtfully. If she was as affected by his story as she'd looked in the beginning, she was hiding it better now. "Does that mean that you know how to make the collars?"

Wellesley's eyes grew cold, then lightened to icy gold. "It is something that does not concern you."

She put her hand up. "I only ask because if someone thinks you know how to make them, you have a target on your back the size of Texas."

Anna remembered Charles saying that there were wildlings here who knew secrets that people would kill for. If Wellesley was the only one who knew how to make those collars . . . he'd be hunted by every black witch on the planet.

Wellesley didn't seem worried about it. His shoulders relaxed as he told Sage, "We all of us werewolves have a target on our back. It's not a matter of if but when someone pulls the trigger."

"Cheerful thought," drawled Asil. "But let us put that one aside—since there is nothing we can do about it that we are not already doing. What does that have to do with Rhea Springs?"

Wellesley shrugged. "I don't know. Charles said to begin where my wolf told me to—and that's where my wolf told me to begin."

Charles was watching Wellesley with a thoughtful expression.

Wellesley shrugged. "As I told you, I really don't remember a lot more about Rhea Springs than I did before Anna broke the curse. Not much at all, really. I remember going there—and I remember your spiriting me out of that jail. But I still don't remember much in between, just bits and pieces." He bowed his head. "I remember the witch's face but nothing else about her."

Charles said, "Maybe you should—"

The phone rang.

Wellesley rose from the table and glanced at Charles—who shrugged. He put in an earpiece and hit a button on the phone.

"Hello?" Wellesley said, and listened a moment.

He'd found a way to have a private conversation in a room full of werewolves, Anna thought, delighted. She'd have to find out what he used.

He hit another button, and asked as he lifted the handset, "Could you repeat that, please?"

Leah's voice, breathless and hoarse, replied, "I asked, are Asil and Anna there?"

Asil took the phone from Wellesley. "We are here."

"I'm calling from Jericho's phone," she said. "We've got bodies here but no Jericho. You should come."

"Charles and Sage are here, too. Do you want us all?"

She made an exasperated sound. "What did you do? Decide to get together for a party? Never mind. Yes. Everyone should come and help me search for Jericho. We don't want him running around loose—or in someone else's hands, for that matter."

She left them in a fit of dial tone.

"Are you up for this?" asked Charles.

It took Anna a minute to realize he was asking her.

She put her feet on the floor and stood up. "I'm okay," she said. "I won't be up to a Wild Hunt, but I'll be fine."

Wellesley said, "I need to eat and rest."

Asil gave him a frown. "You weren't invited, my friend. I'm very glad that your wolf has evidently been freed from a witch's curse— but that's a long way from being safe and dependable."

Wellesley laughed, but his eyes were wary. "I suppose it is."

"I could stay with him to make sure he's okay," offered Sage. She gave the artist a brilliant smile. "I've been a fan for a long time. I'd love to commission something if you are willing."

Wellesley shook his head. "I'd rather be alone if you don't mind. I have a lot to absorb. A little rest and a lot of food will see me right as rain. As far as a painting is concerned—I'll get back to you on that.

Most of my paintings were done to stave off madness. I don't know what I'll want to paint now."

"Leave him," said Charles.

"Come on, children," said Asil. "You are dawdling."

WITHOUT DISCUSSION, CHARLES climbed into the driver's seat of Sage's SUV, setting the Viking's axe in the back. He nodded to Anna to get into the passenger side. Evidently, the keys were in the SUV because it started right up. Sage didn't look happy about her car being co-opted—or maybe just about being left to ride with Asil. But when Anna started to get out, Sage waved her hand and gave her a quick grin.

There was no room to turn around, which didn't seem to bother Charles a bit. He gunned the engine and backed up the twisty, scary, narrow track up the cliffside at about thirty miles per hour.

Anna choked back a laugh, made sure her seat belt was tight, and closed her eyes. "I hope Sage has good insurance," she said.

"I don't like this situation at all," Charles said instead of responding to her banter—unless he had flashed her that quick grin of his. Had she missed it by being a coward?

The SUV took a sharp turn and reversed directions. She opened her eyes, and they were back on the safer track, headed down it at what would have been a crazy speed if anyone else were driving.

"Which situation?" she asked. "Wellesley's unexpected curse? Missing werewolf? Or bodies at the missing werewolf's house?"

She couldn't find it in herself to be as concerned about the bodies as she would have been before Hester was killed. They could have been random hikers who had gotten way, way, way off the beaten path and run into a crazy werewolf. But she was making the assumption that they were the enemy because cooler heads than hers were considering other possibilities.

"What are they trying to accomplish?" Charles said. "It's bad to have an enemy with the kinds of resources these people apparently have—but it is infinitely worse to have crazy people as enemies."

"Evidently," Anna said, "you also consider it a certainty that the bodies that Leah found belonged to our enemy and not Canadian hikers who have been wandering around the mountains lost for a few months."

He started to say something, then closed his mouth. He gave her an assessing look. "Why Canadian?"

She held up a finger. "Local hikers would figure out that downhill and south mean safety, uphill and north just gets worse. Downhill and south would take them away from our territory." She held up a second finger. "Casual hikers would have fallen down and died before they ever reached anywhere near here—I don't know exactly where Jericho lives because I've never heard his name before, but I'm assuming it's in this general direction."

"And lost Canadian hikers are the only ones who could get here by going downhill and south," he said. He grinned at her. "It's not quite true, we run hikers out of our territory all the time, and there's a lot of federal land between us and Canada."

"*And,*" Anna said, holding up a third finger, "Canadian hikers would be too polite to end up as bodies. Thus the bodies must not belong to random hikers."

He gave a shout of laughter. "I love you. I came to the same conclusion by a different path. I'm pretty sure the bodies at Jericho's belong to the same group who went after Hester and Jonesy."

She looked at him. "How did *you* get there?"

"There are no such things as coincidences. The last time one of our wildlings interacted with a normal human was six months ago. Now we have two in two days."

"Leah didn't say how old the bodies were," Anna commented. "When was the last time someone heard from Jericho?"

He shrugged. "Da has kept me busy with other things. I haven't talked to any of the wildlings since last winter."

The Marrok used Charles, Asil, and a couple other of the older wolves to check on the wildlings once a month or so as soon as the snow flew, saving a few of them to visit himself. Not that the wildlings couldn't take care of themselves, most of them—it was what they would do to take care of themselves that worried Bran.

"Why do you think going after Jericho makes no sense?" Anna asked. "They went after Hester. What makes him different?"

"They have werewolves, so they don't just need genetic samples." A deer stepped onto the road, and he braked, slewing the big rig sideways in an effort to miss the doe. He stopped about three feet from the deer, who had frozen.

"Go on, little sister," he told her. "There is no one hungry today."

Released from whatever instinct had caused her to plant her feet and remain still, she bounced up the hill and into the trees.

Anna looked behind them, but there was no sign of Asil and Sage.

"There are several ways to get there from Wellesley's," said Charles as he put his foot down on the gas again. "I expect Asil hopes to beat us there."

The race is on, thought Anna, but she didn't say it. It was either a guy thing or a dominant-werewolf thing. Either way, Charles and Asil would enjoy the challenge.

"So why does Hester make more sense than Jericho?" she asked.

"Jericho is an atomic bomb waiting to go off. Questioning Jericho makes no sense at all."

"I'm not familiar with him," Anna said. "But if he was on Leah's list—didn't she have the safer wolves?"

"Jericho was on Sage's and my list," Charles said. "One of the dangerous ones. I don't know what Leah is doing there."

"If they are recruiting," said Anna thoughtfully, "they are being stupid about who they are choosing."

"Lethally so," agreed Charles.

"The only thing that makes sense from our end is that they want to cause chaos while Bran is away. But even that doesn't quite work," she said. "Because then all the surveillance equipment at Hester's is a lot of risk and money for an end that is easier to reach different ways. If they have a helicopter, they could just drop something nasty on your father's house from the air. More effect and less risk."

"They want something," Charles agreed.

"Maybe Jericho will know what they wanted," she said.

Charles made a noise.

"That wasn't a hopeful grunt," she said.

"Jericho can barely communicate on a good day," Charles told her. "If there are bodies around, it isn't a good day."

"We don't have enough information to make sense of what they want," said Anna.

Charles nodded. "I don't like being in this position. Reacting and not acting. We can't get to an offensive position until we know more."

"Speaking of knowing more," Anna said. "What exactly happened at Rhea Springs? Asil gave me what he knew—but there wasn't much of it." She tapped her fingers on the witch gun lying on the seat between them. "Witches seem to be cropping up all over the place."

Charles pursed his lips. "They do, don't they? There is no reason that Rhea Springs has anything to do with our current situation, though."

"Maybe not," Anna said. "But Wellesley certainly has knowledge that someone might be looking for. If Wellesley is the wildling our enemy questioned Hester about, then maybe Rhea Springs has more to do with our situation than we think."

Charles nodded. "Wellesley didn't remember anything when I got there," he told her. "Most of what I know comes from the newspapers. Rhea Springs was a small town of about a hundred people in 1930, three hundred if you counted the people who lived in the general area. A hotel and a hot spring with reputed healing powers was the major source of economy. I don't remember exactly what year it was, but the Alpha of the Tennessee pack sent us some newspaper articles about a naked black man found with the bodies of some white people. The details varied from article to article—one said four young women. Another claimed it was fifteen children. The naked black man, our informant told us, was a werewolf and gave us a name that wasn't Wellesley. Da knew the werewolf in question, told me his story, and sent me out on the next train."

Charles quit speaking for a while. Anna waited, content to watch his big hands steadying the SUV as it bounced and slithered on the rough road. She loved his hands, broad-palmed and long-fingered. They were adept on the steering wheel, the fretboard of his guitar, or her skin.

"News didn't get to us up here in Montana with anything like swiftness. By the time I got to the town where he was being held—a slightly larger town some miles from Rhea Springs—his trial was already over. Considering the era, the place, the color of his skin, Wellesley's fate was determined no matter what his defense. I'd known before I got on the train what the result would be. Capital punishment was the electric chair. I don't know that electricity has ever killed one of us—but I doubt it would make him very happy. Leaving him to the authorities just wasn't possible. My orders were to kill or rescue him, depending upon what he told me."

He fell silent again.

"What did he tell you?" she asked.

"That he didn't remember anything. He wasn't in good shape—his wolf . . ." He paused. ". . . what I thought was his wolf, anyway, would break in and babble some crazy stuff. A witch. Witchcraft. I didn't smell the witchcraft on him—and I'd like to know how they did that. That had to be a major working to hold his wolf this long, and I didn't catch the scent of witches anywhere."

"Did you check the crime scene?" Anna asked.

He shook his head. "I knew his story. I thought he was talking about earlier. A stray Indian wasn't much better off than a black man in that time and place, so I didn't do a lot of wandering about. In the end . . ." His voice trailed off, then he shook his head. "In the end, I figured that Da could keep him safe with the other wildlings if he never recovered."

"His story was so close to what happened to your da," Anna said softly. "You couldn't bear to kill him—innocent or guilty."

"And once I realized that," Charles said, "I didn't bother investigating it further. I got him out of there and on a train to Montana." He glanced at Anna and smiled. "No, I didn't buy tickets. We rode freight to Billings, then took horses the rest of the way."

"I think," she said slowly, going over what Wellesley had said—and what he hadn't—in her head, "that he believed you broke him out of jail because he was innocent."

"I know," Charles said. "I wish I could go back and investigate for him. I don't even know, really, who the victims were. At the time, I didn't care. Maybe he'll remember more when he rests up."

"You didn't want to find out that he'd killed fifteen children," said Anna. "Because that would mean you'd have had to kill him."

"Yes," agreed Charles soberly.

"That briar curse is interesting," she said. "More interesting as you think about it. Asil said there was supposed to be a witch in the vicinity. I wonder if the dead people were *all* witches."

"I wonder if they were all the victims of a witch," Charles said, "including Wellesley. I wonder if I let a witch free because I didn't investigate further—and how many more people she killed before she died."

"Oh," Anna said, understanding how Charles operated. He was responsible for the world, her husband. She couldn't change how he felt. She put her hand on his leg. "I hadn't thought of it like that. I understand. Maybe you should do a little research on Rhea Springs? A place where the hot springs were supposed to be magically healing sounds like somewhere a witch might have set up shop, do you think?"

"Black witches seldom do healing," he said dryly.

"Black witches have to start out somewhere, don't they?" she asked.

The next mile or so was traveled in thoughtful silence.

"Not a lot of information left on Rhea Springs, I imagine," Charles said. "And any human still alive who once lived in that place would have been a young child."

"Still," Anna said, "maybe one of the wolves from that neck of the woods will remember something."

"Maybe," he said. And from Charles that was as good as a declaration that he'd pursue the matter. He sounded as though the thought made him feel better.

She only hoped that he didn't find out that there had been a witch and that she *had* killed fifteen children. Witches had the same life span as any other human, though—with very few exceptions. The witch who cursed Wellesley, no matter what she'd done, was beyond justice now.

Leah's truck was parked at the trailhead of the path to Jericho's. Asil's Mercedes was parked beside it.

"Ha," said Charles as they got out of the car. "I talked too much. Slowed me down."

Anna laughed, as he meant her to. Charles didn't really care who got here first, and Anna knew it. Brother Wolf was grumpy about losing, though. *He* thought it would have been better to have been first.

Anna hopped out of the car and waited while he looked around the interior of Sage's SUV until he found the key fob so he could lock it. Maybe he was taking unnecessary precautions, but he wasn't going to leave Jericho an easy way out. He also grabbed the axe. He left the witch gun, though. Jericho was crazy—but he would listen to an axe better than a gun.

He checked the other two vehicles; they were both locked. Anna turned to start up the trail.

"Hold up," he said. "We have a missing werewolf. He could have come this way as easily as any other."

She stood quietly and waited while he examined their surroundings. She took in deep breaths herself but didn't offer any opinions, so he could safely assume she didn't detect anyone, either. If Jericho was hiding around here, he was doing a good job of it.

A better job than Charles thought the wolf was capable of.

"Okay," he said. "Let's go—but keep an eye out."

Anna nodded. She'd been quiet the last part of the trip here, a thoughtful quiet that meant she was thinking. As they started up the trail, she linked her hand on his elbow—that was okay; he trusted her to drop her grip if they met danger. And he liked her hand on him.

"Charles," she said, "if our traitor isn't one of the wildlings, who do you think it is?"

"What has convinced you that it isn't one of the wildlings?" Charles asked.

She made a *hmm* sound, tightening her arm. "I don't know. Wellesley, maybe. Unless you think there are more wildlings who are capable—like Hester."

Charles shook his head. "No. Hester—there were reasons for Hester."

"Jonesy," said Anna.

"Jonesy," agreed Charles. "And Da certainly knew about her—he would. He probably knew about the flyovers, too. I just wonder . . ." He stopped talking as a few thoughts crystallized into a whole.

Anna started to say something, but Charles held up his hand, because . . . he didn't want to be right.

"There is none so blind," he murmured as all of the oddities of the last few days fell into place. The enormity of it all brought him to a stop as he broke out in a cold sweat.

"Charles?" Anna asked.

Brother Wolf saw it as Charles had, understanding what it meant. He went wild with denial—and for a moment, it was all Charles could do to restrain the wolf.

Not now. It's not now, he told his brother. *We will do what we have to do, but not yet.*

"Charles, what's wrong?" Anna asked, beginning to sound worried.

"I know why Da isn't here," he told her. Sick horror gripped him.

"Charles?" Anna asked again. She leaned against him, and Brother Wolf quit fighting and simply braced himself.

He breathed in her scent, and told her, simply, "He thinks Leah is our traitor."

She stilled against him. "Why do you think that?"

He laid it out for her as he saw it. "If Hester was as normal as we all think, she'd have called Da as soon as she started to get flyovers. That would have alerted him of trouble. A month ago, Da asked Boyd for the files the Chicago pack has been putting together in their search for what Leo had been up to."

"Okay," Anna said. "We knew all of this."

"I don't know that he knew we had a traitor at that point, just that our enemy was active again," he told her. "I think that Da was looking for that enemy with the threads we've been able to collect."

"Thus the files from Boyd," Anna said.

Charles nodded. "Then Mercy got into trouble—and he took those files with him. He might have other sources of information, but the files make the most sense."

"Okay," Anna said. "But why Leah?"

"Because he was headed home—and out of the blue he called up and told me he was taking a vacation in Africa with Samuel," Charles said.

Anna drew in her breath, seeing what Charles had seen. "He's afraid to come home because he thinks the traitor is his mate."

"Africa, because he needs to be as far from here as he can get," Charles told her.

She stiffened because she realized what it meant if Leah was the traitor.

He said the whole thing out loud anyway. Just to make sure. "If he's right, I am going to have to execute his mate." He drew in a breath, his chest tight. "And probably my da. Because even if Leah has betrayed us, if I execute her, he'll come for me. His wolf spirit won't let him do anything else."

And he's not in Africa, said Brother Wolf somberly. *He's somewhere a lot closer than that.*

Anna nodded jerkily. She'd met his da's wolf, the monster the Marrok held leashed with his mating bond to Leah. She knew what they'd both be facing after Charles killed Leah.

"Leah is just about the most straightforwardly honest person I know," Anna said. "Every thought that crosses her mind comes out her mouth. How could she keep a secret like that from Bran? From her mate? I can't even keep a surprise birthday party from you. There's no way I could keep a bigger secret."

Brother Wolf sent his apologies through their bond to Anna. He hadn't known the party was supposed to be a secret.

"My da's bond with Leah isn't like ours," said Charles with certainty. His da didn't talk about his mating, but Charles knew his da well enough to know that he wouldn't want anyone else rummaging through his mind, least of all Leah. And his da had the abilities necessary to make certain his bond functioned just as he chose. "And suspecting she is a traitor isn't going to encourage him to open that bond any further than he can help."

"That's why he's closed the bonds to the pack down so tightly," Anna said.

Charles nodded.

"Could he be wrong?"

"I hope so," Charles said.

"What are we going to do?" asked Anna. He didn't think the question was directed at him.

He tried to draw serenity from the forest around them. It didn't work, but it helped.

"We are going to find Jericho and take care of the immediate problem," he told her. "We're then going to finish warning the wildlings. I don't think we need to consider them suspects anymore. But they do need to be warned nonetheless. Then I'm going to sit down with the files that Boyd sent me last night and see if I can figure out what set my da off."

Anna nodded. "Okay. That sounds like a plan of attack."

She was quiet all the way up to the small cabin that was Jericho's home—thinking things through.

Charles hoped that she'd think something different than the scenario that was playing out all too clearly in his head. He did not want to face off with his da. Though he had known, from the time he understood what happened to old wolves, that eventually the duty of killing his da would probably be his—it was not something he was resigned to.

They smelled the bodies well before they reached Jericho's cabin.

"These people died before the attack on Hester," Anna said.

Charles nodded. "By a couple of days, I'd guess."

She reached out and took his hand, holding it tightly in hers. He was so blessed in his mate, who understood when to talk and when not to.

Asil, Sage, Juste . . . and Leah were waiting for them next to a line of dead bodies—obviously werewolf kills—that they had laid out neatly. Sometime during the trip here, Asil and Sage must have worked something out, because Sage was standing so her shoulder brushed Asil's.

Anna dropped Charles's hand and went to look at the faces of the dead to see if she knew any of them without anyone's saying anything. She was young to have such an understanding of necessity.

They weren't pretty corpses—and so badly rotted that he didn't think Anna had the experience to tell what they might have smelled like when they were alive.

"This one was one of . . . of the men I knew in Chicago," she said finally, pointing at one of the dead werewolves. "And maybe this one." Pointing at another—his face was pretty badly torn up.

"The last one is human," said Juste. He wasn't doubting her—just advising her.

She sighed. "He was human then, too." She frowned unhappily at the dead man in question, then bent and quickly ripped open the dead man's jacket and shirt, exposing the front of his chest.

The tattoo must have been a beautifully rendered dragon. Charles could see it in the delicate skill used on the parts he could distinguish. It didn't look so good now, distorted by death and by the ragged wound that cut through it.

Anna coughed at the additional smell she'd released, putting her hand over her nose. "Yes. This one."

When she finished coughing, she said, "He used . . ." She stopped speaking, glanced at Charles, and closed her lips.

He could take a good guess at what she would have said if she hadn't been worried about setting him off. This was another of the men Leo had allowed to abuse her. Charles did her the courtesy of swallowing his rage as best he could.

"Too bad they are dead," said Asil, with a growl. So Charles wasn't the only one who had heard what she didn't say.

Anna looked at Asil, and said firmly, "No. It's a good thing. I don't need more avenging, Asil. Charles did that. *I* am thriving. But these men are bad men, and I am glad they are dead."

"Where is Jericho?" Charles asked. They had all been standing around the bodies instead of searching for Jericho. That could only mean they had already found him.

He assumed that Jericho was dead—since *everyone* had been waiting with the bodies—but Juste said, "Devon has him located in a cave about a half mile from here. Asil told us to let Devon hold the fort until the two of you could make it up here."

"Devon told you that Jericho had had trouble?" Charles asked. Devon was a wildling—and he'd have been on Leah's list, the group of the safest wildlings.

"Not exactly," said Juste. "Devon didn't change to human for us, but he scratched Jericho's name in the dirt. Leah and I decided to check it out since Devon's place isn't far. We found no Jericho and these, the dead."

Leah, looking tired and smelling of rotten corpses, said, "A few minutes after we got here, Devon showed up, too. He's the one who ran Jericho down—probably he just knew where the likely places to look were. We left him to make sure Jericho didn't run again, but we didn't approach."

She did not say that they were waiting for Charles, so that he could do his job: kill Jericho.

Asil looked at Anna, then met Charles's eyes. "You and I should go up."

Yes.

"No," said Leah in a low voice. Then more clearly. "No. We have already lost Hester. We have to try to save him."

She looked at Anna thoughtfully, and Charles had to fight back a growl as he realized that she hadn't been waiting for him. She'd been waiting for Anna.

"She's tired," said Sage, before Leah could say anything.

Leah closed her mouth, but her body was tight with some strong emotion. He couldn't tell what it was.

Grief, said Anna's voice through their bond. *She does not want to lose another wildling.* Her voice was accompanied by a surge of hope.

It does not mean she is innocent, said Brother Wolf. *Charles is grieved by those he sends on.*

"No doubt," said Anna aloud, answering Brother Wolf, but it sounded like a reply to Sage. Maybe it was both. "But there has been too much tragedy around here. If we don't try, I'll always wonder if I could have made a difference."

"If you do try," Asil told her, "and you succeed in giving him back a little control of his wolf, Jericho still will not last another five years."

"Do you know him?" Anna asked.

Asil shook his head. "No. But I have talked about him with Devon in better times. Devon and he were friends, once. Closer than brothers.

Now Devon is . . . Devon." There was a wealth of sadness in Asil's voice because Asil and Devon had once been very close as well. "And Jericho is so near to madness that he cannot even use words most of the time. The man he once was may not thank you for your help, Anna."

Sage said, in a low voice, "I know him. The first year I was here, I got lost for three days in the middle of an ice storm. I didn't know it was possible to be that cold and live." She looked away. "I found out later that Bran had called all the wildlings, to send them out looking for me. Jericho found me and brought me to his cabin." She rubbed her eyes. "Sorry. He was . . . sweet and shy. Brought me here, dried me off, and called Bran. I know his reputation—even then he was pretty bad off. But he lit a fire in the little stove—and went outside to wait for Bran to come and pick me up."

Sage met Anna's eyes. "I'm telling you this so you know I'm not just being expedient. He treated me well—and it surprised Bran that Jericho was able to do that. That was twenty years ago. And every day of those twenty years, Jericho has spent fighting with his wolf." She waved her hands to indicate the dead. "This time it was the enemy. But next time it might not be. Jericho needs to die." Truth rang in her last sentence—truth as she saw it, at any rate.

"'Fighting' is the right word," said Leah in a grumpy voice. "Since when is fighting a horrible thing? We are werewolves—fighting is what we do."

Sage gave Leah a sad smile. "Sometimes, Leah, the kindest thing is to let them go."

A long, wailing howl echoed through the trees.

Charles raised his face to the sky and answered in a like voice so that their lone soldier understood there was help coming. Of one sort or another.

"If I take Jericho," Charles told Asil, "it's like as not I'll have to do the same with Devon."

The words were a blow—even though Charles knew Asil was well aware of that. Charles had only known the broken wolf his da had brought here sixty years ago. But he knew that Devon, in his glory days, had had a knack for making and keeping friends. Jericho, Asil, and even Bran had been friends of his.

"Devon will defend him," said Asil, giving Charles a half smile. "Devon defends those he loves. That's part of what made him the man he once was."

Leah stepped closer to Anna. "You and I don't always see things the same way," she said.

"That is true," his mate answered, meeting Leah's eyes.

"I know you are tired," Leah continued. "I know that this will only be a stopgap, but my mate gets so sad when the wildlings go on. He breaks his heart over them."

"It would take more than those two," said Anna, indicating Asil and Charles, "to keep me from trying to help. Bran isn't the only one who gets sad when the old ones die."

Leah would think that Anna was speaking only of herself, but Charles knew that Anna was talking about Leah, too.

And us, said Brother Wolf. *We regret, too.*

After saying her bit, Sage had moved away from the dead. She wrapped her arms around her middle and frowned off into the distance. The dead usually didn't bother her much—a result of her early life as a werewolf, Charles had always supposed (it hadn't bothered him at all to take care of most of that rogue pack). Maybe it was just that she was upset about Jericho, who had saved her life once upon a time.

Asil addressed Charles. "I've seen your mate almost die once today. That is enough times, I think."

Charles agreed with him wholeheartedly . . . but he knew what Anna would do. He knew it was not his job to make her smaller, safer. It was his job to lift her up as high as she wanted to soar—and to kill anything that tried to interfere.

"She'll be safe enough with all of us there," Charles said. "And—"

There was a sharp yip of pain, and all of them ran toward the sound. Brother Wolf chose the change before Charles could decide if it was a good idea or not.

There are two werewolf wildlings nearing the end of their days, Brother Wolf told him. *We are all of us wolves, but sometimes the only answer is fang and claw, and we can do this faster than the others.*

More and more, Brother Wolf spoke to Charles in whole sentences, when previously he was more likely to communicate with emotions or wordless gestalt statements that conveyed an entire conversation as a whole. Charles thought that it was the need his brother had to speak to their mate that was causing the evolution.

Leah had taken the lead. Brother Wolf contented himself with running beside Anna and following those who knew where they were going.

The cave where Jericho had retreated wasn't a real cave, but a sheltered place where two great boulders rested against each other. It smelled lightly of Devon and more heavily of Jericho. From the scent layers, this was a place where Jericho slept more often than he used the small cabin they'd just left.

"Jericho," called Leah.

"Coming," said a man's voice. Jericho's voice.

I have never heard Jericho sound like that, said Brother Wolf in surprise.

Anxiety peaked in the whole group. In Brother Wolf's shape, Charles's nose was sharper. What had happened to Devon? Jericho's voice had sounded almost casual, and Jericho was never casual.

No one liked where they saw this going.

There was a shuffling noise, then a muscled man emerged. He had to crawl to get out of the sheltered space, but he stood as soon as there was room. He had a cloth wrapped around his loins in a fashion that Charles hadn't seen in a long time. It gave Jericho the appearance of wearing baggy shorts instead of an old bedsheet.

Jericho looked much as he had the last time Charles had seen him. His beard and hair were long and scraggly, with bits of leaves and other forest detritus caught in it. His hair was tangled every which way and randomly hacked shorter here and there. His eyes were ice blue—the wolf dominant, in that moment at least. There was something odd about that cool stare, but Jericho looked away before Charles could put a finger on what bothered him.

Jericho's body was fit and strong. Which was a good thing—hunger tended to destabilize even the most controlled werewolf, which none of the wildlings were to begin with. He hadn't, Charles thought, eaten any of the dead men—though it was usual for an out-of-control werewolf to eat his victims.

Most of the wildlings were twitchy in human form, as if the wolf were ready to climb out at any moment. Jericho's body was very still and balanced on the balls of his feet. He glanced around at their group with his wolf-blue eyes, then away. He shivered.

"Where is Devon?" asked Leah.

"I . . ." He stopped, swallowed, and began again. "He wanted me to run. He doesn't want me to die. But I killed those men. The only rule is no killing. I had to tie him up in the cave."

And that was more coherent sentences in a row than Charles had been able to get out of him in ten years. To top off the performance, Jericho walked up to Charles, dropped to his knees, and presented his throat.

"Well," said Anna briskly after a moment of silence. "That's all very dramatic and heartfelt, I'm sure. But we're pretty sure those men attacked you. Self-defense is always legal."

Jericho eyed Anna. "No killing. The Marrok was very clear."

Behind Jericho, Asil crossed to the cave and ducked in.

"Those men belonged to our enemy," said Leah. "A similar group killed Hester yesterday. Her mate followed by his own hand."

Jericho swayed a bit then, and his eyes darkened to human blue. "Felt that," he said. "Hester . . . didn't like me at all." For a second, he grinned widely. "Damn near killed me first time we met." Then he blinked, and the human left his eyes again. "Not sorry I killed them. But the rule is no killing."

"How did they find you?" asked Anna. "Do you know? Did you hear anything that can help us find them?"

Jericho growled at her.

Brother Wolf growled more savagely, and Jericho subsided.

"Don't do this," Sage said, apparently to herself because her voice had been very quiet. "You don't need to do this."

Charles gave Sage a sharp look—but her attention was on Jericho.

Jericho's attention was on Charles.

Asil exited the cave and a very thin, patchy-coated wolf followed him, head low and tail tucked. Asil nodded at Charles—he'd found Devon just as Jericho said he would. Charles looked carefully at

Devon, but the wildling seemed unharmed—if not particularly happy.

"Assume that we'll take care of an execution if it needs to happen," Anna told Jericho dryly. "Moving on to a different topic. Did you overhear anything they might have said? Any clues to who or what they were?"

Jericho focused his ice-blue eyes on Charles's mate. Charles would have been happier if he hadn't done that.

"She said not to come here. To wait. That this attack is too likely to give her away," Jericho said, in a hard, oddly deep voice. His voice changed again, becoming both lighter and quicker. "She is not in charge; she is not the boss. And I don't know about you, but I'm more afraid of the boss than of her."

And Charles realized that Jericho had taken Anna's question literally. He was repeating back exactly what they had said in his presence.

And they had been talking about a "she."

Charles looked at Leah—he couldn't help it. But she was watching Jericho with her brows furrowed—Charles didn't think she'd quite figured out what Jericho was doing.

"Our job," continued the wildling coolly, "is to get the information from this one if he has it. No one will miss him for a long time. If we can't get it from him, then we hit the other one." Jericho sighed loudly and dropped into the first voice. "And that will be a cluster because someone keeps taking out our surveillance equipment, I know. I don't like going in blind, eith—" Jericho stopped speaking.

"Anna can help you," said Sage intently. "She just broke a hundred-year-old curse on another wildling. I was there."

The first statement was a lie. Charles turned his attention to Sage—because he'd never heard her lie before. Even more interesting than the lie was the implication that she didn't believe Anna could help Jericho.

Even though he'd once rescued her—and Charles remembered the incident pretty much the way she'd told it—she was scared of Jericho. Charles could tell that much, though her control was very good. Probably he and Jericho were the only ones who could smell it. Charles because he had Brother Wolf, and Jericho because he was mostly wolf even when he wore human skin.

"Eith—?" asked Anna.

"I killed him before he finished the sentence," said Jericho smugly. "He was probably going to say 'either' but you asked me what they said. Not what I thought they were going to say."

Asil said, "You are feeling talkative tonight, my friend." He sounded a little suspicious.

There is something going on, said Brother Wolf. *Something is wrong with Jericho.*

Well, yes.

More wrong, said Brother Wolf intently. *Differently wrong.*

He just killed seven people and has been waiting for two days for his death sentence, Charles reminded him. *But I agree.*

Satisfied, Brother Wolf fell silent.

"Did you kill them before they attacked you?" asked Leah.

"Don't," Sage whispered.

Jericho gave Leah his ice-blue stare. "They invaded my territory. They came with guns and sharp things. With wires and switches and buttons to make me tell them things. They wanted to take Bright. I couldn't let them do that. They said, 'Sage can't figure out where Frank Bright is, and she's had years. How hard is it to find the only black man among Bran Cornick's misfits?'"

Charles bolted, but it had taken him an extra breath to realize what Jericho had said. That short space of time allowed Sage to get a head start.

As she ran, she grabbed her necklace. He had time to see her shift to her wolf as quickly as he could, felt the wave of witchcraft that allowed her to do so.

Then a puff of smoke billowed in the air right in front of him. The acrid, greasy cloud filled his nose and mouth and left him coughing and gagging and trying to breathe. He plowed to a stop and tried to clean his nose with his paws, wiping his face on the ground when that didn't work.

Asil passed him without hesitation, Leah and Juste on his heels. Anna stopped and pulled off her shirt. She wiped his face and paws with it. That did the trick, and he could breathe again.

"Witchcraft," she said. "I saw something burst right in front of you."

Smelled stale, said Brother Wolf. *The magic was trapped in an object. We would have known if she were witchborn.*

"If she had that with her," Anna said, "then she was prepared for us to find her out."

Yes.

Sage was their traitor. He'd let himself process that, to grieve over that, later. He got to his feet and shook himself, trying to decide how to proceed.

"Heyya," called Jericho.

The wildling had Devon beside him, and they were walking along the side of the mountain about twenty feet above where Charles and Anna were. Devon still had his tail between his legs and was watching Jericho with uncertain eyes—probably wondering why Jericho had tied him up, though it was hard to be certain with Devon.

"She's following a trail," Jericho said. "I know where it comes out—there's a shortcut. If they don't stop her before she gets that far, we can take her at the other end."

Charles and Anna made short work of climbing the slope until they were up on the path the wildlings were on. It didn't take them long to catch up. Jericho was not in an apparent hurry because he waited for them.

As they neared, Jericho tilted his head and frowned at Anna. "I don't know you," he said. "Should I know you?"

"Hello," Anna said as they drew close. "We haven't met. I'm Anna, Charles's wife."

Jericho looked at her with blue eyes that shifted from wolf to human with an unhealthy speed. "The Omega?"

She nodded.

Without tightening his muscles in warning, without a word or a sign, he jumped her.

They rolled down the steep side of the mountain so quickly that Devon and Charles didn't catch up with them until they were nearly to the bottom. They rolled up against a tree and slammed into it, Anna letting out a grunt that had more startle than pain in it.

Charles would have snapped Jericho's neck if Devon hadn't knocked him sideways, then stood in front of the tangle of bodies. His head was lowered, tilted submissively, his tail was tucked, and he was shaking like a wet horse in a snowstorm, but he still stood between them.

"Second time in one day," Anna complained with a tremor of shock in her voice. "What is it with people? Did they forget their manners? Hello, how are you? No, I get the full tackle like I was a quarterback."

If she was complaining, she wasn't badly hurt—though rolling down that rocky mountainside wouldn't have done her any good.

"No manners at all," said Jericho's muffled voice. "Oh God. Oh God. You don't parade surcease like this in front of wildlings, you young idiot. What were you thinking?"

It took Charles a second to realize that he was the young idiot Jericho was talking about.

Charles growled.

Jericho gave a shaky half laugh that was full of tears. "I'm sorry. So sorry. God. I can think. I can *breathe*." There was a little pause, and he said, in a lost voice with a touch of panic, "What I can't do is let go. It doesn't *hurt*. It doesn't *hurt*."

"Well, I hurt," Anna said in a grumpier voice than before. "We just rolled down the side of a mountain." This time there was a thread of panic in her voice. "Don't get me wrong, but I would really, really be grateful if you would let me up."

"I *can't*," Jericho said.

They were so fragile, these wildlings of his da's. Dangerous as all get out, but they were fragile.

He is frightening our mate, growled Brother Wolf. *If he doesn't stop, it won't matter how dangerous or fragile he is—he will be dead.*

Devon whined anxiously—and Brother Wolf nosed him to reassure him that they wouldn't kill Jericho unless they had to.

Talking seemed like a good idea if no one was to die, so Charles changed. He let his human shape come upon him more slowly than usual. That way he could do one more quick change if he needed to be wolf again without pulling on the pack.

Fully human again, though the stress of the last minute or so showed in that he was wearing buckskin and moccasins instead of jeans and boots, he stood up and shoved Devon aside.

"It's okay," he told Devon, "But I need to sort this out."

Anna's eyes were panicky, and he could see that she'd about reached her limit. Understandably, she didn't like anyone on top of her at the best of times. Brother Wolf would have just killed Jericho and been done with it. Death was coming for that one sooner rather than later anyway.

But with his stepmother's accurate assessment of Bran's sorrow at losing another wildling and the understanding that probably, unless Leah beat him to it, he was going to have to kill Sage, Charles had little taste for more death. Though at least, he thought with some relief, he would not have to kill Leah nor meet his da in mortal combat.

Not yet.

Instead of killing Jericho, Charles peeled the werewolf off his mate while Anna helped by scrambling body parts out of reach as soon as he'd freed them. When Jericho's skin lost contact with Anna's, he screamed, his whole body locking up in agony. Charles finally took him all the way to the ground and pinned him, facedown.

Wrestling with werewolves was complicated by the fact that weight didn't hold a werewolf unless his opponent was the size of an elephant, maybe. Joint locks still worked, though.

"Move again," Charles snarled, letting Brother Wolf's dominance color his voice, "and I'll break your neck, and you won't have to worry about touching my mate ever again."

Devon made a soft, frightened sound.

Anna, on her feet and winded, said, "Don't worry, Devon. He doesn't mean it."

But he did. Fortunately, the right person believed him, and Jericho subsided, panting and sweating. And sobbing.

Anna crouched and touched the skin on his arm with her fingers. She frowned a little, reaching with her other hand to touch Charles. Her pulse was still fast, and her grip was just a little too hard—she was using Charles to calm herself down.

Jericho was lucky Charles didn't break his neck anyway for the way the wildling had made his Anna's heart race with reflexive panic.

As soon as Anna touched him, Jericho's whole body relaxed, though he still panted with stress.

"Gods," he said, again.

Carefully, Charles let him go, keeping himself between Anna and Jericho without breaking Anna's grip on Jericho's arm. Which left him too close to the other wolf. He liked to give himself a little distance if he might have to kill someone. A little distance gave him more options.

He saw Jericho's eyes do the weird blue-swirl shift to the ice of his wolf again. And for some reason, his long-dead grandfather's voice echoed in his head.

You can always tell them by their eyes. The old medicine man's hushed voice rang in his ears as if his mother's father had been standing right behind Charles. He could picture where he'd been when he'd heard those words the first time—ten or eleven and huddled by the fire with a handful of other boys his age as his grandfather taught them the things they would need to know when they were men.

He had no idea why he was thinking of that tale right at this moment.

Hadn't Sage said that werewolves were just the tip of the iceberg as far as monsters were concerned? And she had been right.

Anna said, "Some days, this Omega gig sucks worse than others. What is it with everyone's throwing themselves on me?"

"It's the wolf," said Charles absently. "The wildlings, most of them, have worn out their ability to control their wolf. The wolf spirit wants to be close to you—and their human half cannot restrain it."

"Sorry," said Jericho, closing his eyes. "I'm sorry."

Charles could hear it in his voice, smell it in his scent. Jericho was sorry.

So why was Charles feeling like he was overlooking something important? He asked Brother Wolf, who understood what he was feeling but didn't know what it was, either. He was no help at all.

"Sage will be long gone," Anna said. She didn't sound too unhappy about it.

He appreciated how she felt—a lifetime of never hearing "Hello, hello, Charlie" again. But they could not allow a traitor to live.

Devon made a noise—and then Jericho said, "No. No. We can still get there—" He started to get up, moving away from Charles to do so. He also moved away from Anna.

And Charles had to put the wildling back down on the ground to keep him from attacking Anna again.

"No," growled Charles firmly.

"You and Devon go," said Anna. "If Devon knows the shortcut?"

She put her hand on Jericho's. He gripped her—and relaxed again.

Devon yipped.

Anna looked at Charles. "You and Devon can go and help them with Sage." Tears welled up, and she wiped them off impatiently as she continued urgently, "Sage. Of all people. Damn it. I know she can't be allowed to live. I know that. But you can make it quick. Leah won't. You know Leah—she plays with her prey as if she were a cat rather than a werewolf."

Jericho, released from Charles's hold again, sat up but made no other move.

"Jericho and I will stay here," Anna continued. "We will wait for someone to come back and tell us what happened. Then we can figure out something to do about this." She made a waving motion to indicate their joined hands.

Rare—his grandfather's voice—*but deadly.*

Charles, watching Jericho's icy wolf eyes, abruptly remembered the story his grandfather had been telling that day when Charles had been a child.

"SHE WORE THE skins of her victims," his grandfather told them, his voice shaky with age. "She wore the spirit and memories, too, as if they were clothing. She cried when my aunt would have cried, laughed when she would have laughed. Her own husband and their children could not tell that the monster in their home was not their beloved one. Only I saw the monster wearing my aunt's skin—and I was only a little boy younger than any of you are now. I had no one to show what I had seen because there was no one else in the village to see her for what she was. My mother's uncle, who was our medicine man and my first teacher, had died the year before.

"That fall, though, a trading party came to camp, and their shaman came with them. I told him about my aunt and asked for his help. He came with me to the fire where my aunt and uncle were sitting—and he told my uncle that his wife had been taken by evil. My uncle, he did not believe the strange medicine man, nor the affidavits of his power that the man's companions were quick to give. The thing who wore my aunt's face cried and begged my uncle not to hear the stranger's words.

"While she was pleading, this medicine man walked up and placed his hand on my aunt's head. She quit talking, frozen in place by the great power he held."

Charles's grandfather sighed. "I was there, and still, what happened is so strange that I do not know how to build the picture for you." He'd fallen silent and watched the fire as if he had not noticed the terror he'd inspired in his audience. For weeks afterward, he would be asked to examine someone's mother or aunt or uncle to make sure they had not been taken.

"That old man," Charles's grandfather said, "he sang a song to her in a language I had never heard before—and have not heard since. After a moment, he raised his other hand and put it out so." He put one hand down as if it rested upon the head of a woman. He put the other one up. "Then he tipped his hand over slowly until it was palm down, too. And under his hand another person formed, as real as you or I, an old woman, naked, sitting in the same position as my aunt. Then my aunt fell to the side. For a moment I thought he had saved her, but she was truly dead. Her corpse rotted until it was as any body that had been dead over a year would have been. The medicine man changed his song, and he sang for a very long time. Eventually, the naked woman disappeared, and the medicine man was left with the feather of a bird in his hand."

Charles's grandfather looked each boy in the eye. "Afterward, that old man sat down with me and explained what the monster who took my aunt was. He said, 'A medicine man, healer, or shaman who has given up his connection with the way of the earth is more evil than anything I have ever met—and in my youth I hunted the stick men and three separate times I brought down the Hunger that Devours. When those who are sent to do good turn from that path, when they gain power and long life by stealing life from others—there is no evil greater.' He had, he told me, seen only one other such. The creature who took my aunt is the only one I have ever seen. They are rare and dangerous. Hard to see them—but if you look in their eyes . . . If you keep watch, it is their eyes that give them away. There is only one way to kill them, if you are not a medicine man such as he or I. That is with fire."

"JERICHO," SAID CHARLES softly.

A quick change, my brother, he asked the wolf. *As quick as we ever have. For Anna's sake.*

Then, opening his mating bond as widely as he could, he said, *Anna. I need you to do something for me.*

The wildling looked at him, and so did Anna.

"Jericho," said Charles again, heavily. This time, it wasn't a request for the other's attention. "Jericho's wolf's eyes are yellow."

Run, he told Anna. *Run and do not stop.*

Anna bolted before her brain caught up to her feet.

Skinwalker, Brother Wolf breathed into their bond. *The Diné would call him a skinwalker. Such as he can only be killed by fire or a medicine man's magic.*

And then Brother Wolf drove her to her knees with the sudden, complete memory of a smoky, dimly lit place where eight boys listened in terror as an old man told them a warning tale about a monster. And the information the old man had given those boys terrified her, too.

Devon whined. Anna turned her head to see that he was trotting back and forth, watching the battling wolves—because apparently whatever wore Jericho's body didn't have a problem making a quick shift to wolf.

Given what she now knew about Jericho, she should be running.

"Devon," she said. "Devon—that's not Jericho." She remembered what Charles had said before he attacked. "Jericho's wolf had yellow eyes."

Devon froze and looked at her.

"Skinwalker," she told him. "They kill the people whose form they want, then they steal it. They wear their whole person like a coat. It's not Jericho, Devon. He's dead, and the skinwalker stole his body and his memories to wear."

Flesh and spirit, Charles's grandfather had said. That must be why the blood bonds between the Marrok and the wildlings had not warned him and, through the Marrok, the rest of the pack. But the thought of it made her want to be sick. How much of Jericho was left? Did he understand what the skinwalker was doing? Or was he truly dead and "spirit" meant something different?

Anna, said Charles, *I cannot defeat him. I have magic, but it is not the kind that my grandfather meant. He meant the magic of a holy man. Get out of here, my love. Get out of here and warn the others. Call my da and tell him he—*

His voice in her head broke off as the air around the thing that was Jericho rippled where the werewolf had been. And in its place was a bear far larger than the grizzlies that roamed the pack territories.

Anna, please, Charles implored.

You must survive to tell our da—in case he takes us, said Brother Wolf. *He won't be able to tell until it is too late.*

Charles expected to die. He expected to die and that the skinwalker would take his shape. As the skinwalker had probably been planning on doing to Anna after separating her from the others by sending them off after Sage.

Sage had known what the skinwalker was—had known *who* it

was. That's what those strange-at-the-time requests had been while Jericho had been talking. Sage and the skinwalker knew each other—and Sage had been asking Jericho-who-was-not-Jericho not to betray her to them.

They had been looking for Wellesley. Jericho-who-was-not-Jericho had called him Frank Bright—the name Wellesley had used before he'd come here. They'd gone to Hester and to Jericho because—Anna would put money on this—those were the only two wildlings whose homes Sage had been to. But sometime during the attack on Jericho, the skinwalker had seen the chance to do more than that, to become one of the Marrok's pack.

Anna tried to visualize what she'd seen when that stink bomb had gone off and driven Charles off the trail. Had it come from Jericho—who had been on the trail above Charles? Charles, in wolf form already, was the one most likely to catch Sage. But the distraction had also allowed the skinwalker to isolate Charles and Anna from the rest—and ultimately, Jericho had been trying to isolate Anna.

And then there was Sage. Had she been looking for Wellesley for over twenty years? Or had her primary purpose been as a spy?

Later, Anna told herself, she'd figure it out later. She would not allow the skinwalker to have her mate. Charles had to keep fighting while she looked for a way to kill it.

Anna didn't know where a holy man was to be found, but she did know that they had just burned down a cabin, and all three of the vehicles parked only a couple of miles down the trail had been at Hester's cabin yesterday—and Asil had been in charge of the fire.

While she'd been thinking—only a second or two, she was pretty sure—Devon had disappeared. Apparently, the Kodiak bear that had appeared in Jericho-the-wolf's stead had convinced him when she had not.

Anna rolled to her feet and sprinted for where they'd left the vehicles. There wouldn't be a holy man waiting for her, but maybe someone would still have things that she could use to set a skinwalker on fire. She tried not to remember that she'd ridden in two of those vehicles and didn't recall noticing the smell of anything volatile.

THE CARS WERE all locked. Since Asil had been in charge of Hester's pyre, his was the first car she assaulted. She could probably have broken the latch on the back hatch but wasn't sure enough to try it. If she failed, she might just jam the stupid thing—and that would slow her down further.

So she broke the driver's side window with her elbow. A rock would have saved her some pain, but she was too worried about time to look around for a rock.

"Keep him busy," she muttered to her husband, but she didn't send it along their bond. She didn't want to distract him. That Kodiak had been as big as a truck and unholy quick.

Charles was the bogeyman of the werewolves. He could take a bear, no matter how big it was. And all he had to do was hold on until she got back.

She popped the back hatch of Asil's Mercedes open with a button and found a barbecue lighter but nothing else. Nor was there any sign that there had ever been anything else. Knowing Asil, he probably had C-4 stashed in sealed containers along with detonators somewhere in the car. But no one but Asil would be able to find it.

She wondered if C-4 would kill the skinwalker as well as fire would.

"Come on, come on," she said, frustrated at the empty vehicle. "It's a start, but I need something bigger."

Not too far away, she heard the sound of a motorcycle and wondered if Sage had planned far enough ahead to have stashed a vehicle to use—or if she had just found it somewhere. Anna supposed it might be someone else, but the wildlings lived in the most remote corners of the pack territory, so it was unlikely.

She broke the window on Sage's SUV with her left elbow since her right was still sore from Asil's car. A quick search, during which the motorcycle appeared to be approaching closer, showed her that there was nothing in Sage's car that would be useful. But she grabbed the witch gun and tucked it into the back of her jeans. She was pretty sure that the old shaman who talked to Charles's grandfather would have tried a witch gun on a skinwalker if he'd had one.

The motorcycle rider must be coming here because this was remote enough that there *wasn't* anywhere else. That seemed to indicate that whoever it was, it was not Sage after all. If she had a motorcycle to escape on, Sage would be riding away from here as fast as she could go.

The shell on the back of Leah's pickup wasn't locked. In the bed of the truck, bungee-corded to the side, was a battered, metal, five-gallon can of gasoline.

"Hallelujah," she said. "Just keep him busy, Charles, I'm coming."

She hopped out of Leah's truck with the full gas can in one hand and the lighter in the other just as the motorcycle—carrying a helmet-less Wellesley—roared up the track. He slid the dirt bike to a stop with all the aplomb of a motocross maven.

"What's wrong?" Wellesley asked at the same time she asked him, "What are you doing here?"

He waved at her to get her to answer his question first.

"Charles—" She started to tell him, then realized how long *that* would take.

"I don't have time for this," she told him impatiently, and took off up the trail, carrying the mostly full five-gallon can and the lighter.

She didn't care if she lit the whole forest on fire just so long as she saved Charles. Wellesley ran beside her. He made no effort to take the gas can from her.

"Talk while you run," he said.

"If I can talk," she retorted, increasing her pace, "then I'm not running fast enough."

Apparently, he could run and talk at her fastest pace because he said, "I'm here because my wolf spirit woke me up from a sound sleep and told me that our enemy was this way. So what are you trying to burn, Anna Cornick? Why are you in such a hurry to do it?"

"Skinwalker," panted Anna. Deciding talking might be useful after all, she slowed enough that she could manage short sentences. "I think that's the Native American version of a black witch."

Wellesley smiled, his eyes bright gold, and when he spoke, his voice had a rasp of wolf in it, too. "I know what a skinwalker is. There was a skinwalker at Rhea Springs. She is here."

"It is a him," Anna huffed.

"Doesn't matter to her what form she takes," said Wellesley. "Male or female."

There was a lot of confidence in his voice. "You remembered what happened at Rhea Springs," she said.

"I did," he said. "I remembered—"

Pain hit her through her mating bond, sharp and sudden. She put a foot wrong and tumbled into a tree, unable to catch her balance while her mind was consumed with agony that had nothing to do with her fall.

THE THING THAT wore Jericho's flesh had not been a werewolf for long enough to figure out how to fight in that body. It didn't take the skinwalker long to figure that out and take on another form.

The Kodiak, the grizzly's bigger, stronger brother, outweighed Charles five to one, and it was very nearly as quick as he was. But it wasn't the first bear Charles had fought, not even the first Kodiak. He preferred to leave them alone if he could—even a werewolf had its limits, and a Kodiak was very close to them. But there were times, like now, when the fight could not be avoided.

Charles was more maneuverable and—Brother Wolf was certain after the first few minutes of battle—more experienced at utilizing the abilities of Brother Wolf's form than the skinwalker was used to using the bear's form.

Even so, the bear made the skinwalker much more formidable and less clumsy than he'd been as a wolf. This bear form was something he'd fought in before.

When dealing with a predator larger than he, Charles liked to use the hit-and-run method of fighting. It was less effective against the bear than he liked—the bear had a thick, tough hide covered by thick, tough fur and a layer of fat beneath that. Although Charles was able to get a lot of surface cuts in, they weren't deep enough to be anything more than annoying. But engaging the bear fully was likely to end up with Charles flattened under the bear's greater strength. The trick to fighting bears was to tire them out.

The single hit the bear had gotten in had cracked three ribs. Charles, remembering just in time that he could draw upon the pack's strength for healing, managed to stay maneuverable, though he didn't heal them entirely.

Even with pack magic, the bones were likely to remain fragile for a day or two, and a little pain would remind him of that. Additionally, he didn't want to use up all that he could draw from the pack. It had taken a lot of power to free Wellesley, and although there were some real heavy hitters in his pack, he didn't have the experience to know what the limits were.

He learned something about the skinwalker in the opening bit of hit-and-run, too. Most of the time, Charles was fighting the bear's intelligence and not the skinwalker's. Most of the time, the bear fought like a bear. Which was smart on the part of the skinwalker because that bear knew how to fight.

But if he was fighting a bear, there were some things Charles could do.

He got in a second deep bite on the bear's flank, right on top of a previous wound—and this time his fangs dug into meat. It was also a place the bear couldn't reach him, so he held on until the bear's flesh began to give under his fangs.

He waited until the bear started to move, just before the meat would have given way and dumped Charles on the ground. Then, digging in with all four clawed feet, Charles scrambled right over the top of the beast.

He took the opportunity to attempt to dig into the bear's spine, just behind the ribs, where there was the least flesh protecting it. His teeth closed on bone, but when the bear rolled, he let the grip go.

Charles ran and turned to face the bear from a distance of about twenty feet. It wasn't a safe distance—he didn't want a safe distance. His only intention was to fight as long as possible, to give Anna time to warn everyone.

He'd done more damage than he'd thought. A chunk of bear hide the size of a hand towel had been pulled to the side, flapping like a loose horse blanket. Blood scented the air and dripped onto the ground. But when the bear moved, it was clear that, gruesome as it was, it was only a flesh wound, impressive but minor, and it wasn't bleeding enough to weaken him.

But it hurt.

The great bear reared up and roared, its upright form nearly ten feet tall. Any creature more intelligent than a bear would have been too smart to do that with the steep slope of the mountain behind it. Charles took a running leap and hit the bear in the face with his body, sending the bear tumbling backward down the side of the mountain. The beast's teeth opened a gash in Charles's shoulder, but it hadn't been expecting the move, so it was slow. It wasn't able to get a good hold, and Charles fell free.

Charles tumbled a few paces but was back on his feet and harrying the bear as it rolled the fifty yards or so of very steep, rocky ground all the way to the bottom. When it rolled to a stop, before it could get its feet under it, Charles landed on its back and went for the spine, now showing whitely in its bed of flesh.

He closed his jaws on bone and shook as hard as he could. Beneath him, the bear tried first to get to its feet—and then just to roll over. But it had fallen awkwardly, and Charles was able to keep it from finding the leverage to do much more than wiggle. It gave a hard lurch . . . and the spine separated with a pop and a grisly crunch.

The bear's rear quarters fell limp, and Charles bounded away from the still-dangerous front end. The bear's blue human eyes regarded him balefully as it roared and snapped its teeth together.

Charles growled, showing the skinwalker his own fangs. He stayed back as his opponent thrashed and struggled—apparently paying no attention to anything other than reaching Charles. Charles gradually became aware of aching muscles, stiffness in his left shoulder, and the persistent ache of his ribs.

Eventually, the blood loss, made worse by the bear's refusal to be still, won out. The giant beast gave one last heave and collapsed on the torn-up ground. It breathed four times, then the air whooshed out with a sigh, and the blue eyes glazed over.

Charles waited. He did not remember a time that his grandfather had been wrong about something. Charles was not a holy man, and so he should not have killed the skinwalker. But unarguably, the skinwalker in the bear's form lay dead. Charles's ears could not pick up the sound of his enemy's heart beating. He waited until his nose told him that death had begun its work, the body had started to decompose, before he decided that his grandfather had been mistaken. Werewolves were not native to this continent; perhaps that was why his grandfather had not mentioned werewolves as a way to kill skinwalkers.

Charles looked for Devon. He'd have thought that the wildling would have joined in the fight—on Jericho's side. Jericho was Devon's friend, and Charles and Devon were only acquaintances. But Devon was nowhere to be seen, his scent just a hint on the wind.

Whatever Anna had told Devon when she wasted time that she should have used to get away had been effective.

Now that he had scared her to death, he supposed, he'd better let her know that—

Fifteen hundred pounds of Kodiak hit him like a bulldozer. His shoulder crunched against a tree, and screaming agony flared throughout his body. Somehow, the skinwalker's magic had concealed the sound of movement, the rebirth of the bear, and the feel of blood magic at work, so the bear had taken Charles completely by surprise.

In his head, a quavering old man's voice said, *My grandson, why do you always have to learn the hard way?*

LEAH RAN, FOCUSED on her goal. She was taller than Asil and Juste both, and she outpaced them.

She was a skilled hunter, and she learned from others' mistakes. She did not allow herself to get close enough to Sage to fall victim to one of her witchy tricks as Charles had. But she kept Sage in sight.

She had the advantage on this ground, she thought. With her mate, she had traveled every foot of their territory, stayed up late at night discussing the topography, its strengths and weaknesses. She knew, for instance, that Sage was trying to take them on a roundabout route to the cars. Sage was hoping that they would let her get far enough ahead that she could take one of them and escape.

Never had Leah so resented the protocol that forbade cell phones. It would be nice to alert the pack, so that they could set up roadblocks on all of the ways that Sage could take her wussy SUV out of these mountains. Maybe even get someone up here in time to disable Sage's car. But the nearest phone was at Jericho's cabin, and that was too far to do them any good.

Leah was pretty sure that Sage didn't have the knowledge to start one of the cars without a key—thank heavens that Charles had left his old truck at home. Even Leah could hot-wire a truck from that era in about ten seconds flat.

She had a gun, concealed in a shoulder holster, but didn't bother to take it out. She was a decent shot, but at this pace she would be unlikely to hit Sage. Besides, killing Sage with a gun would be so much less satisfying than killing her with her knife.

She jumped a tree, tucking her feet up so as not to catch a toe. Sage was keeping to rough ground where she could because Leah was faster, even on two feet, than Sage was on four.

Some of that was because Leah ran in her human form every day. Some of it was that Leah was built like a runner. But most of it was that, as the Marrok's mate, second in the pack, she could draw on the strength of the pack to aid her muscles.

She kept Sage's wolf in sight, though the light and dark golden brown coat was better even than Leah's own tawnier fur at blending in the light and shadow of the forest they ran through. After a couple of miles, Juste and Asil were some distance behind them, and she was just settling into her stride. But that was all right.

She could take Sage.

Her mate told her that her attitudes were stuck in the nineteenth century. She knew that Bran worried that her lack of confidence when facing down a male opponent would get her hurt someday. But she had him for that—and there wasn't a female werewolf on the planet she was afraid of.

They were nearly back where they had started—a trick of the trail

Sage had been taking. That meant they were about two miles from the cars.

Sage tossed a look over her shoulder, and Leah could see the consternation wash over her when she saw Leah. She'd really thought she could outrun Leah. She wasn't the first person to underestimate Leah. Most of them were dead.

Her mate was the only person who truly saw her. He might not like her—Leah knew that, and it didn't bother her. Much. But Bran Cornick appreciated her skills and her strengths, and he respected her. He didn't truly respect many people. She would make do with that.

She increased her speed, narrowing the distance between them. Even Bran would be surprised that it was she, and not his son, who killed their traitor.

She was barely a hundred feet short of Sage when she felt a shivery light in the pack bonds that told her one of their pack had been gravely injured. Who? She slowed her approach, letting Sage's lead grow again, as she searched through the ties that bound her to her pack.

Charles.

How did Charles get hurt? It doesn't feel like magic, so it isn't an effect of whatever Sage threw in his face. Leah had been a werewolf a long time, and she knew how to read the bonds. This was a physical hurt, grave enough to mean death.

A bear roared its triumph—from the direction of Jericho's cave. *What in the world made Charles take on a bear when we have a traitor to catch?*

She set one foot down and pivoted on it. Sage would have to wait.

No, it would not hurt her if Charles died. She didn't like him, and she'd never made any bones about it. He was sullen and silent, and she was more scared of him than she was of anyone, not excluding Asil.

But if a death of another wildling would hurt her mate, the death of his son would do far worse. And though she knew Bran did not love her, knew that love had no part in their long-ago bargain, it didn't matter. She loved her coldhearted, flawed bastard of a husband and mate with all of her selfish heart. If she could save Charles, she would.

And wouldn't Charles just hate that. She smiled widely as she ran, sweeping up Asil and Juste in her wake with a gesture of her hand.

CRUMPLED AGAINST A tree, Anna looked up at Wellesley with tears in her eyes. "He's hurt," she said, too frantic to wonder if Wellesley would even know who she was talking about. "He's hurt. Nothing can kill it. Only a holy man or fire—and Charles has neither."

Instead of answering her, Wellesley gathered the five-gallon can and found the lighter where it had landed when she fell. Anna scrambled belatedly to her feet, feeling dizzy and light-headed, though the pain had dimmed a little. She couldn't tell if it was because Charles had tightened down their bond or because he was losing consciousness.

But pain meant he was still alive, and if he was still alive, there was no time to stand around. Save mourning for when it was too late to do anything.

"Get me there," said Wellesley. "I can help."

And that's when she actually looked at him and paid attention to what she saw.

Sometime between when they'd left him at his home, tired but whole, and now, he had resettled his person. This man was no harmless artist. Here was the man who had survived slavery of the worst sort, who survived a curse for nearly a century and emerged sane. Such a man could command armies—or a slightly battered Anna who had a skinwalker to kill.

Despite the pain that drifted to her through the mating bond, Anna allowed herself a little hope. She took off again, trying to build her speed back up to where it had been. She didn't quite succeed—she'd twisted her ankle pretty good, and even with the increased healing her werewolf gained her, it hurt. Wellesley caught her elbow twice when she would have stumbled.

Eventually, though it was probably only a couple of minutes, the pain faded, and she resumed her breakneck pace. They passed Jericho's cabin. Charles was still alive—even if their bond was so quiet it scared her.

SHOTS RANG OUT. Anna hesitated—who was shooting? Charles didn't have a gun with him. Shaking off her surprise, Anna ran to the trail where she'd left him, but the fight had gone downhill and into the trees.

She and Wellesley scrambled down until they could see over a second, even steeper drop-off to the battle royal below.

Charles was crumpled in a heap, and Leah, Asil, and Juste were fanned out between him and the bear. Leah had a gun in one hand and a wicked-looking knife in the other. Asil had a bladed weapon somewhere between a knife and a short sword in length—it was dripping blood.

Juste threw a fist-sized rock at the bear's head. A major-league pitcher couldn't compete with a werewolf for speed or force. The bear tried to get out of the way, but the rock hit it in the head with a crack that knocked it off its feet.

Anna would have plunged down the hill, but Wellesley caught her arm.

"Wait," he told her, his eyes on the bear. "I need you to stand guard. She will try to stop me when she notices what I'm doing."

She pulled her eyes off Charles and turned them to Wellesley and demanded in a voice she barely recognized as her own, "Are you a holy man?"

"Are you asking if I can end this creature? I am the last descendant of the holiest family in my clan. The earth speaks to me. Can I end this creature?" His smile was fierce. "I don't know, but I have dreamed of trying for a very, very long time."

Wellesley pulled out a cloth folded into a pouch that smelled of garlic, chili, lemon, and some unfamiliar things. He crouched and gathered old leaves, dried grass, and a few sticks. He quickly cleared a space of anything burnable and used the fuel he'd gathered to build the makings of a miniature fire, dumping the spice mixture on top of that.

Below them, Leah put three rounds into the bear—and Juste hit it with another rock. Of the two bullets or rock—the rock seemed to do the more damage. But it was light-footed Asil who made the killing stroke—leaping on top of the wounded bear and sliding his blade between its shoulder blades and through its spine.

Wellesley knelt on the ground and, though Anna had brought him five gallons of gasoline and a barbecue lighter, he lit the fire by holding his hand over it and murmuring a word that made the hair on the back of her neck stand up. He closed his eyes and began to sing—more of a chant, really—in a liquid language she'd never heard before.

She looked around for something to help her defend him—and ended up piling stones of an appropriate size. Juste's rocks were proving effective—and she knew how to throw a baseball.

It was too bad, she thought ruefully, that she wasn't witchborn. The gun would probably be a much better weapon than—

"You have something that belongs to the skinwalker," said Wellesley—chanting the words in the same rhythm he'd been using so that she almost missed that he was talking to her.

"I have this," she told him, and pulled the gun out of the back of her waistband.

He didn't open his eyes, just inclined his head. "Please place it in the fire," he asked.

Anna eyed the fire. The gun was made mostly of metal—and Wellesley's fire wasn't that hot. But she didn't argue with him, just slid it cautiously into the fire.

She kept an eye on the fight.

The bear had collapsed after Asil's blow. Asil had continued forward, driven by his own momentum to take five or six strides away from the bear. He turned to regard the fallen beast. Leah and Juste closed in on it warily.

Charles stirred, then staggered to his feet. The sensation of his pain made her gasp. He looked up to where Anna and Wellesley were, and she could feel his consternation.

Anna, he told her, and she could feel his despair, *run, my love. This thing cannot be killed.*

I found a holy man, she told him a bit smugly despite her worry.

He's a little broken, I think. But he believes he can do this. If not, I have gasoline and a lighter.

Behind him, the beast's form blurred, shrank, and a little girl, no more than six or seven, rose to her hands and knees where the bear had just been. She wore a ragged dress of unbleached cotton, and her dark hair was matted. She looked around her with wide eyes, and her mouth trembled.

"Don't hurt me," she said, scrambling away, her eyes on Asil. "I ain't done nothing to you. Don't hurt me."

Sometime, somewhere, the skinwalker had killed and skinned a child. For a moment, Anna could barely breathe.

Charles had turned at the child's first words. Like Anna, he froze momentarily.

Warn them, said Brother Wolf, as their pack mates were pulling out of battle mode. *It's not a child. Anna, warn them.*

"It's a skinwalker," she called out. "A shapechanger, a witch. It's not— *Watch out, Asil!*"

Flowing out of the child's form, the bear, now unharmed, rose again, mad blue eyes sparkling in a stray bit of sunlight. He swatted at Asil, who, warned by Anna, ducked under the swat and went for the bear's underside. But the bear had seen Wellesley. Ignoring the huge wound that Asil had made in its abdomen, which left entrails escaping, ignoring the werewolves attacking it, the bear began running up the side of the mountain toward Wellesley and Anna.

SAGE DIDN'T KNOW what had distracted Leah. She had hunted with the Marrok's mate for two decades or more and would have sworn that nothing could pull that one off a trail once she'd chosen it—but Sage wasn't going to look gift horses in the mouth.

Her car was parked next to Asil's Mercedes, though someone—Anna, by the scent of the blood—had broken the window. Just as well, because Sage would have had to do the same thing. She took the token that hung from the leather thong around her neck and bit it again.

The speed of the change made her grit her teeth and shudder. She didn't make any noise, though. She didn't know where the werewolves were and had no intention of drawing their attention if she could help it.

Hopefully, they would be fully occupied with Grandma Daisy. Shivering and naked, Sage opened the door of her SUV and grabbed the backpack from the backseat. She pulled on the spare set of clothing she kept there.

Dressed, spare key to her SUV in hand, she drew her first deep breath since she'd looked into Jericho's eyes and realized what Grandma Daisy had done. She was an old creature—Sage didn't know how old because her own grandmother had called her Grandma Daisy. Old predators knew how to be patient. But evidently, her patience had run out at last.

Ironic that it had happened on the day that Sage had finally found their quarry. Decades of searching because the Marrok kept his wildlings secret from everyone except for his mate and his two sons. Then Asil had come to the pack—and he also had been sent to deal with the wildlings. She'd attached herself to him to see if he could be persuaded to tell tales—and because he was beautiful.

And he *was* beautiful.

She would regret Asil, she thought. Maybe once her grandmother had the pack under her control—assuming she could torture the secret of the collars from Wellesley, and Sage never underestimated her Grandma Daisy—maybe Sage would take Asil and use him for a while.

The thought made her smile.

She had worried when Grandma had outed her, worried that she somehow had displeased the skinwalker. But when Grandma had detonated the stink bomb in Charles's face, Sage had understood. If Grandma Daisy could get Charles alone—if she took *Charles*—then she could take the whole pack, Wellesley and all.

Grandma Daisy wouldn't mind throwing away Sage for a chance at the pack, at the Marrok himself. Sage couldn't blame her, really. But since the chance presented itself to *not* be a martyr, Sage intended to take it.

She tossed the backpack into the rear seat and started to get into her SUV.

A low growl stopped her.

She grabbed the knife she kept in a sheath beside the seat and turned to face—

She had worried it might be Asil or Charles, but the wolf who had broken through the greenery next to her car was skinny and ragged, his ribs moving harshly with the exertion of intercepting her.

Devon. And he was alone.

Gunshots sounded, a roar rose in the forest—Grandma Daisy's bear. And Sage had her explanation for why the pursuit had broken off. Evidently, everyone except Devon had gone to fight the bear.

Sage was realistic enough to know that she wasn't a match for Bran or Charles. Still, sometimes in her dreams she plunged this very knife into their bodies and heard them scream in payment for the pain she'd had to suffer for their actions. If they had not interfered in Grandma Daisy's plans, Sage would have simply been one of the many children who had no magic and therefore served as helpers. Grandma would not have picked Sage to be her werewolf spy. Her life would have been normal.

The pain of the Change, the torture of being the plaything of Grandma's picked group of rogue wolves—that was all the fault of Charles and Bran Cornick, who had robbed Grandma Daisy of her prey and hidden him away. Even using his hair and blood, they could not find him.

Sage knew now that it was because Grandma Daisy's own half-failed binding spell, now broken, had changed the artist beyond recognition. If Bran had not changed Frank Bright's name, though, they could have found him by his true name. All of Sage's suffering was the Marrok's fault.

She could not kill Bran or Charles. But Devon, friend of Asil and Bran's special pet, who was weakened by his inability to eat enough to keep himself healthy? Once he had been a formidable warrior, she knew, but now?

She smiled at the weakest and most beloved of Bran's wildlings. She would take her revenge where she found it.

"Hello, Hello, Devon," she said.

CHARLES FOLLOWED HIS pack mates, who were running after the bear as it charged up the side of the mountain, though if dragging its insides up the rocky slope didn't slow it down, he wasn't sure what he could do about it.

He was too slow. Even drawing on the pack's power, he couldn't heal broken bones three times in a row and get wonderful results. His right front leg hurt so much when he ran on it that he just tucked it up against his body and ran on the other three.

He leaped onto the flattish stretch of ground where Wellesley had set up his fire and took in the scene in a single glance.

Wellesley, eyes closed, was chanting over a fire—where it appeared that he was trying ineffectually to burn the witch gun. Whatever he was doing, the skinwalker evidently thought it was dangerous enough that it was trying to get to Wellesley through Leah, Asil, Juste—and Anna.

Leah, Asil, and Juste looked as though they were engaged in the hit-and-run technique Charles had begun with, harrying the bear and trying to distract him from his target.

Anna was pelting him with rocks—and doing a damn fine job of it. White bone showed on the bear's head as it roared at her.

There's not enough space, said Brother Wolf—though he knew that Charles already understood that. The rocks were a distance weapon, and the bear was closing in on Anna.

There wasn't time for an easy change, and he didn't have strength to change fast enough with his own power. But his da had left him in charge of the pack. Without consideration for the limits of that power this time, he pulled on the pack and donned his human shape between one stride and the next.

He felt the drain of it in the reluctant slowness of his muscles and the bone-deep ache in his joints. He was going to have to eat a feast and sleep a week to recover from this. If he lived another five seconds.

Still running, he used the momentum to fuel the left-handed blow as he brought Ofaeti's damned big axe down between the bear's ears and buried it there, up to the haft, in the bear's skull. Sometimes, especially when they needed to, objects he was holding when he shifted from human to wolf came with him when he made the change back to human.

"Heal *that*," he growled.

"Get away," called Wellesley, scrambling to his feet. "Get away from the bear."

Charles started to take a step back, but an unexpected and sudden weariness caught him. He stumbled, and his mate steadied him and shoved him farther back at the same time. For thirty or forty seconds, nothing more happened.

And then the gun burst into white flames—and so did the body of the bear.

Wellesley raised both arms to the sky and sang a song in some strange, twisting tongue. But it didn't matter that Charles could not understand the language. He knew a prayer when he heard one.

CHAPTER

12

One of the most amazing things about the past few days, Anna thought, was that the whole mountainside didn't go up in flames when the skinwalker burned. They didn't have a fire line, they didn't have a backhoe, and that bear went up with a ton more heat than Hester's house had.

The bear burned to ashes in about five minutes, smelling disturbingly—given the nature of the beast—like bacon as it did so. When the fire had ended, there was only a pile of bones left on soil that looked as though a molten rock had pressed into it and left it blackened and shiny. The bones themselves weren't blackened—they were white and clean, and they belonged to a human.

Wellesley knelt and pressed his hand on top of the skull—and the bones melted into . . . well, into nothing.

Anna thought of his story, of the spirit of the hurricane who had called this man its brother. She thought about what it had said about

Wellesley. Something about how Wellesley carried the blood of earth magic and was descended for a thousand years from a lineage of priestesses, whatever that meant—other than being able to resist a blood-magic curse for as long as he had.

No one said anything about going after Sage. They weren't in any shape for a pursuit—and besides, they had all heard the sound of Sage's SUV starting up and driving away.

Tiredly, quietly, thoughtfully, they took the trail down to the cars.

ANNA AND CHARLES stayed in their own house that night—Bran's orders be damned. Charles looked like he'd gone forty rounds with a meat grinder. She wasn't going to bring him into the middle of pack HQ looking like that. He wouldn't sleep there when he was hurt, for one thing.

And she needed to get him alone.

Anna fed him frozen pizzas while she worked on something with more protein that would take longer. And she joined him in eating the pizzas and the steaks.

Anna wasn't going to say anything, but her mouth said, "She called you Charlie." It had bothered her—that another woman had a pet name for Anna's mate. She hadn't realized how much it bothered her until she said it out loud.

Charles put down his fork and nodded. "She had a bruise that covered most of her face when Da introduced us. She was terrified and half-starved—which is why the bruise was still there. I let it go—and she continued to use the name. I thought at the time that it was a prod—a check to see if we were as bad as her first pack. If we would hit her for not following the rules."

"And now?" Anna asked.

He shook his head and started eating his steak again. "That might still have been the case. She was brutalized—no question about that. Even if she volunteered . . . and I don't think a skinwalker asks for volunteers any more than any other witch who uses black magic does."

Anna thought about that for a while. "So maybe she didn't want to betray us."

"Anna," Charles said in a gentle voice, "she was here for twenty years. She could have come to my father for help at any time. She gave Hester, Jonesy, and Jericho to the skinwalker."

"And then there was Devon," Anna said.

They had found Devon's body when they returned to the cars. Evidently, he'd decided to go stop her. She'd killed him as painfully as she could manage without delaying too long. The Sage that she had known would never have done that.

"There never was a Sage," Anna told him.

He put his hand on her knee and kept eating.

He was healing as she watched him. Bruises fading, cuts mending themselves.

"It almost killed you," she said. And she hadn't meant to say that, either. She tried to lighten the stark terror she heard in her voice with a little humor. "No more fighting bears for you."

He set down his fork and squeezed her knee. "I killed it," he told her. "It was dead and rotting when I turned my back. It used magic to conceal itself, or it would never have taken me by surprise."

"No more fighting dead things," she said, but her voice wobbled on the last word.

He reached for her—and she crawled on his lap, burrowing into his arms. He rested his chin on the top of her head.

"I will probably have gray hairs tomorrow from the moment when I saw you throwing rocks at the bear," he told her. "No more throwing rocks at bears for you."

Eventually, she slid back into her seat, and they both ate some more. When neither of them could eat another bite, she left the mess in the kitchen and they leaned on each other all the way to their bedroom.

In the darkness, while he slept, she cried silently on his shoulder—tears that she would never have allowed herself had he been awake. He worried too much over her tears. But in the darkness of their room, surrounded by his warmth and his scent, it seemed the proper time for tears.

They could have lost him today. She wondered, If the skinwalker had taken him, would she have noticed? Would she have, like his grandfather's uncle, lived for months without understanding that Charles was dead?

Skinwalker, the old medicine man's voice rolled through her head. Though she didn't think he'd ever used that word in the . . . in the vision that Brother Wolf had sent her.

She cried because she didn't know what else to do with the roil of fear and just-missed grief that was bound up in the thought of what the skinwalker could have done.

And when she was done with that, she cried for the woman she had thought was her friend. Thinking back over all the time she'd known Sage, Anna couldn't decide if Sage had been very good at deception or just very good at avoiding things that were lies. Maybe Charles would know. Maybe it didn't matter anymore.

She cried for Asil. For the romance with Sage that had been something else and for the friend that he had lost.

When they had found Devon, Asil went very still. He picked up Devon's body without a word. He laid the bloody mess on the leather of the backseat of his Mercedes without any hesitation. Then he'd sat in the back with Devon's head on his lap. He had not protested when Anna got in the driver's seat, with Charles taking shotgun.

They had taken both of them, Asil and Devon's body, to Bran's house, where the rest of the pack would take care of them. Then she and Charles had gotten into Charles's truck and driven home.

Anna cried for Devon, too, though she hadn't known him well. She'd never seen his human form—only known him through the stories of others. Asil had liked and respected him—and goodness knew Asil didn't respect very many people on the planet. Bran. The mysteriously amnesiac Sherwood Post. She couldn't think of anyone else offhand.

Jericho, the real Jericho, she had never met. Charles said that he was pretty sure that he'd been taken the same time all of the enemy soldiers had died. Hard to tell if those men had been killed by Jericho or by the skinwalker, to draw Charles to Jericho's home. She thought that they would probably never know for sure.

Hester, Jonesy, Jericho, and Devon—they'd lost so many in a very short time. Anna put her ear to Charles's chest, listening to the steady beat of his heart.

Suddenly, every muscle in his body tensed, and he sat up. He gave her a wide-eyed look. It seemed like an overreaction to her tears.

"Leah saved me," he said in a disgruntled voice.

She couldn't help it—she laughed. And then she cried a little more.

He made love to her—which helped both her tears and his ruffled feathers.

But before he went to sleep, he murmured, "Leah is never going to let me live this down."

"That's okay," Anna told him. "If you were dead, you wouldn't be bothered by anything Leah had to say. I hope she torments you good and proper."

He laughed then, a warm, sleepy sound that followed her into her dreams.

BRAN PARKED THE rented silver Camry on the road outside his house—there was no room for it any nearer. He left his suitcase where it was and walked home.

The lights told him that everyone was awake. He felt the subtle expectation that told him the pack could feel him, even if they didn't know what was causing their restlessness. Standing on the porch, he straightened his shoulders and opened the bonds, accepting back the responsibility that he had handed to his son.

For a moment, the sensation was overwhelming. He took a step sideways to balance himself. Then everything settled back into place, and it was as if he had never left—except for the missing pieces—no Hester with her tie to Jonesy, who lit up Bran's feel of that tie like a nuclear explosion; no Jericho, who could have taught Tag a thing or two about berserker fighting; no Devon, whose sweetness had survived the years that had robbed him of all else.

As Bran walked into the room, an expectant hush filled the air.

Juste, looking exhausted, rose from his seat and went down on one knee before Bran. "We have failed you, sire."

Yes. They ran their packs differently in Europe.

"Get up," he said, trying not to sound irritated. It had, after all, been he who had failed them. But this pack could not deal with doubts about their leader, so he could not apologize to them—as much as it would have relieved his guilt to do so.

"Get up, man," said Tag. "We don't bend our knees around here. If he wants your throat, you'll know it. Otherwise, we can say we're sorry while standing on our feet."

Bran looked around the room—Asil met his gaze with wry sympathy. According to the pithy report Charles had left on Bran's message app, Asil didn't know that Bran's absence was because he thought Leah was their traitor. But Asil was a wise old wolf, and it looked as though he'd worked things out.

"I think," Bran said, "under the circumstances, we are lucky we didn't lose more of the pack. Thank you."

They had Devon's body laid out on the bar, the dead wolf curled up as if he were merely asleep. Bran bent down and kissed his forehead.

For a moment, he saw a wild, laughing young man, full of joy and adventures. "Come on, Bran," he'd said. "It'll be fun. We're all werewolves—let's join the Wild Hunt!"

Tag, standing at Bran's shoulder, said, "Do you remember the day he talked us all into trying to find the Wild Hunt?"

Bran's memories sometimes leaked out through the pack bonds if he wasn't careful.

Bran shook his head. "Reckless idiot."

"And so you told him," agreed Tag. "But you came with us anyway."

That had been . . . six hundred years ago, give or take fifty. And now, of those who had run that night, only Bran and Tag were left.

"So I did," agreed Bran.

He stayed there for a little while, feeling his presence settle the pack down until they left by twos and threes, going home to rest. Until only he was left.

He found Leah in her bedroom. She was curled up in a chair, reading a magazine that she put down when he entered the room.

"You," Bran said, "I can apologize to. I thought you were our traitor."

"I?" she said. Her expression of astonishment changed to comprehension. "That's why you left. If I had betrayed you, betrayed the pack, you'd have had to kill me."

He nodded. "I can't do that. You know why. So I left it to Charles." He apologized again. "I am sorry."

She raised her eyebrows. "Whatever for? I'm flattered that you thought that I was our traitor. It would take a lot of ingenuity and ability to be this close to you and betray you."

She didn't lie. But he knew her well enough to read the hurt in the set of her jaw.

"I should have known better," he said. "You have always been driven by the good of the pack."

She shrugged. "I never suspected Sage. That's the nature of traitors, isn't it?"

She stood up and strolled toward him, leaned into him, and kissed his mouth softly. "I accept your apologies—though I don't need them. You look tired. Come to bed."

He unbuttoned his shirt, and she took it from him to put in the laundry hamper. She came up behind him and put her warm, skilled hands on his shoulders and kneaded them as she kissed his spine.

"Come to bed," she said again.

He did.

* * *

WHEN CHARLES GOT up, he checked his cell phone and found he'd slept thirty hours.

Charles showered, brushed his teeth, and braided his hair, listening to his da, Anna, and Wellesley in the kitchen—cooking breakfast, if his nose was any judge. Charles left the bedroom, sauntered into the kitchen, and wrapped his arms around his mate from behind while she scrambled eggs. He kissed her ear.

Charles looked up at his da, who was leaning against the wall next to the back door with his arms crossed over his chest. Bran Cornick, the Marrok, leader of most of the werewolves in North America, looked tired.

"Morning, Da," he said. "Wellesley."

The artist smiled at him from the other side of the kitchen, where he was buttering toast. "Good morning, Charles. Your timing is excellent. Your father was just going to tell us why he was so certain it was Leah who was our traitor."

"You were right," Anna said. "It was in the files Boyd sent over."

Charles glanced at his da—who gave him a rueful smile.

"There were interviews Boyd conducted with each of his pack members about Leo's dealings with our enemy. One of Boyd's people overheard a conversation about ten years ago. One of our enemy's people said something about a female werewolf they were getting information from," Da said.

"So not the financials?" Charles had been sure there had been something in the financials. Something more substantial than an overheard conversation that might or might not be relevant.

His da grimaced. "It was more damning than I made it sound. The information was something that only Leah and I knew."

"And maybe Leah's best . . . not best friend. I'm not sure Leah has a best friend. But best confidant, anyway," Anna said.

Bran nodded.

"You didn't make it to Africa before you set me up to kill Leah—and"—Charles hesitated, then shrugged—"whatever happened after that?"

"I had plane tickets," Bran said. "But the monster"—he tapped himself in the chest—"wouldn't allow me to leave. My wolf decided we needed to protect Leah. I had a time keeping him contained in a hotel in Spokane. That's as far as I could get."

His da's belief in Leah's guilt had really thrown him for a loop.

"Do you know where Sage is?"

"Not at present," said Wellesley peacefully. "But I'm sure she will turn up."

"You told me," Anna said, "when we were running up the trail, that you remembered what happened at Rhea Springs."

He nodded. "Yes."

Anna made an impatient sound, and Wellesley grinned at her.

"So what happened to you?" she said.

"After my wife died, I traveled a bit," he said, "as men did in that time. And I found surcease of a sort by helping other people. I garnered a reputation among the powerless and the poor."

"He was a hero," said Da. "He healed people. He killed people who needed killing. He saved people who needed saving."

"You knew that when you sent me to him?" asked Charles.

Bran nodded.

"And I caught the attention of a woman who called herself Daisy Hardesty," Wellesley said.

"Hardesty was Sage's last name when she came to us," Charles said softly. "Before she changed it to Carhardt."

Wellesley nodded. "Daisy owned Rhea Springs. Everyone who lived there was a member of her family. People came from all over the country to be healed of their disease. Some of them disappeared—including the brother of a woman I'd helped. She got word to me, and I went to investigate."

He grimaced. "I thought I was walking into a den of murdering thieves, and instead, I found a town practicing blood magic. There was a battle. People died—some by my hand. I hurt her, and she cursed me. I think she assumed the authorities would take care of my continued existence for her, and she didn't need to kill me herself to profit from it once her spell was in place."

"Instead," Anna said, "Charles came and spirited you away."

"Indeed," said Wellesley.

SAGE DROVE TO Missoula. She'd changed to her second spare set of clothing—Devon's blood had made her look like the victim of a serial killer. So she stopped in a mall and bought two or three sets of clothing with cash. She had several credit cards and a hefty bank account under the name Samantha Harding. But she didn't want to take chances.

She was certain no one knew about those accounts. Very certain. Still . . . Charles Cornick was good with electronic money. Better to wait until Grandma Daisy contacted her before she used credit under any name.

She stole a car from the airport's long-term parking lot, after switching plates with another car of the same make and color. Driving a silver Toyota Camry was as close to invisible as she could get.

Deciding that she'd best avoid the bigger towns for a day or two, she pulled into a hotel in Deer Lodge. Not that Montana had many "bigger" towns. She'd get an apartment in Billings, she decided, getting out of "her" car.

The hotel wasn't happy about the cash, but her spare ID and the fact that she didn't fit any criminal or terrorist profile helped her—as did her story that she was trying to get away from her husband, running to her sister in Canada.

People always liked to feel like they were helping someone escape something bad—especially if they didn't have to risk anything or make any effort to do it.

The water in the shower was hot, and the sheets were clean. She slept deeply.

And when she awoke, she was not alone.

"Hello, Hello," said Asil.

TWO WEEKS LATER

Charles was following his mate into his da's kitchen when his da grabbed him and pulled him into the office. And that was how neither he nor the Marrok attended the first and last pack barbecue and music social.

By the time Charles came out of the office, Leah was just wiping down the countertops, and no one was around.

"I know we were in there for a few hours," he told Leah, "but weren't there supposed to be activities until dark?"

It was not dark yet.

She looked at him. "Tag took out his bagpipes and played 'The Wild Hunt.' The new one, by The Tallest Man on Earth."

Tag had gone through a new-folk phase, and The Tallest Man on Earth had been one of his favorites.

"On bagpipes?" He tried to imagine it. The effect would have been a lot different than the original. Especially with Tag playing. Tag could play—but he liked to embellish.

"It wasn't that bad," she said. "Not that good, mind you. But not that bad."

"It didn't drive everyone away?" Bagpipes weren't everyone's cup of tea. Especially if most of the people here were werewolves— bagpipes were loud. His da's office had some serious soundproofing if they hadn't heard bagpipes.

"No," she said. "It made everyone want to go for a hunt. My back- yard is full of piles of clothing. Anna and I pulled all the instruments inside—and then we turned the sprinklers on."

She smiled in satisfaction—and Charles grinned at the thought of the two indignant women plotting how to get back at the people who spoiled the musical part of their barbecue.

He and Leah happened to be looking at each other when they smiled. Leah looked startled, and he imagined he did, too. It had probably happened, but he didn't remember the two of them ever smiling at each other.

It would probably be a long time before it happened again.

"I take it that this will be a onetime thing?" he ventured.

She shrugged. "Maybe. Anna suggested we make Tag plan it next time."

He started to go, but Brother Wolf prodded him.

"I have never told you thank you," he said.

Her eyebrows raised—though he knew very well she understood what he was talking about.

"If you had not come back," he told her, "the skinwalker would have killed me."

She folded up the wet cloth and hung it over the faucet to dry. "I don't know about that," she said. "You weren't dead when we got there. If there is one thing that I have learned over the time I've spent here with your father, it is that it doesn't do to under-estimate you."

He folded his arms and looked at his father's mate, and for the first time, the reason he was glad he had not had to execute her for being a traitor had more to do with Leah and less to do with his da.

"Thank you," he said, "for coming back to help when I needed you."

She considered it a moment. "I didn't do it for you." She opened a drawer and took out a clean dish towel and set it out beside the sink. With her back to him, she said, "I do not like you. I have never liked you—and it is not your fault. He loves you. And he does not love me."

She turned around and looked at him with clear blue eyes and an expressionless face.

Charles thought about how his da's wolf had fought Bran to a standstill in Spokane, unwilling to leave Leah to her fate. When Bran knew that the safest place for everyone, if Leah had been their traitor, would have been Africa. His father, who had controlled that wolf for a very, very long time.

Maybe it hadn't been just the wolf who couldn't leave.

"What," Charles said carefully, because he tried very hard not to interfere in his da's marriage "would be different if he loved you?"

She stared at him. "You cryptic son of a bitch," she said.

And that's why he didn't interfere in his da's marriage.

"Do you know where Anna is?"

"She left," Leah said coolly, as if the brief moment of accord over wet clothing had not happened. "I presume she went home."

HE FOUND HER working her little gelding in the arena—she pointedly ignored him. Anna stiffened a little, though, and when she asked the gelding for a transition from canter to trot, she bumped down on his back, off balance.

The cheery little gray took a few more strides—and when it was obvious she wasn't fixing matters, he stopped.

"You forgot to sit a couple of strides before you started posting," Charles said cautiously, climbing on top of the arena fence. If she was mad at him, greeting her with an instruction seemed to be a bad way to make things right—but he couldn't help himself.

Rather than responding—or trying it again—she walked Heylight over to where Charles sat, and said, "Think carefully over your next answer. Your father's life might just depend on it."

He met her eyes, but he couldn't tell how serious she was. "All right," he said.

"Did he pull you into his study so neither of you had to participate tonight?"

"I will answer that," Charles said. "But first let me say that the pack has been wounded by Sage and by the death of the wildlings. Badly wounded in some cases."

Asil had disappeared for a few days. When he returned, he had retreated to his roses and only come out when Kara went and got him.

Bran had been shaken badly—first discovering that they had a traitor, then that business with Mercy's kidnapping, then believing that Leah was their traitor. But the worst issue, as far as his da's confidence was concerned, was the way Sage's betrayal had totally blindsided him.

"This party was just what the pack needed—Wild Hunt and all," Charles told her. "Did Asil go with them?"

Anna nodded. "He said someone had to mind the children."

"Da isn't at a point, yet, where a good run would do him any good. If he had gone out, no one would have played. And they needed to play."

Anna pursed her lips, her body swaying a little as the gelding shifted his weight. "Okay," she said. "I can see that. What about you?"

"I would have loved to go chase the Wild Hunt," Charles said truthfully. "But Wellesley sent my father a bunch of names and social security numbers. So I spent the afternoon working."

Wellesley was keeping his home in the Marrok's pack. But he'd asked, and received permission, to go out hunting witches. He'd left a few days ago with freshly minted identification, credit cards (which he now knew how to use), and a mission to drive him.

"What did you find?" she asked.

"This is bigger than the skinwalker—or at least bigger than just one skinwalker. It looks like the Hardesty family has managed to stay under everyone's radar. They own a fast-food chain, large tracts of land, and a few buildings in New York City. And they are witches. The first powerful witch family for three hundred years—that we know of, at least."

Heylight threw his head up and blew, as if challenging a strange horse. Anna petted him.

"And they are aimed at us?" she said in a small voice.

Charles nodded. "Looks like. But maybe not. Asil—" He sighed. "Asil found Sage."

"No wonder he's been troubled," Anna said somberly. Charles knew he didn't have to tell her that Sage was dead.

He nodded. "Asil told Da that the skinwalker was chasing down rumors that Wellesley, who was once Frank Bright, was here. She had targeted him originally—back in the thirties—because she knew about the collar spell. That was the main thing she wanted. But once she was here and she captured Jericho, the skinwalker thought she might try to take over this pack—and use it as a weapon against another branch of the family."

"Sage told Asil all of that?" Anna asked.

Charles shrugged.

Anna liked Asil. And even if it made Brother Wolf crazy, Charles was not going to interfere with that unless he had to. When she was ready to hear about how much of a monster Asil could be, she could ask him. Or Da. But Charles expected that she wouldn't.

She looked toward the tree-covered mountains, and they were worth looking at. "You know?" she said. "I have been wondering what I'm going to do with my life. But meeting some of the wildlings taught me something."

"What's that?" When he looked at her with his grandfather's gift, he could see the connections that centered in her: connections from the horse, from the trees, from the mountains—and from him. She was so beautiful.

"I may not know, right now, what I want to do with my life. But I have a long time to figure it out. I decided—at the party actually—that learning some things is a great way to start. Before I came out to ride, I signed myself up for online classes." She frowned at him. "Do you speak Japanese?"

Brother Wolf said, *No.*

Charles laughed at his wretched tone. Brother Wolf did not want to disappoint Anna.

A wolf's cry echoed from the mountain behind their house—and before it died away, it was answered by many throats. They had not found prey, Charles could tell, just joy in the run.

"Hey, pretty lady," he said, leaning forward. "Does that horse sidepass?"

She gave him a demure smile. "Maybe," she said.

"Why don't you try it?" he asked.

She stepped the gelding sideways until he stood next to the fence, and raised herself in her stirrups. Charles had to bend down some, because her gelding was really short, but it was worth it.

Kissing Anna was worth however much effort he had to make.

We will learn Japanese, said Brother Wolf.

ACKNOWLEDGMENTS

My thanks to those who helped me shape this story: Collin Briggs, Linda Campbell, Dave and Katharine Carson, Michelle Kasper, Ann Peters, Kaye Roberson, Bob and Sara Schwager, and Anne Sowards. As always, any mistakes that remain are mine.

ABOUT THE AUTHOR

Patricia Briggs lived a fairly normal life until she learned to read. After that she spent lazy afternoons flying dragonback and looking for magic swords when she wasn't horseback riding in the Rocky Mountains. Once she graduated from Montana State University with degrees in history and German, she spent her time substitute teaching and writing. She and her family live in the Pacific Northwest, and you can visit her website at www.patriciabriggs.com.

Find out more about Patricia and other Orbit authors by registering for the free monthly newsletter at www.orbitbooks.net.